BOOK FIVE: THE WEIR CHRONICLES

DIM THE LIGHTS

OTHER BOOKS BY SUE DUFF

The Weir Chronicles
Fade to Black
Masks and Mirrors
Sleight of Hand
Stack a Deck
Dim the Lights
(available February 2018)

Short Stories
"Duo'vr"
a short story in the anthology
TICK TOCK: Seven Tales of Time

"A Mistake"
a short story in the anthology
OFF BEAT: Nine Spins on Song

BOOK FIVE: THE WEIR CHRONICLES

DIM THE LIGHTS

SUE DUFF

CrossWinds Publishing
P.O. Box 630223
Littleton, Colorado 80163
www.sueduff.com

Publisher's Note: This is a work of fiction. Names, characters, places, and incidents are a product of the author's imagination. Locales and public names are sometimes used for atmospheric purposes. Any resemblance to actual people, living or dead, or to businesses, companies, events, institutions, or locales is completely coincidental.

Interior Design by NovelNinjutsu.com

For Adversity

Like the forces that have carved this planet,
You've shaped me into the person I am.

DESTRUCTION

I stand steadfast, with purpose in this here and now while my gaze remains on the horizon. In the distance, the power of earth and moon unite and a wave ignites. I watch with bated breath for its swell as apprehension engulfs me at the realization we are destined to meet.

The wave connects with forces unseen, building and gathering upon itself until it reaches its apex. A liquid thunder fills the air and drowns out the squawk of seagulls flying overhead. The wave drives forward along its inevitable path and I steel myself to meet its strength.

It strikes as a drenching fist, engulfing me with a tremendous thrust. The sand beneath my feet recedes and I'm tossed about like a puppet. Seconds morph into eternity, then the imposing wave disperses around me and I'm deposited prone upon the shore, unable to breathe, think, or feel. The power has washed away my mere existence. Yet, I remain—transformed.

Unknown Author, Book of the Weir, Vol. II

PART ONE

Be careful what you wish for.

ONE

Ian stepped into the steam and turned his back to the shower head. He leaned against the stall and dropped his face, tuning into the stinging spray across his shoulders. When he opened his eyes, a muddy creek curved in a gentle flow beneath his feet, headed toward the drain. The grime of Thrae slowly cleared, but he could never erase the bloody impact the planet had left upon his soul. His trip to Earth's alternate universe had been a devastating lesson of good versus evil. It substantiated who his enemies were. What they were capable of.

He opened his mouth and it overflowed with pristine water. The abundant fluid came from the auditorium's well, drilled beneath the massive structure located amid the desolate tundra of Greenland. The rebel's hideout was his only haven from Aeros and the Primary, two ruthless brothers bent on draining Earth's energy and regaining their grip on the universe. Their destruction of Thrae proved not enough, and they now had their sights on his beloved home world.

Ian pressed his forehead against the cool tile, overcome with guilt at leaving so many behind. It was impossible to send Earth's water to the Thraens trapped on the dying planet. The memories of his trip squelched the comfort he'd sought from the shower, and he shut off the water, abandoning his futile attempt to ease the pain.

A clean sweat suit sat folded on the locker room bench with a note beside it. MEETING IN 15. It was written in Eve's elegant handwriting.

The clothes were still warm from the dryer and brought a crumb of comfort to Ian's troubles. He walked barefoot down the sleeping-quarters hall, listening to subtle, and the not so subtle sleep of friends, relishing in the knowledge that for the first time in over a month everyone was safe. Ian matched each slumbering sound to its owner as he had hundreds of times when they resided at his mansion. The only home he'd ever known, discarded along with his previous life as a world-class illusionist for the sake of embracing a destiny he'd spent his childhood running from.

The one sound he'd been searching for halted his steps. He pressed his palm against the door and leaned his shoulder against it, comforted that Rayne was safe. The planet-wide search for her was worth every battle, every scar, and the countless lessons in humility and death. Their survival on Thrae had changed them and drawn them ever closer in a shared goal. But what haunted Ian upon their return was a burning question. Were they closer in heart, or forever destined to stay apart?

When he pushed through the double doors a thick stream of moonlight spotlighted the center of the auditorium's great hall. It gave way to rising, rippling shadows on either side, marking the rows of empty seats. He lay down in the center of the massive wood floor, resting his forearm over his eyes while drawing energy from the tremendous vortex field beneath the structure. The core in the center of Ian's chest ignited as warmth filled his torso and spread to his limbs. The greater the energy he drew, the more intoxicating it became. He didn't stop until his core blistered with renewed vitality.

Ian sat up and rested his forearm on his bent knee, staring out the huge windows at the far end of the hall. What was left of the glacier beyond the building lay in gigantic chunks of ice, piled a few feet from the window. A near miss thanks to the grace of Mother Nature stopping the avalanche when it did.

"What's the meeting about?" Patrick asked from the upper shadows of the seats. A lighter cast his face in a golden glow, then extinguished, but the sizzling tip of his cigar remained.

"I'm guessing your mother will be filling us in on her master plan to defeat Aeros and the Primary." The cigar odor wafted downward and filled Ian's nostrils. He inhaled deep. His best friend's nasty habit brought comfort like nothing else had since his return.

"No rest for the heroes," Patrick said. "Better to be one of the sidekicks. At least they're exempt from board meetings."

Patrick had a point. Was there another agenda for this meeting? "Where's Jaered?"

"With my mother, where else," Patrick said. "They're as thick as thieves, those two."

Patrick's tone made Ian wary. What happened while he was on Thrae? "Jaered's been at the heart of this conflict since the day he was born, Patrick. You and I have been kept in the dark all of our lives," Ian said.

"And lied to by those we trusted the most," Patrick said. "Welcome to the rebel forces. Information doled out by my mother and our cousin to solely guarantee co-operation."

Cousin. The word formed on Ian's lips, but he stopped short of giving it a voice. No one had told Patrick the truth. Why? "How are you holding up?" Ian asked.

"You know me," Patrick said without his typical pinch of amusement. "I do what I can and try to talk myself out of the rest."

Ian picked at a loose thread on his sweat pants. "How's that working out?"

Patrick's silence hung between them as thick as ash from a volcano. Ian's heart reached out to him. "I'm no hero, Ian," Patrick said.

For years, Ian had relied on Patrick to take charge of their business affairs, yet their roles had reversed in the space of a month. He stared at the rising chunks of the glacier. "From what I've seen, you've come a long way. I have to believe we can take them on if we learn to work together." Ian caught the lack of conviction in his voice and hoped it was exhaustion.

A shadowy image made its way down the aisle from where Patrick sat. Saxon's silent descent reached the gym floor and approached with scuffling scrapes. Ian's beloved companion whimpered. The wolf licked Ian's face and with a *humph*, settled on the gym floor, resting his head in Ian's lap. He stroked Saxon and for the first time since returning from Thrae, found some peace.

A ball of sparkling energy formed ahead of Ian and he shot to his feet, backing up while Saxon sprang to action. Two figures took shape at the center of the vortex field. It was his missing brother and Eve. Her short stance was exaggerated by Jaered's height and they solidified like mismatched bookends.

Eve met Ian's gaze and gave him a guarded smile that quickly morphed into all business. At Saxon's hunched growl, Jaered spun around on the ball of his foot and headed for the double doors in silence. The wolf followed the rebel out of the room, nipping at his heels.

A greeting froze on Ian's lips at Jaered's slight.

"He's back to normal," Patrick muttered from up in the stands.

"He's not part of this meeting?" Ian asked.

Eve shook her head. "He's already briefed me about what happened on Thrae."

"And you've come for the rest of the story," Ian said.

Movement in the stands. "I'll leave you and my mother to your powwow."

"Patrick, you need to hear what Ian has to share," Eve said. "And I'll fill in the rest."

Patrick slumped into the nearest seat and rested his feet on the edge of the chair in front of him.

"You start," Ian said under his breath. "He deserves the truth about Aeros."

"What about Aeros?" Patrick asked.

Ian cringed. Not only had Patrick's core blast and shyfting powers developed while Ian was on Thrae, his keen hearing had also kicked in.

Eve took a couple of steps toward the railing. "Ian learned about the Weir heritage on Thrae from my sisters."

"Which makes us cousins. I know all of this," Patrick said.

"You're more than that, Patrick. You, Jaered and Ian are . . ." Eve paused and looked up at her son. "You're brothers. Halfbrothers."

Silence. It took but seconds for the core at the center of Patrick's chest to glow beneath his shirt. He bolted to his feet and descended the steps with his eyes searing hot. He forgot about the Curse. Patrick inhaled deep and pressed a fist against his chest, but his steps didn't slow.

The triggered Curse took hold in Ian's chest and he bent forward with a groan as an elephant's weight crushed his ribs and stole his breath.

"Patrick! Get a hold of yourself!" Eve shouted with raised hands.

"Aeros!" A roar detonated from Patrick's lips. "My father?" Patrick stumbled on the bottom step and lurched forward, but managed to grab the railing before he plowed face first onto the wood floor.

Vibration beneath Ian's feet, subtle at first, but then it multiplied exponentially with each beat of his pulse. A wooden-slatted wave rose at the center of the vortex in the massive hall, floorboards separated one after the other as the wave traveled outward across the room toward the stands. The crushing Curse prevented Ian from drawing enough power to shyft. Ian and Eve were swept off their feet by the displaced boards and they landed against the crumbled floor with a forceful *thump*. Sizable chunks broke away from the glacier beyond the window and slammed against the reinforced glass with nature's angry fists.

Patrick wrapped his arms around the railing at the base of the steps, tossed back and forth with each convulse of the building.

The lights shut off at the same time a shrill alarm blasted over the loudspeakers. Ian rolled on top of Eve when several ceiling panels ripped off and crashed down around them. Patrick let go of the railing, dropped to the floor and cowered against the onslaught of raining ceiling. One of the panels fell on top of him and he disappeared beneath it.

A moment later, the earth's plates stilled and the quake eased, then came to a halt. The alarm shut off, but the red strobing lights continued.

Ian scooted away until he'd gained enough distance between him and Patrick to stop the Curse. The pressure in his chest eased and he sucked air back into his lungs, choking on the plaster dust that came with it. "You okay?" he directed at Eve once he gained his voice. She nodded. "Patrick!" he called out.

"Shit!" It came from beneath a huge ceiling panel. Patrick crawled out and got to his knees, coated in debris but otherwise unscathed. "It's a miracle this place didn't come down on top of us."

"Built with the best earthquake engineering money could buy," Eve said. She stood, brushed herself off with irritated swipes, and then threw her son a furious glare. "You've got to control your anger, Patrick!"

He paused in mid-cough. "You don't mean—"

"Your Duach core's been activated. It has direct ties to Earth's core," she said. "Any more outbursts like that and you'll do more damage to this planet than our enemies."

Jaered banged open the double doors that led to the sleeping quarters. He glanced between everyone and his expression relaxed. "Aeros?" he asked.

"Stupidity," Eve snarled.

"More like ignorance!" Patrick shouted, but closed his eyes and drew a deep breath when the windows rumbled in angry protest. "Why didn't you tell me I could do that?" He fell into a choking fit and waved at the plaster cloud floating around him.

"Stay or go?" Jaered directed at Eve.

She stilled as if mulling it over. "Go," she announced with the firmness of a CEO. "Pack up. We're out in ten."

"I'll alert the others." Jaered took off through the double doors.

"Why?" Patrick asked.

"Because your tantrum has put us on the seismic map," Eve said. "If Aeros and the Primary don't take heed, the world's scientists will." She left Ian and Patrick with a silence that bespoke volumes.

Patrick stared at the ceiling. "I can't believe I did that."

"Bound to happen," Ian said. "It's why I was raised in seclusion."

"Milo warned me." Patrick ran his fingers through his hair. "Unchecked power is a dangerous thing."

"Unleashed secrets are just as dangerous," Ian said, wanting to believe that Eve had her reasons for keeping so much from Patrick all these years.

"How long have you known?" Patrick asked. "About Aeros."

"I found out on Thrae," Ian said. "I'll fill you in on what I know."

The crushing pressure in the center of Ian's chest returned, more intense than ever, and it dropped him onto his hands and knees. "Ugh!" Crimson sparks formed in the vortex ahead of Ian. "Patrick!"

It took a moment for Patrick's face to lift in alarm. Duach Sars were shyfting to their location. The quake hadn't gone unnoticed.

TWO

Patrick took off at full run toward the emergency power jam button on the wall beside the double doors. When he slammed his palm against it, nothing happened. "Fuck!"

"Go! Warn the others!" Ian rasped as the shyfting bodies solidified in front of him.

A crimson blast plowed into one of the Duach Sars and the intruder doubled over with a groan. Another blast ripped open his skull and he slumped to the floor. Core blasts came rapidly, scattering the remaining three Duach Sars. The distance diminished the debilitating effect of the Curse, but the second it eased in Ian's chest, the pressure returned. Patrick came toward Ian with raised palms, swirling scarlet balls of core energy in his open hands, focused on keeping the intruders away from Ian. As closer Patrick came, his steps slowed and he, too, doubled over with a groan. The blasts in his hands snuffed out as the Curse took full effect.

A huge Duach core blast hurled toward Patrick and he dove to the floor. It missed the top of his head by inches, but left a smoldering strip across his scalp. The odor of burnt hair filled the air as Ian scrambled far enough away to stop the Curse effect. He sprung to his feet and delivered his own emerald core blasts aimed at their attackers but from that distance, the blasts slowed and the Duach Sars easily sidestepped them.

A shotgun blast ripped into the intruder closest to Ian. The man's chest tore open and he fell onto his back. At the cock of the shotgun, Ian directed his focus on the farthest intruder, pulling his hand back with a massive core blast. His met the Duach's blast it hurled toward him in midair and the colliding blasts cancelled each other out in a violet cloud.

Jaered followed up with a shot to the man's head. "Go! We've got this!" he yelled in Ian's direction.

Patrick faced off with the last intruder. As Ian slipped through the doors, Patrick spun around and landed a solid kick to the man's head. The Duach Sar bent over, spitting blood. Patrick fell to his hip, taking out the man with a scissor kick. Ian pushed through, and the doors shut on the fight scene beyond. He leaned against the hallway wall, never prouder of his brother. Patrick had come a long way in Ian's absence, thanks to Jaered.

Footsteps approached from deep in the dark hallway. "Ian!" Rayne shouted and came to a standstill, inches from him. "Are you hurt?"

Ian shook his head. "They're Duach Sars. Jaered and Patrick are finishing off the leftovers," Ian said. "Where's everyone?"

"Eve's resetting security. Tara and Milo are grabbing more weapons from the arsenal." Rayne stepped away and raised her handgun when Jaered pushed open the door.

"They were just round one," Jaered barked. "We're not staying for round two." He jerked his chin at Rayne. "Find Eve. Tell her we need to blow this location, fast."

Ian and Rayne took off down the hall and sped around the corner, but came to a jarring stop when they were met with raised guns pointed at their chests. Milo and Tara dropped the barrels when they recognized who it was.

"Where's Eve?" Ian asked.

"She's in the control room behind us," Tara said. "Where's Patrick?"

"He and Jaered are holding down the rear," Rayne said.

"Grab only what you can carry." Ian rushed past them and ran into the control room. "Jaered said we have to—"

"Blow up my two-point-five million-dollar hideout," Eve said with her finger resting on a button. She stroked Saxon with the other hand like she had all the time in the world. Jaered entered the control room at a full-out sprint with Patrick close behind. "Take everyone to the tunnel," she said.

Jaered's eyes widened. "You're not staying."

"Don't be so dramatic," Eve said. "I've got it set on a timer."

"I'll stay with her," Patrick said.

Jaered nudged Ian. "Come on, I'll show you where."

"Saxon, stay with her," Ian said.

"He goes with you." Eve patted the wolf's head and Saxon took off, out the door.

Ian and Jaered returned to the waiting group and Jaered took command. "Go to the walk-in pantry downstairs and push against the back wall. First on the upper left corner—"

"And then the lower right," Ian said. "Same as the escape tunnels on Thrae."

Jaered stole a deep breath before continuing. "I'll make sure Patrick and Eve get out and we'll be right behind you. There's only enough snowmobiles for half the group, so double up."

"I have no idea how to drive one of them buggers," Milo said.

"You're about to get a crash course." Jaered disappeared down the hall with his shotgun pointing the way.

Milo grunted. "Let's hope that was a figure of speech."

They followed Tara to the back stairs and made their way to the lower level. A red strobe light lit their way, and Ian took the lead, using his keen vision to make it to the rear storage pantry. The walk-in freezer hummed as they passed by it and Milo paused long enough to glance in the freezer's window and stare at a hanging side of beef.

"What?" Tara asked.

"I had such plans for that." Milo turned away from the window. "A delicious welcome-home feast for Ian and Rayne."

"It's the thought that counts." Rayne gave him a grateful smile.

Gunshots rang out overhead. Everyone turned toward the ceiling.

A bright flash came from the freezer window. Jaered shyfted inside with an intruder in each hand. Ian pressed his face to the window. "Lock the door!" Jaered shouted, but it came out muffled through the thick glass.

Everyone scrambled to find something to stick in the empty padlock hole. Tara handed Ian a screwdriver and he jammed it in place.

One of the intruders brandished a knife from his leg sheath and lunged at Jaered, but Jaered shoved the side of beef at him. The man dropped the knife, grabbing the huge hunk of meat with both hands to stay upright. The other intruder wrapped his fingers around a hanging hook and tried to pull it off, but it held securely in place.

Jaered backed up and shyfted outside the freezer as both men slid on the frosty floor in a scramble to reach him. The second Jaered reappeared next to Ian, he rubbed his upper arms. "When the first wave of Duach Sars didn't check in, they sent powerless Duach with guns."

Tara stepped in. "Where's Patrick?"

"He's locked in the control room with Eve." Jaered ushered Milo and Tara toward the pantry. "Follow directions for once and get them out of here!" he yelled at Ian.

"They can get themselves out of here." Ian snatched Milo's rifle out of his grasp. "I'm staying. If they're powerless Duach, I can help." He gestured for the others. "Go! We'll buy you some time." When Rayne didn't budge, Ian gave her a pained smile. "We'll catch up, I promise."

"The tunnel ends at an ice cave dock with a boat moored there, but be careful," Jaered said. "They may be covering the waterfront, too."

The others filed out the back of the pantry and Saxon took off down the tunnel. By the time Ian closed the escape hatch, snowmobile engines turned over in the tunnel. The ensuing noises weren't the expected grinding of metal, but a deafening *hum.*

"Eve turned off the jam long enough for me to shyft those two down here." Jaered loaded fresh cartridges in the chambers of his shotgun. "We're doing this old school."

They hurried up the stairs and paused at the door leading onto the upper hall. It placed them about twenty yards from the control room door. It might as well have been twenty miles. The corridor beyond the door was filled with armed intruders lying in wait with their guns pointed at the control room.

The squad members were crouched low and hadn't noticed Ian and Jaered taking turns glancing through the slit window high in the stairwell door. Jaered wrapped his fingers around the knob, but shook his head. The door was locked. So much for a surprise attack from the rear.

Jaered raised two fingers and motioned for Ian to keep climbing. They made it to the upper floor without resistance, and discovered an unlocked door leading onto a narrow hallway. Ian followed Jaered around the corner and they came to a dead end. A steel ladder was bolted to the wall. It rose to a catwalk overhead providing access to the auditorium's infrastructure near the ceiling. Jaered pointed up.

On the climb up, Ian had no idea how this would give them an advantage over the death squad one floor below.

Plaster chunks and pieces of ceiling tile littered the catwalk. Ian and Jaered stepped gingerly to not dislodge debris on the unsuspecting men keeping guard in the auditorium's great hall below. Jaered held up his closed fist and they stopped, dead center where the catwalk spread in all directions like spokes on a wheel.

About ten feet away, a camera lens turned in slow motion with a soft *whirrr*. A moment later, it pointed directly at them. Its blinking red penlight turned to a steady green. Jaered handed Ian his shotgun and leaned forward using sign language, but it was so rapid, Ian couldn't make out most of the message. The green light turned off—on—off, and then turned back on in a steady green beam.

Jaered reached toward Ian, and he handed the rebel his shotgun. "Go back the way we came," Jaered said quietly. "And cover me."

Ian never got a chance to ask why. His core ignited. Eve had turned off the jam.

"Hurry!" Jaered hissed. "Before they send reinforcements."

Ian took off down the stretch of scaffolding, gaining as much distance between Jaered and the end of the cat-walk as he could. He'd barely made it before Patrick shyfted his mother next to Jaered. They hunched down and spoke so softly Ian couldn't make it out.

The mad dash to avoid triggering the Curse came at a price. Bits of debris had been kicked off and had landed on the uprooted wooden floor below. A couple of the nearby men standing guard looked up at the catwalk. One of the guards shouted, lifted his automatic rifle, and let loose a hailstorm of bullets at Jaered, Patrick, and Eve.

THREE

Ian opened fire, killing the gunman and wounding another. Return fire ricocheted off the underside of the cat-walk and took out chunks of the wall behind him. He ducked and fired again. "We're about to have company!" Ian yelled.

"Get to the snowmobile!" Jaered shouted, rushing toward Ian.

Scarlet sparks encircled Patrick and Eve and they disappeared.

Ian shyfted in an emerald cloud and reappeared inside the pantry far below. He listened at the closed door, but didn't detect anyone waiting in ambush. Pressing fingers to release the latches, he swung the rear pantry wall open and entered the ice tunnel.

To his dismay there was only one snowmobile. He spun around when Jaered shyfted behind him.

"This is why I wanted you to go with the others," he snarled. "Pur and Duach Sars just get in each other's way!"

Ian straddled the vehicle and turned over the engine. Jaered jumped on. "Get this thing moving. We don't have much time."

The *hum* Ian heard earlier turned deafening when he tightened his grasp on the accelerator. Instead of the expected jerk, the snowmobile lifted as air released below the vehicle.

Ian took off down the narrow ice tunnel. His years of dirt biking and motorcycle stunts helped, but it still took a few minutes for Ian to learn how to control the hoverboard-like contraption, especially on the tight curves. He found that he could sweep further up the sides of the tunnel than on a typical bike. He did his best to keep their speed at maximum.

At the third tight curve, Jaered reached around Ian and signaled to slow down.

"Why?" Ian shouted over his shoulder.

"We need to make a pit stop," Jaered said. "It's somewhere in here."

A control panel sat a few yards down the next stretch. When Ian pulled up beside it, Jaered hopped off the bike and opened the panel. He flipped a switch.

An explosion rang out behind them. The walls of the tunnel rumbled and shook but held. Despite the thickness of the tunnel, fiery flashes could be seen overhead in succession. It wasn't until then that Ian looked down. The entire tunnel was supported by steel platforms. He reached out and discovered that the tunnel wasn't made of ice, but a clear, flexible plastic. No wonder the tunnel hadn't collapsed during Patrick's quake or the destruction of the facility above. Jaered got back on the bike and patted Ian's shoulder. "Go."

The tunnel dropped in a gradual slope and soon ended in a large reinforced cave made of the same tunnel material. Rayne, Tara, and Milo were on a large fishing boat moored next to the water's edge. Their guns were aimed at the tunnel opening. They stood and smiled in relief.

Ian brought the snowmobile to a stop beside the others. When Jaered dismounted, Ian grabbed his arm. "What was that about? I thought the explosion was on a timer."

"She used herself to bait Aeros. But when he didn't show, we had to go to Plan B." Jaered slipped onto the boat and climbed to the upper deck. "We're not in the clear, not yet. Cover the tunnel entrance." He turned on a sonar and the beeps echoed off the frosty walls while the lapping waves kept the boat in constant motion. Saxon emerged from below deck. He stood at the base of the ladder and growled up at Jaered. "Get Fido out of my face or I'll lock him below," Jaered said without turning around.

"Saxon!" Ian called. The wolf joined Ian on the pier and sniffed about.

"Where are Patrick and Eve?" Rayne asked.

"They've gone to secure a new location," Jaered said. "If the coast is clear, we'll take off for open water and wait for new instructions."

"We'll need coffee. Tara, help me find the galley on this tugboat," Milo said.

"There's more weapons below," Jaered said. Tara tossed her rifle to Ian, and she followed Milo.

Ian crouched behind stacked crates on the dock and pointed his weapon at the tunnel. Saxon lingered to the side of the entrance at the ready.

Rayne held position at the rear of the boat. "And I thought Thrae was exciting," she said with a bemused grin.

The gentle lapping against the boat turned to pounding. "What's happening?" Rayne asked, steadying herself against the rear seat cushion.

"The explosions must have triggered an avalanche of ice." Jaered grabbed the railing next to the control panel with one hand while he held a headset next to his ear. "If I don't hear from Eve soon, we might have to shyft out of here."

Ian looked at Rayne. Her power drain would compromise shyfting with this large of a group. Jaered would have to take her.

Distant rumbling morphed into a looming freight train of twisting metal and broken struts. "Hang on!" Ian shouted. He waved at Saxon to move.

A tremendous cloud of silt and plastic burst out of the opening when the escape tunnel collapsed, sealing them off from any potential pursuers.

At the same time, a tremendous roar came from further down the icy channel as a wall of water rushed toward them. The wave lifted the boat toward the ceiling of the cavern and tilted it sideways. With a deafening creak, it headed for where Ian crouched, its whirring propellers chopping nothing but air. He dropped the rifle, raised his hands, and summoned as much power as he could to keep the boat from smashing onto the ice dock and splitting in two.

Jaered clung to the upper railing with both hands and swung wide, scrambling for a foothold.

Saxon swam toward the crates, but they washed away as the ocean swirled around Ian's knees. Rayne disappeared beneath the churning mass and she clamored to grab onto the moor post. Her head bobbed above water, gasping for air, a moment later. Saxon swam past. She grabbed the wolf with one hand and hung onto the post with the other.

A power drain ignited every nerve in Ian's body and he winced. Ian's hold on the boat waned as his core rapidly lost power. Rayne wasn't touching him. What was draining his core?

The second the ocean receded, Ian lowered the boat and fell to his knees, trembling.

"Are you all right?" Rayne spit salt water. "I felt it, too. What happened?"

Ian pushed his confusion aside at the clicks and metal of grinding gears coming from the rear of the boat. A barrage of curses floated down from the upper deck. Jaered threw Ian a concerned glance. The engines had flooded.

Rayne and Ian slipped back onto the boat. "Check on the others," he said, and she disappeared below deck. A moment later her fist appeared in the open doorway with a thumbs-up.

Ian opened the hatch and discovered a third of the engine was encased in salt water. He closed his eyes and concentrated, creating a water funnel below. It encircled the engine, sucking the water up in its swirling mass. The funnel rose above deck and when he spread his hands, it splashed off to the side. He summoned tremendous amounts of air, as powerful as a wind tunnel, and directed it over the soggy engine until it sputtered to life. He closed the compartment door.

"We're out of here!" Jaered shouted.

Ian leapt off the boat, untied the mooring, and returned with Saxon. He climbed the ladder and joined Jaered at the controls.

"We've got a new heading," Jaered said, setting the headset on its hook.

"Boat or shyft?" Ian asked.

"It's an approximate location, so we have a watery ride ahead." Jaered turned the wheel and the fishing boat swerved away from the remains of the dock.

The boat chugged along the narrow water passage for about a quarter mile, pushing floating ice chunks, many the size of small boulders, against the channel walls. The opening in the underground inlet was camouflaged by netting attached to the upper cave wall. One corner had detached and hung like a torn curtain. Jaered accelerated and the boat entered open water beyond. He spun the boat parallel to shore.

Ian took in the splendor of the calving glacier and its jutting, snowy spires rising a hundred or more feet to the sky. The moonlight cast varying shades of shadows in vertical lines, outlining the ancient ice finding its way to the sea. Thanks to global warming, at a faster rate than Mother Nature intended, Ian thought.

Flames danced above the ridge, consuming what was left of Eve's safe house and rebel training center. The boat slowed and everyone's faces were captured in a fiery glow as they stared at the destruction. Ian searched for survivors, but couldn't see anything through the roiling smoke.

The engines raced at top speed. Ian slumped onto a nearby cushion as Jaered swung the wheel and the boat headed into the ocean beyond.

FOUR

Around four in the morning, they abandoned the fishing boat about fifty miles off shore and shyfted to an oil tanker in the port of Hellissandur, Iceland. Ian took Saxon, Milo, and Tara. Jaered shyfted Rayne. When they reappeared, Jaered hid his discomfort, but Ian knew all too well what it felt like. Or was his power that much greater than Ian's? He wondered.

Within the hour, the tanker left port and slipped into the North Atlantic Ocean on schedule. The tension Ian had carried around eased and he gave into the fatigue. Eve controlled one of the largest shipping fleets in the world and the skeleton crew were members of her rebel forces. They were safe at the moment.

Ian leaned against the railing of the tanker and peered into the murky depths of the ocean below, curious how long the tanker could keep up the speed that Eve had commanded of the captain. They needed to keep one shyft ahead of Aeros launching another blitz attack.

Eve joined him at the railing and readjusted her shawl to better cover herself against the wind whipping across the enormous, weathered ship. Hair fell across her face, but she didn't pull it out of the way.

"Where are we headed?" Ian asked.

"South of the equator," she said. "But we'll be gone long before the ship reaches its destination."

"We can't keep running," Rayne said, stirring from under the thick blanket.

Ian had found the beat-up deck chair and claimed it for her a couple of hours before. It hadn't taken her long to fall into a deep slumber.

"There's got to be a way to take the fight to Aeros," Rayne said on the tail of a yawn.

"How many rebel troops do you have?" Ian asked.

"About one thousand," Eve said. "Scattered across Earth."

"And another four hundred from the Primary's penal colony. The ones you helped rescue from Thrae," Rayne said.

"They're not in the best of shape," Ian said. An uncomfortable pause heightened his concern.

"We'll meet after breakfast in the mess hall." Eve left them with a casual stride that did little to hide the frustration she must have felt.

Ian lifted his face to the cool gusts and inhaled the salty air. The squawk of a seagull split the calm. "Did you get much sleep?"

"A little." Rayne shed the blanket and stretched. "You look wiped, Ian."

"I'm not the only one." He rubbed his finger across the moist railing separating them from the vast ocean below. "You're different," he said a moment later.

"How so?" she asked.

"Your time on Thrae . . . hardened you." He tilted his head toward her, but the noise of the engines forced him to keep his voice raised. "You're tougher, more confident."

From her stare, she'd drifted miles away. "I'll never be able to forget what I saw and how Aeros massacred so many for the sport of it. Earth can't suffer the same fate."

"What about our fate?" Ian asked. "I've felt it over-taking us for the past couple of months. I blamed Jaered, but he's only one of the reasons."

"Jaered isn't your enemy, Ian," Rayne said.

"I know," he responded, but couldn't shake the feeling that his brother was his rival.

"I love *you*, Ian," she said gently and turned her brilliant blue eyes upon him. In the dark, they appeared as mirrored crystals, and he saw the truth to her words. He'd always been able to read her eyes. "There's been so much separating us," she said. "Right now, our focus needs to be Earth, not each other."

"I have to believe there's more out there than the next battle," he said.

Her heavy sigh grounded him like nothing else could. "What's more important than saving the planet, and with it, humanity?" She gripped the railing tight. "Isn't that enough?"

"Not since I met you." Ian fought not to pull her close and feel those soft lips upon his. How he longed to run his fingers through her silky hair, fill his lungs with her scent and lose himself to the woman he'd loved since opening the door to her, so many months ago. More than the Earth itself, Ian was prepared to die for Rayne Bevan.

The pain at their inability to touch reflected in her face. She pushed away from the railing and walked past him. Ian barely made out her parting words before they were stolen by the breeze. "I don't want to spend what time we have left, aching for what can never be."

Ian stared at the horizon trying to ease his shattered heart. A golden glow highlighted the edge of the vast ocean, a promise of a new day taking hold and pushing the darkness away. They had survived another day to fight the good fight, but even Rayne knew their days were numbered.

The ship's engines dropped to a crawl an hour later, long enough to allow Marcus to safely shyft onto the tanker. The old general arrived with an off-balance stumble. Ian and Jaered ran up to stabilize him before he landed on his derriere.

Milo's breakfast was devoured in a fraction of the time it'd taken to prepare. Tension revved faster than the ship's engines and their conversation raised to a deafening pitch. Marcus stood and cleared his throat, with his hairy caterpillar eyebrows bunched together. Saxon scampered out from beneath the kitchen table and sat at the alert.

"We don't have enough man power to launch an attack on Aeros and the Primary," Marcus said, giving voice to what Ian had already surmised.

"But there is a plan," Ian said. "You said as much when we returned from Thrae."

"We know *how* to defeat them, we just don't have the numbers to mount the assault," Eve said.

"Once the Pur army learns that Marcus is back, we can use them." Ian hoped Marcus wouldn't come to regret molding the Primary's army into such a skilled foe. "Your soldiers respected the hell out of you."

Marcus's jaw bulged. "The Primary made me a spectacle when he condemned me to his Thrae prison." Sadness crept into the general's face. They had rescued so many from that hellhole, but the general's son, Vael, hadn't made it.

Patrick's voice sounded in their ears. Thanks to the ship's cramped rooms, intercoms were the only way to communicate as a group. "If we can get most of the Pur army on our side, then we won't be battling them, too."

"The Primary cut off all communications with my former troops." Marcus rubbed his unshaven chin. "Scroll messages don't work. He's left me no choice but to arrange clandestine meetings with my most trusted lieutenants."

"A guaranteed trap," Jaered said.

Ian stared at his partially consumed breakfast. "How have the rebels kept in communication?"

"Unlike the antiquated Pur, we employ modern methods." Jaered withdrew his burner cell from a back pocket and placed it on the table.

Heat bristled at the back of Ian's neck and spread to his cheeks. "It's not the Pur's fault for living in the dark ages. The Primary kept them that way."

"Get on the same page, everyone!" Marcus roared. "This is no longer about Pur and Duach squabbles."

"We need all Weir to not only raise awareness, but bear arms against Aeros and the Primary," Eve said from the head of the table. "We're here for ideas."

"On Thrae, the penal colonists worked together for the good of the whole, and they were both Pur and Duach," Ian said as an idea took birth in his thoughts.

"How did they get past the Curse?" Rayne asked.

"The jam shut down their cores enough that they didn't affect each other," Ian said.

Marcus nodded. "Which in turn built up communication between them. They didn't coexist as opposing clans."

Ian stood and paced around the table. "Survival at its best."

"The penal colonists have sworn their allegiance to the rebels," Marcus said. "We can use them to help spread the word."

The renewed energy in Marcus's voice stirred Ian's excitement. "Most of them hailed from Earth. They have families, friends, acquaintances."

Eve sobered. "We need to be cautious. As word gets out, the more likely the blind and loyal will leak information to

Aeros, or the Primary. I've taken great pains to keep the rebels hidden and protected."

"Your caution has kept us from recruiting effectively," Jaered said. "We can't afford to do business as usual, not any longer." He pushed back his chair and stood. "I'll get word to my fellow Thraens here on Earth. Gather as many Pur and Duach as you can, then choose a location large enough that we can safely meet as one."

"We'll need a pretty powerful jam for that large of a group," Ian said.

"Leave those logistics to me," Eve said.

Jaered regarded Eve. "We need a common leader. With you at the helm—"

"I'm not your leader," she said. "When we give them not one, but *three* Heirs, only then will we unite all Weir."

"The Pur are loyal to the Primary," Ian said. "Not me."

"You're wrong, boy," Marcus said. "The Pur looked the other way when captured Duach went missing, but the Primary shot himself in the foot when he tortured and killed his Pur enemies. You're the one who saved them."

"Where do I come in?" Patrick's voice piped up. "The Duach don't know squat about me. I'll hardly come across as their leader when the time comes."

"Duach rebels understood the need to keep your existence hidden. Soon, everyone will know who you are," Eve said.

"Knowing isn't the same as loyalty," Patrick said.

"Then prove yourself the best way you can," Ian said. "I saw you in action last night."

The clatter of dishes stopped. Milo half-turned from the sink and touched his ear with a sudsy finger. "When you were Ian's manager, no one handled the press like you. For all your bullshit, you can give a hell of a speech."

"This is what you three were born to be," Eve said with more conviction than Ian had ever heard her use. "It's time you act the part."

Memories of the previous night's battle returned in the form of a nagging naysayer, and Ian shook his head. "Uniting the Pur and Duach won't do us any good if we can't fight together. A jam might help build communication, but it prevents us from using our core powers side by side in battle."

"Meaning?" Rayne asked.

"We've got to find a way to negate the Curse." As soon as it passed his lips, Ian realized how ludicrous it sounded.

"That's like proposing we change our eye color," Marcus said. "We're born this way."

"Ian's right." Jaered said. "What good are those two by my side if they keep getting in each other's way."

"What about the Book of the Weir?" Patrick asked. "What does it say about the Curse?"

"My sisters and I only documented Weir history, the coming of the three Heirs, and compiled Sar powers in the Book," Eve said. "Once Aeros stole it, nothing else was added."

"We don't have the Curse phenomenon on Thrae. Why?" Jaered asked.

Eve pursed her lips and leaned back in her seat. "Centuries ago when Aeros turned his attention to Earth, the two brothers came to an accord. Aeros and the Primary devised a way to keep their two factions separate, to prevent one group from defecting to the other."

The room quieted as several pairs of eyes stared at Eve. Marcus's face turned a bright pink. "The Curse was . . . *created?*"

"Aeros and the Primary found a way to separate Earth's energies," she continued. "Aeros paired the Duach cores directly with Earth's planetary center. That's why so many Duachs possess core blast power."

"What are Pur cores linked to?" Marcus asked.

"The Primary has always feared loss of control over his chosen world of Earth," Eve said. "He made sure no Pur would ever develop greater power than his. The Pur cores pull their energy from the surface of the planet."

Ian stilled as the last of the truths, and misinformation about Weir history, fell into place. "We have to stop the Curse if we're going to win this war. It's the only way to unite all Weir." "I'll return to Thrae and convince my mother to come back with me," Ian said. "If anyone can figure this out, it's her."

"What you're proposing could still take years, Ian. Earth doesn't have that kind of time," Rayne said.

"Nor does Thrae," Jaered said.

"There is one other option." Eve hesitated as though choosing her next words carefully. "We make the Primary do it for us."

FIVE

Patrick's thoughts swirled faster than his pulse, and he removed his earpiece to ease the rising headache. Marcus and his mother locked themselves behind closed doors, devising a plan that wouldn't get everyone killed. Eavesdropping at the door was impossible over the grinding of the ship's engines and the vibration it caused throughout the ship.

Two days later, their rested and well-fed group stood on the main deck of the tanker, divided into sub-groups. Jaered oversaw Tara and Patrick. Marcus was paired with Ian and Rayne.

Eve and Tara spoke in hushed whispers off to the side. Patrick's curiosity was piqued when he saw his mother touch Tara's forearm like something were there. Tara kept nodding at whatever last-minute instructions his mother provided. A moment later, they joined the rest of the group. If Tara noticed Patrick's questioning stare, she ignored it.

Milo clasped Eve's hand and they shyfted.

Marcus checked his watch. "We're to give them a head start," he said.

"Other than the big picture, we still don't know anything," Ian said.

"The squad leaders have the preliminary info," Marcus said. "At each step, we'll get the next phase of our mission."

"Kept in the dark as usual," Patrick muttered.

"This was put together on the fly," Marcus said. "For some of this, we're making arrangements on the go."

"At least let me shyft us there," Ian said. "Rayne's energy drain is greater than you realize. I'm the more powerful shyftor."

"No worries. I've got this covered," Marcus said, checking his watch. "Jaered, you're on."

Tara and Patrick huddled together with Jaered and the they clasped hands. Tingling. Jaered shyfted them to a storage room in the heart of a commercial office building. They exited onto a hallway lined on one side with office doors. The surroundings gave Patrick pause. He turned, taking in the familiar carpet, walled art, and views outside the floor-to-ceiling windows across from the offices.

"I know this place," Patrick said. "My father's office is on the top floor."

Tara's eyes widened. "Aeros?"

"His other father," Jaered said. "Meet us under the Arc de Triomphe." Jaered tugged on Tara's sleeve and they headed for the stairs, leaving a bewildered Patrick standing alone.

"What am I supposed to do?" Patrick said.

"Eve said you'd figure it out," Jaered said, entering the stairwell with Tara in tow.

Two businessmen rounded the corner and strolled toward Patrick, engaged in conversation. *Ding.* The elevator doors opened and a woman stepped out. Patrick slipped inside a second before the doors closed.

He pressed the button for the topmost floor and was thankful when the rising metal box took on additional passengers for three more floors. It'd been over two years since Patrick had seen his father, and it didn't take family counseling to know where his mother's head was at. There hadn't been a chance to talk with her, ever since she dropped the bomb of the century on his head that Aeros was his biological father. She expected Patrick to come to grips with that on his own. Typical.

The other passengers were deposited on upper floors and by the time the elevator's *ding* announced the top floor, Patrick was alone. At a *swish*, the elevator doors opened.

Patrick exited and his core's energy swirled deep inside his chest. He took deep breaths to gain control of his emotions.

Like everything in his life, he was under his mother's control. He stood mulling over what to do next. The receptionist behind the counter eyed him with a mixture of curiosity and concern.

"*Puis-je vous aider?*" she said. When he didn't respond, she stood. "May I help you?"

"Is Simon Langtree in today?" Patrick asked.

"Do you have an appointment?" When Patrick shook his head, she pursed her lips. "His schedule is quite full." She adjusted the slim microphone on her headset. "Who may I say is calling?"

"His son," Patrick said. For the first time in his life, it felt disconcerting to say aloud. Did his father know the truth about Patrick's conception? Was his father Weir or human, or both? Was he another servant to his mother, or a convenient figurehead, helping to keep up appearances? Did any of this matter in the bigger scheme of things?

The emotions playing across Patrick's face must have piqued the receptionist's curiosity, and she glanced at his father's portrait hanging on the wall next to where Patrick stood. From the flicker of her gaze, she seemed to be weighing the truth that Patrick was indeed her boss's son. Did the woman notice the facial dissimilarities between him and his father that never occurred to Patrick until this moment?

"Was he expecting you?" Her attention fell to her computer screen.

"No, I've popped into town for a couple of hours, and thought I'd stop by," he said.

She sat down, speaking in French into her microphone. Patrick wandered into the waiting room with its modern décor of leather chairs and glass tables. No surprise his father choose style over comfort.

How easy to slip into a disgruntled mood. It was only two days earlier that Patrick had thought of himself as the son of a billionaire. He reminded himself not to draw undue attention, to relax and not think too hard. He swiped his sweaty palms across his pants and hoped the receptionist didn't notice.

The view of the Champs-Élysée below bustled with midday shoppers, lunch-goers, and tourists. Patrick searched for Jaered and Tara in the crowd, but didn't spy Tara's cascading white hair, or Jaered's scowl.

"Patrick?" came from behind. Simon Langtree stood next to the receptionist's desk doing his best to hide his irritation. His father's coiffed hair was unkempt behind one ear, and his shirt was loose around the middle, like it'd been hastily tucked back into his pants.

Patrick's surprise visit had interrupted something other than a business meeting. "Hello, Dad."

"Come, I can only spare a few minutes." His father led him down the long hallway to his executive suite. His private secretary stuffed a compact in her desk drawer when the door opened, and she gave Patrick an awkward smile.

"Ginette, hold my calls for a few minutes." His father stepped inside his office and leaned against the edge of his desk. "Close the door, son."

Patrick shut it and hesitated. He'd never known what to say to his father.

"What brought you to town?" his father asked. "The last I heard, you and your magician friend were taking some time off from doing tricks."

"I've been spending some time with Mother," Patrick said, dismissing the slight as he'd done most others. "I'm in town with friends and thought I'd pop in." When his father didn't respond, Patrick blamed his mother for their lifelong inability to communicate. "You look good," he said.

"As do you," his father replied, glancing at the clock on the wall. "I don't have time for lunch. If you'd let me know you were coming, I could have had Ginette move my calendar around."

"No worries," Patrick said, anxious not to drag the encounter out. "I wanted to see you one last time."

The choice of words didn't slip past his father, and he rose to his full height with genuine concern deepening the lines of his face. "Are you okay? I get the impression there's something you're not telling me."

"Why haven't we spent more time together, Dad? What went wrong between you and Mother?" Patrick asked.

His father inhaled so deep it could be heard across the room. Or, was it obvious because of Patrick's enhanced hearing? "I suppose I knew this conversation was inevitable. I'm surprised it took this long." His father sobered and turned toward the window. "I married your mother for her money, Patrick. It may sound heartless and cold, but she was no fool and knew who, and what, I was, maybe even better than I knew myself."

"Mother isn't sinless," Patrick said and clenched his fists to stop the rise in his core temperature.

"No, but whatever agendas take her away for days or weeks at a time, she always comes back to me. And make no mistake, she has been one hundred percent devoted to you since the day you were born. I've often thought you were all she ever wanted, perhaps needed. It wasn't me. I was lucky enough to go along for the ride." He turned and approached Patrick, grasped his son's shoulders and gave him a genuine smile. "You're loved by both of us, in our own way, son. Never forget that."

Patrick embraced his father. The man returned with a gentle pat on Patrick's back. When Patrick didn't loosen his grip, his father returned the hug with greater emotion.

"I'm sorry we weren't more of a close-knit, traditional family for you. I do regret that, truly."

Patrick pulled away and wiped his nose with the back of his hand. "I've got to go. My friends are waiting."

"I'll take that rain check on lunch," his father said. "Next time you're in town."

"Next time." Patrick walked out of the office, passing the befuddled secretary and wondered what were the odds he'd ever see his father again. He rode the elevator down, inwardly damning his mother for setting him up. Yet, by the time the lift reached the lobby, he'd forgiven her, thankful for the opportunity to see his father for what might be the last time.

Patrick found Tara taking pictures of the Arc de Triomphe with her phone. He wasn't sure if she was acting the tourist to blend in, or if she was relishing in the history of the structure. No matter the reason, the weight that Patrick carried with him lifted the moment he set eyes on her.

A few feet away, Jaered stood with his back to them. He'd pulled his visor over his face and kept his head down.

"I'm hungry," Tara announced. "Your mother said to grab lunch while we were here."

"I know a place," Patrick said, and he grasped Tara's hand. "You're going to love it. It's one of the few places I spent with my father and mother whenever we were in town."

SIX

Marcus shyfted Ian and Rayne to a tree line near a small lake. As Ian suspected, it took a couple of minutes for Marcus to recover from Rayne's energy drain to his core. When Ian realized they'd returned to his former estate, he placed himself between Rayne and the open grounds.

"Why the hell are we at the mansion?" Ian asked the ashen-faced Marcus.

"We're meeting Eve and Milo here," Marcus said.

"But doesn't the Primary have Pur guards patrolling the mansion grounds?" Rayne asked.

"According to her intel, they were pulled out when you went to Thrae. They haven't returned."

"Still, it's a huge risk for us to be here," Rayne said.

Ian peered over the lake. The site of his abandoned home shattered his world. He rose to his full height, stunned.

"Ian, what is it?" Rayne asked.

On the other side of the lake, Ian's childhood home, the only one he'd ever known, was in shambles. The mansion roof looked like it'd been ripped off by a giant hand, leaving a gaping hole and exposing the inner rooms to the natural elements. The outside brick walls stood with a jagged upper edge where the roof had caved in.

"What happened?" Rayne asked.

Ian made his way toward the ruins along the path at the lake's edge. The reason the Primary withdrew his patrols was clear. There was nothing to come back to.

The lake glistened in the afternoon, California sun. Memories of swimming with Tara and Mara returned with a gut-wrenching, painful blow, and tied knots in Ian's gut with each step. Shock gave way to anguish and he slowed his steps, unsure if he could bear to see what was left of the mansion.

They approached the devastation in silence. Ian bent down to touch a piece of the front door, splintered into wooden slats and scattered across the porch. Slivers of his ancestral, stained glass that used to line the doorway lay in shattered pieces at his feet.

"Who could have done such a thing?" Rayne asked.

He stepped into what used to be the two-story foyer and paused at the sight of the sun inlaid table. It rested on its side against the far wall. The intricately crafted table was broken in two and ruined beyond repair.

Ian entered with slow steps and raised his face to the gaping hole overhead, by sheer will keeping the despair from taking hold. He closed his eyes against the destruction, drawing upon happier memories and struggling to wake from this nightmare.

"I'm not sure who is ultimately responsible," Eve said from the balcony where she and Milo stood. The old caretaker trembled with white-knuckled fists. The moment their gaze met, the two shared their suffering in silence.

"Why?" Rayne asked.

"It could have been Aeros," Eve said.

"It was the Primary," Milo said. "He's not keen on defectors."

Ian wandered into the shell of the great room. Chunks of the stone fireplace mantel lay among the wreckage. Perhaps the Primary and Aeros destroyed Ian's home together. He imagined them dividing up the mansion, room by room. Or had they simply unleashed their tremendous fury on whatever surface caught their eye?

The others joined him and they stood in shocked silence.

"Why bring me here?" Ian asked a moment later.

"Closure," Eve said. "To give you a chance to say farewell to your human side. The Pur rejected you because you chose to live as human these past few years, Ian. You must become who you are, if the Pur are to follow you."

And set aside childish things, Ian thought. For most of his life, he'd walked in both worlds, human and Weir. He soaked in the memories of growing up in the mansion and the life he'd enjoyed. Milo snapping kitchen towels at the chasing children. Playing hide-and-seek with Mara and Tara in the escape tunnels below the mansion. He'd spent many of his teenage years believing this place to be a prison. How wrong he'd been.

"Thank you, Milo," Ian said.

"For what?" He gave Ian a puzzled look.

"For giving me a childhood I failed to appreciate at the time," Ian said.

The old caretaker's chest heaved. "The pleasure was all mine."

Milo, Ian, and Rayne gathered a handful of pictures but left everything else they found where it lay. The group wandered along the foot path in an impromptu vigil and came to the gravesite of Galen, Ian's mentor, and Mara, Tara's twin.

Ian surveyed the surroundings, thankful the Primary and Aeros's wrath had left their graves intact. It was not long ago that they'd lowered their bodies into the ground, returning them to the earth from which all living things came. When his thoughts touched upon the Primary, and the memory of him standing at the foot of their graves giving their eulogy, Ian's resolve crumbled and the wind picked up, becoming a forceful gale. He rocked on his feet as the wind tore branches off nearby trees and whipped up waves on the lake.

A lightning bolt struck the lake. "Ian!" Rayne shouted over the thunderclap. Eve stopped her from reaching for Ian. Milo stepped up beside him and laid a gentle hand on his shoulder.

"The Primary was responsible for Galen and Mara's deaths," Ian yelled over the lightening. "I see that now."

"Calm yourself, Ian," Milo shouted over the storm. "Save it for when it matters most. Don't say your good-byes to them in anger."

The tears weren't to be denied. They streamed across Ian's cheeks, moistening his face and washing away the worst of his rage. The lightening ceased at the same time the winds faded into gusts. "They won't have died in vain," Ian whispered.

Milo's grip on his shoulder tightened. "No, boy. We'll both see to that."

Eve linked arms with Ian and led him farther down the path as if taking a leisurely stroll. She must have signaled the others, because they remained at the gravesite.

"I have a secret I need to share with you," she said.

"There's no structure on Earth that's large enough to hold your secrets," Ian said. He stopped and faced her.

"It's about Jaered." She averted her eyes. "I've kept something from him because I needed him to stay focused these past few years. I couldn't afford for him to be distracted."

"You needed him compliant," Ian said. He thought of how the Primary had fed him lies all his life. Patrick and Jaered were no exception. Manipulation was second nature to the Ancients.

"I'm sending you and Rayne back to Thrae," Eve said.

Ian's breath caught in his throat. "Are you mad? We barely escaped with our lives a mere two days ago. Aeros killed dozens of people chasing after us. And you want to repeat that carnage?"

"You need to convince Oocaw to come to Earth." Eve's gaze hardened and she widened her stance. "The dragon knows you and Rayne. If anyone can convince her, you can."

"You're condemning the Thraens to death."

"If the data your mother sent back with Jaered holds true, Aeros isn't their biggest threat any longer. The planet is about to implode. You need to evacuate the remaining populace. Her voice lowered and she leaned close. "And there's someone who's been hidden there, out of Aeros's reach, who must be escorted back."

"The secret you've kept from Jaered," Ian said. Eve's next words boiled the blood in his veins. He'd been wrong and had grossly underestimated how manipulative Eve could be.

SEVEN

Patrick continued to enjoy the exquisite aftertaste of the Bordeaux he'd treated himself to at lunch in the Renaissance Paris Vendome Hotel, overlooking the Eiffel Tower. He couldn't help but think of it as his last meal.

He paid the bill with his mother's credit card per her instructions, and while he waited for the waitress to return with the receipt, he wondered why Jaered chose not to join them. Patrick had never seen him this antsy before and wasn't sure if Jaered felt out of place in such a high-society environment, or was anxious to connect with their rebel contact, someone who worked in a dress boutique in the heart of the Champs Élysée

Jaered didn't return, so Patrick and Tara hurried to the boutique to make the rendezvous as scheduled. A smiling woman greeted them at the door, but her welcome drooped when Tara asked for their contact by name. The saleswoman gestured toward an older woman handing a customer a bag.

Their contact walked her satisfied customer to the door, then whisked Tara out of sight with the promise that matters were expertly in her hands.

The longer Tara was gone trying on clothes, the more Patrick's tapping foot and twitchy hands fed his unease. Where the hell was Jaered?

A woman in business attire strolled into the boutique and set down her briefcase next to Patrick's chair. She bent down, perusing the jewelry draped on a miniature replica of the Eiffel Tower. Having found something to her liking, she wandered to the sales counter and made the purchase, then exited the boutique. She'd left the briefcase behind.

The curtain *swished* open to reveal Tara and her new outfit. The saleslady had indeed transformed her into a chic businesswoman. The gushing woman twirled her finger at Tara to show her gentlemen suitor with the Platinum Card the full ensemble. Tara obliged with a disgruntled expression. Her long snowy hair was twisted in a wide braid and fastened at the back of her head with a metallic comb that came to a sharp point. Patrick didn't doubt Tara had picked that one out herself. She could turn it into a lethal weapon at a moment's notice. They'd chosen a short-skirted suit, enhancing the curves of Tara's hips with a deep slit up the side that wouldn't impair her during a foot chase. The low-heeled pumps could be kicked off if needed. Her face was radiant thanks to full makeup behind wide designer glasses.

It clicked. His mother's credit card, familiar haunts. It wasn't Patrick the Duach Heir and rebel that Eve wanted on display. It was Patrick Langtree, son of billionaires, with his girlfriend. Patrick stared as Tara strode toward him with the grace of a well-bred collegiate. As they turned to leave, the saleslady handed Patrick the briefcase.

Tara linked her arm in his and ushered him out the door with a grateful smile tossed at the saleswoman. "Close that gaping mouth, my love. It's your turn."

"What do you mean?" Patrick asked.

She handed him a slip of paper. "The contact said to go here."

They found the custom tailor's shop halfway down the street, and separated just inside the door. Tara flipped through the assorted silk neckties near the counter. Patrick recognized an older gentleman, down on one knee, tugging at the bottom of a man's pant leg. He couldn't remember the man's name, but he was someone his father used for most of his custom-made suits. Other than coming to the shop, Patrick was unclear about his next step and went about the motions of choosing a suit material from a display of bolts.

"Buy yourself a suit off the rack, then meet me in the coffee shop across the street in twenty minutes," a voice said from behind. It was Jaered.

"Where the hell have you been?" Patrick hushed.

"I can't be seen with you for this to work," he said. A moment later, the bell at the door signaled he'd left.

Any tension Patrick had been carrying dispersed by the time they crossed the busy street and entered the local café. He hated to admit it, but he felt safer with Jaered around. Movement at the back of the café. Jaered tossed down some cash and let himself into the rear storage room.

Tara and Patrick followed. Even before he stepped inside, Patrick's core came alive. There was a powerful vortex between the shelves lined with cans and boxes. Jaered closed the door. Bright sparks appeared while an intense tingling formed in the center of Patrick's chest. They grasped hands. Patrick filled his lungs in preparation for Jaered's powerful shyft. "Where are we going?" Patrick asked.

"South of the equator," Jaered said. "Hope you put on fresh deodorant with that new suit." They shyfted and reappeared in the outdoors. "Welcome to Brazil," Jaered announced.

The morning sun blistered Patrick's cheeks. Jaered had shyfted them to a secluded airstrip, surrounded by thick trees and shrubbery. Patrick brought the edge of his hand up to his forehead, searching for a control tower, any vantage point where someone might have noticed their sudden appearance. Except for the crumbling runway, the airstrip was isolated.

"It's typically used by drug smugglers," Jaered said. The rebel walked to the far side of the tarmac and lifted a rock the size of a toaster. It proved hollow, and he removed a walkie-talkie hidden beneath it. When Jaered brought it to his lips, he wandered away from Tara and Patrick.

"You look, uh, different," Patrick said, nudging a chip of concrete with his shoe.

"You don't," she said, eyeing his tailor-made suit.

He gave a slight bow. "Patrick Langtree, manager of Fade to Black Productions, at your service," he said, overcome with melancholy.

She straightened his tie though it didn't need it, and gave him a reserved smile. "Are you ready for this? We can't have your powers going berserk."

"I'm as cool as a cucumber," Patrick said. "You should be worried about Grumpy Dwarf over there." He tilted his head in Jaered's direction.

"He's got skills that amaze even me." Tara grew serious. "I trust him, and your mother trusts him even more. You should, too."

"I do," Patrick said. From Tara's raised eyebrow, she didn't believe him. "But trust isn't the same as like," he muttered under his breath.

Jaered stopped several feet from them, staring at a line of trees. A few minutes passed. The humidity had to be close to a hundred percent and beads of sweat dripped down Patrick's chest beneath his two-hundred-dollar shirt. He wiped perspiration from his forehead, but not before it dripped and stung his eyes. Tara didn't appear phased by the heat. Flapping wings and squawks came from a flock of birds at the tree line. A helicopter flew toward them.

"That's our ride," Jaered said. He returned the walkie-talkie to its hiding spot.

The aircraft approached, then hovered until Jaered waved with bent fingers. It must have been a signal because the whirlybird lowered, touching down with the blades whipping up dirt around them. Tara pressed her hands at her sides to keep her skirt from flying up. Patrick grabbed the briefcase when it fell over.

The helicopter's paint job glistened in the sun. From its size, it could easily seat six or more. It spoke money and prestige.

Jaered opened the side door to reveal an opulent, leather interior. Other than the serial number on the tail, there were no other markings. The pilot wore dark reflective glasses, a lightweight, and a black baseball cap. He resembled a bush pilot and seemed out of place in such a fancy bird.

Jaered assisted Tara with getting in and then offered a hand to Patrick, who declined the help. This wasn't Patrick's first helicopter ride. Jaered left him and chose a seat next to the pilot up front. Patrick closed the side door and sat across from Tara. He gestured for her to put on her headphones, then slid his on and adjusted them over his ears.

"Buckle up and settle in," the pilot said over their intercoms. "We've got an hour flight ahead of us." The helicopter rose high into the air, hovered for a second above the tarmac, then dipped and turned in the direction it had come, flying low over the trees. The thick jungle offered a variety of vegetation with sprawling trees, broad-leafed vines, and some breathtaking waterfalls. Patrick marveled at the variations of greens creating a patchwork across the landscape. The brush dropped off into sparkling waters and the helicopter descended, leveling off over the ocean. When he squinted, Patrick made out the lighter blues of shallow reef with the richer blues of deeper water beyond.

"We've left the archipelago and are headed to the city of São Paulo," the pilot announced.

"Archipelago?" Patrick asked, but he failed to speak into his microphone and he didn't receive a response.

"He means the cluster of islands," Tara shouted. "They're environmentally protected by the State of Brazil." She leaned her forehead against the window, gazing downward. Her curiosity at the scene below confused Patrick. He swung the microphone around to his mouth. "You act like you've never been here before," he said.

A gust slammed into the side of the helicopter and they grabbed the edge of their seats. "You miss a lot when you're always shyfting, you know? This is the first time I've had a birds-eye view, ever," she said. Something below excited her, and she pressed her nose up against the glass. "It's a school of fish!"

Patrick watched Tara experience a new take on the world that she loved and had spent a lifetime fighting to protect. He didn't bother to look out the window. He enjoyed this view just fine.

The helicopter touched down at the edge of the São Paulo Guarulhos Airport where a stretch limo awaited their arrival. Patrick channeled his inner spy and realized tinted windows would allow them the option of shyfting into and out of the limo if the need arose.

Jaered hopped out of the helicopter. To Patrick's surprise, he had changed clothes on the ride, and wore a uniform with a brimmed cap pulled low over his face. He ran around to open the side door and helped Tara from the whirlybird. When Patrick waved him off, Jaered stood his ground.

"From this point on, the more formal the better," he said. "You're here as JoAnna Langtree's son and business representative. Forget that you're a Duach Heir. Be who you used to be."

"Chauffeur, bodyguard or both?" Patrick asked, eyeing his outfit.

"Whichever one gets you out of this helicopter," Jaered said.

Patrick smiled wide. "So essentially you work for me."

"Good luck with that," Jaered said without a lick of amusement. He gestured for Patrick to grab the briefcase.

They headed for the limo while commercial jetliners took off and landed overhead every minute or so. A common occurrence at the busiest airport in São Paulo.

Jaered opened the side door of the limo. "What about luggage? Won't it be suspicious when we check into a hotel without it?"

"You're not used to trusting your mother, are you?" Jaered said.

Tara pulled on Patrick's arm to get into the waiting car. He joined her in the back seat with brewing questions. Jaered shut the door with a resounding *Bang*, then slipped behind the wheel in the front cab.

The limo pulled out of the airport and headed for their hotel in the heart of the city. "Check the briefcase," Tara said.

Patrick discovered it was unlocked. It held information about a local bank, and the name of the bank manager. A time was handwritten at the bottom. Nine a.m. Stapled to it was a prospectus about a mining operation in southern Brazil. "We have a meeting with a banker, first thing in the morning," he said. He pressed the intercom button at his ear. "There's no mention of why I'm supposed to meet with this banker."

"You'll be briefed at the hotel, Oh Impatient One," Jaered said. "Unless you know for a fact the limo isn't bugged."

Patrick looked to Tara for confirmation. She pressed her ear bud. "Understood." She slid over against Patrick and ran her finger across his lips. "I have a few ideas how to quell that anxiety of yours," she murmured. She straddled his lap in one swift move and cupped his face, gazing into his eyes like she would dive inside his heart at any minute.

He appreciated the deep slit in her skirt as his hands moved up her thighs. When she didn't object, he pressed her hard against him. Her tongue parted his lips. In no time at all, they managed to erase everything outside the limo, Jaered in the driver's seat, and their purpose for being there. Tara revealed a side of herself Patrick never knew existed and the rugged, Amazon woman he knew slipped away. Their breaths came as rapid as their pulse and he reveled in her taste, committing her sexual scent to memory. When his fingers found her moist and wanting, a groan rose above their heated breaths. She abandoned his lips, resting her forehead against his. Her passion came out as sweltering gusts against his skin.

His mouth sagged, and he closed his eyes, unable to look at her, hoping the warmth in his face hid any embarrassment that he'd gone too far.

"We can't," she said, brushing her lips against his forehead and raising goosebumps down his arms. "Not here, not like this." Tara slid off him and adjusted her skirt. She clasped his hand tight and brought her mouth to his ear. "We may have an audience," she said for his ears only.

He nodded, wondering if that was all an act. If Tara was simply playing the girlfriend role. God, it sucked to be a spy, he thought.

It took forever for his heartbeat to return to normal as he stared out the window trying to focus on something other than the ache between his legs. In contrast to the dense surrounding forest, São Paulo was the city-state's urban jungle, filled with skyscrapers crafted in the modern amidst the historical buildings of a lost era. The religious, Italian, Portuguese, AfroBrazilian, and American influences could be seen everywhere. They passed what appeared to be a nod to the Brooklyn Bridge in New York, and the Banespa Skyscraper was a clone of the Empire State Building. The limo continued with its picturesque driving tour, taking its occupants past the Monumento às Bandeiras with its stone depiction of Portuguese explorers in a Soviet-style sculpture. Beyond, fountains jutted high above the lakes of Ibirapuera Park.

"What's the sightseeing tour about?" Patrick muttered. A part of him was thankful for the delay.

"Marcus said Eve had to scramble to organize this," Tara said for his ears only. "The rebels probably needed to gather the necessary equipment and sweep the hotel room for bugs."

"We are almost to your hotel. I hope you enjoyed the tour of the city," Jaered said in Patrick's ear.

Patrick cringed. Did he eavesdrop on them the entire time? The heat resurfaced and Patrick rubbed his face vigorously to cover it up.

A few minutes later, the limo pulled to a stop at the Hotel Unique. A bellman rushed up with a brass-plated cart while one of the doormen rushed over and opened the side door for Patrick and Tara. Jaered stepped in and gave the man a cursory pat-down before moving aside to let the man offer a helping hand.

"Don't you think he's overdoing this?" Tara said, standing on the curb.

"It's all about appearances. This is one of the worst crime-infested cities in the world," Patrick said. They approached the hotel lobby while suitcases were removed from the trunk of the limo and loaded onto the cart. Patrick couldn't help but wonder what was inside them.

His mother had chosen a hilltop resort hotel with sleek lines, a fully modern motif and impressive architecture. It was also smaller than other resorts he'd stayed at in the past. From what Patrick could tell, it offered fewer than a hundred rooms.

Patrick approached the receptionist and set the briefcase next to the counter. He relayed the reservation number texted to his smartwatch moments before they arrived.

"Where's the pool?" Tara asked, indicating the sign advertising the hotel's architectural awards.

"It's on the roof, madam," said the receptionist. She gave Tara a wide smile while her eyes drank in Tara's expensive outfit. According to the woman, they had reservations for one of the upper-floor suites with multiple bedrooms.

Patrick finished checking in. When they entered the elevator, Jaered pressed the rooftop/pool button.

"Aren't we going to settle in the suite first?" Patrick asked.

"Bug sweep or not, I'm more trusting of unexpected locales for our briefing." Jaered leaned against the back wall of the elevator and dropped his face.

Patrick glanced up at what Jaered already had surmised. A security camera had eyes on the elevator. "If you're concerned with being recognized, should we?"

"You're the bait. By now, the Primary's wondering why you're here. He won't approach you, not at first. He'll keep a tight leash on you, though." Jaered took the briefcase from Patrick when the elevator opened. They stepped out to blinding sunlight and a panoramic view of the city. The narrow, crimson pool stretched from one end of the hotel to the other. Jaered took an offered towel from a young teenager. "Guard the door," Jaered said.

The white-uniformed youth grabbed a handgun from between the folds of another towel and faced the elevator.

Patrick voiced the obvious. "One of ours?"

"A friend to the rebels. Word is spreading fast among the Duach not smitten with Aeros." The teen stared at Patrick with nothing short of awe. "You're apparently quite the celebrity," Jaered said. He chose a seat at one of the umbrella tables. Towering glass panels separated the pool area from the edge of the building. The heat of the day kept the winds to a minimum. Jaered pushed the towel toward Patrick. "Make yourself useful, Oh Exalted One."

"Those are getting old," Patrick said.

"Too bad, I've got a million of them," Jaered said with a smirk.

Patrick picked up the towel, surprised by the weight. He unwrapped it and discovered a handgun with a silencer attached. A fully loaded clip was next to it. He inserted it and loaded a round.

Jaered removed the paperwork from the opened briefcase and handed the pages to Tara. "The Primary has kept a tight hold on the world economic market, amassing tremendous wealth over the years," Jaered said while searching the pockets of the briefcase. "What has baffled Eve was why the Primary would allow his megalomaniac brother to slowly take control of Earth and ruin what he had built."

"And we're here to find out the answer?" Tara asked.

"We're to verify what her spy suspects," Jaered said. "That he's set his sights on a new planet in a neighboring dimension." Jaered ran his fingers across the briefcase lining.

"When the Primary realized he couldn't stop Aeros from taking over, he chose another planet unmarred by his brother," Tara said.

"And has already begun to transfer his accumulated wealth there," Jaered said. "The problem is, Eve doesn't know which one."

"So where do we come in?" Patrick asked.

Jaered's fingers paused at the base of the briefcase. He raised a switchblade in his other hand and it opened with a *click*. He jammed it into the lining with the skill of an apprentice butcher and ripped it open, then removed a computer chip. Jaered shut the blade by pressing it against his hip.

"What's that?" Tara asked.

"Our ticket into the Primary's bank account," Jaered said. He flipped open a secret compartment in the side of the briefcase and inserted the chip into a slot. A scarlet penlight appeared next to the handle.

"Aren't we in the wrong country?" Patrick asked.

"The Primary's bank is in Geneva," Tara said.

"That's where he does Weir business." Jaered shut the ruined briefcase. "São Paulo is where he keeps *his* wealth." He gave Patrick and Tara a smile which unnerved Patrick more than the next words out of his mouth. "And we're here to steal it."

EIGHT

I t wasn't until Milo and Eve were gone that Ian realized he didn't know how to contact them upon his return.

"All right, we've got a job to do," Marcus announced. "For this next part, I'm going to need you to do the heavy shyfting, boy."

"Where are we going?" Rayne asked.

Ian glared at Marcus. "We're headed back to Thrae."

Rayne's mouth fell open. "You're not serious," she said. "If Aeros finds out—"

"We're parashyfting during an earthquake. Eve swears Aeros won't detect it and come after us," Marcus said. "We're on a recruiting mission."

"Those people have been through hell. We can't ask anything else of them," Rayne said.

"We're not trying to recruit Thraens." Marcus rounded a curve in the path. "We're after the creatures that live there."

Rayne and Ian came to a halt. "Oocaw," Rayne said.

"Aeros's Duach army are mostly Core Blasters," Marcus said. "The dragon and another creature are impervious to the blasts. We need as many of them as we can get." The old general rounded a curve in the path, and then stood, staring at a wide field that Ian didn't recall had been there before.

Ian blinked. The remains of the once lush and majestic forest beyond his home resembled a battlefield wasteland. Charred nubs of centuries-old trees tall enough to block out the sun were downed or missing amidst a desiccated landscape. The small fire that killed Mara a few months earlier had been nothing but tinder compared to the destruction yielded by Aeros and the Primary. Whichever brother was responsible, they'd taken the life of the entire estate.

"This is what we'll bring back to Thrae if we return," Ian said.

Marcus grunted. "Don't kid yourself. Thrae's worse."

Rayne continued walking down the path, taking the lead. "No matter what happens, we'll have blood on our hands."

They reached the northern vortex building and entered the gaping hole where Aeros had ripped off the front wall in his attempt to intercept Ian, Rayne, and Jaered a couple days earlier. Wind whipped through the building with an ear-splitting, whistling tune and left leaves and twigs scattered across the floor. The doors into the vortex room dangled at a severe angle, held upright by bent hinges.

Marcus removed his cell phone from its Faraday case and studied the screen.

"What are we waiting for?" Ian asked.

"Eve has inside intel on the quakes Aeros triggers," Marcus said. "A massive one is expected within a minute or two."

"How massive?" Rayne asked.

"Greater than eight, nine?" Ian shook his head when Marcus didn't respond. "Oh my god."

"We've got to warn everyone!" Rayne blurted.

Marcus didn't lift his attention from his screen. "If we did, Aeros would know he had a traitor."

Rayne stared at Ian, begging for his support. Ian couldn't look her in the eye. "He's right," he said.

She shook her head. "Even if it means hundreds, maybe thousands will die."

A flash came from Marcus's screen. "Fate has made the decision for us." Marcus returned the cell to his Faraday case and took a position in the middle of the vortex. "Ian, we need to parashyft at the peak of the quake."

Despite the ruined building, the vortex energy pulsed as strong as ever. Ian stepped into the center of the field beneath the rising pyramid ceiling that had miraculously survived Aeros's earlier wrath. If the quake was as strong as Marcus predicted, the ceiling wouldn't survive much longer.

Vibration beneath their feet. What was left of the northern vortex structure creaked and moaned as the massive quake hit. The dangling doors fell with an echoing clatter. Marcus motioned for Rayne to hurry. But she hesitated. Ian drew energy into his core at the same time the overhead glass pyramid buckled, releasing an avalanche of glass shards. With a protesting cry, Rayne jumped in between them and they huddled together, clasping hands.

Her energy drain struck with the impact of a rockslide. Ian gasped from the needles of pain, igniting every nerve ending in his body, and he fought to draw energy to counteract his rapidly draining core. The earthquake split the ground in the nearby hallway, and they struggled to stay on their feet. The walls cracked and collapsed toward them at the same time Ian parashyfted them to Thrae.

The trio arrived in the cramped storage room in Thrae's Northern Colony. Ian and Marcus collapsed to their knees from Rayne's drain, and everyone shivered from the intense cold of the parashyft. By the time Ian's clouded thoughts cleared, the flashing amber light and shrill alarm beyond the locked door alerted the colonists to an intruder's presence. Marcus rose to his feet while Ian lingered in the vortex, struggling to pull what energy he could. Thrae's core was weaker than ever.

"Did it work?" Rayne asked.

"If Aeros doesn't come after us, then it worked," Ian said with chattering teeth. Their return would give him a chance to reconnect with his mother, but he wasn't sure what reception they'd receive.

Footsteps approached and the latch to the storage room door opened with a metallic scrape. A woman's skeptical eye peered inside, then widened in recognition. The door swung wide. It was Catherine, wearing saggy, blood-patched clothes. "Sire!" She bent down to one knee and dropped her face.

"Catherine, I'm relieved to see you survived," Ian said, pulling the woman to stand. "Where's my mother?"

"Mother-to-us-all and Keeper of Thrae are tending to the injured." Catherine gestured for them to follow. The woman led them through the darkened hall and to his Aunt Sophenna's quarters. The woman paused next to the door. "Are you in need of nourishment?"

"No, thank you," Ian said.

"Thank you for sending Doctor Mac to help with the wounded. He's a wonderful, tireless healer," Catherine said. "We were shocked, of course, when he first arrived."

"Why?" Marcus asked.

"He's the paral to their previous healer," Rayne said.

Catherine gave a slight bow. "I trust you know your way through the escape tunnels. They are in the assembly cavern. I must retrieve more bandages. I will meet you there." She scurried down the hall.

Rayne led them inside and opened the pantry escape tunnel at the rear wall. She lit a torch from the wall socket and led them through the tunnels without hesitating at the numerous turns, or missing a step.

"Good thing she came along," Marcus said, bringing up the rear.

"She lived among these people for weeks," Ian said.

"And they protected me with their lives." Rayne stopped and turned toward them. "That's why Eve's plan had better work. I won't be responsible for bringing Aeros's wrath down on them, not again."

"Eve must have tested it out with Doctor Mac," Ian said. "Otherwise, she wouldn't have taken the risk."

"Patrick's mother is single-minded, Ian," Rayne said. "Every decision she makes is filled with risk."

"She'll either come out as a hero, or a failure on a universal scale," Marcus said. "Welcome to war, Rayne."

She led them the rest of the way in silence, then paused at the open door to the assembly hall cavern. The blinding glare of the vortex column reached beyond the door and escaped through cracks in rays of pulsating light.

Ian opened the door to the expansive, natural stone cavern. His Aunt Sophenna had her back to them and crouched over an injured man. Doctor Mac appeared to be closing a gash in a woman's leg as his mother assisted.

"I can't believe Doctor Mac is still wearing those filthy pink bunny slippers," Ian said.

"Your mother gave them to him the night the Primary banished her to Thrae," Rayne said. "She told me the story."

Gwynn glanced up and recognition lifted her features. She wiped the blood from her hands on her apron and hurried over. She wrapped her arms around Rayne, and pressed a cheek to the crown of Rayne's head.

"My child, why are you here?" Gwynn said. She let go of Rayne and grabbed Ian, gathering her son in her arms, embracing him as tight as the first time she'd laid eyes on him. "You shouldn't have come back," she whispered.

Rayne made her way among the injured, bending down and clasping their hands, begging for forgiveness at every turn. As she neared, Sophenna stood with open arms and hugged her. A moment later, Sophenna glanced about, but her excitement withered. Rayne must have told her Jaered hadn't come.

Gwynn extended a hand toward the old general. "I don't believe we've met."

Her hand disappeared in his grasp. "Marcus, ma'am. You must be Ian's mother."

"Gwynn," she said. "Among the Thraens, I'm known as Mother-to-us-all."

Dr. Mac gave a brief nod in Ian's direction and returned to his patient. "When did he get here?" Ian asked.

"About twenty-four hours after you and Rayne escaped," Gwynn said. "He's been a godsend. Sophenna and I couldn't have managed by ourselves."

"How many dead?" Ian asked.

His mother ushered them out the door. "Why are you here?"

"We're gathering as many as we can," Marcus said.

Gwynn pursed her lips. "You won't find any Sars left among us. They were the first ones Aeros killed when he took his revenge."

"That's not why we're here," Marcus said. "We need the coordinates to Thrae's animal preserve."

Darkness rose and fell in Gwynn's face. "My sister's idea?" She stepped away and turned her back to them. "Eve is asking us to sacrifice the last of their kind. Guaranteed extinction of their species."

Ian placed a gentle hand on her shoulder. "Mother, if we don't defeat Aeros, every one of them will be lost with the death of this planet. Along with millions of Earth's species."

"At least on Earth, these creatures will have a fighting chance," Marcus said.

"Many on Earth have never seen these creatures. Those who have, have pursued them mercilessly. Who will protect them from humanity?"

"We all will," Rayne said.

"Eve has chosen locations with displaced Thraens already en route to care and train them on Earth," Marcus said.

"The last time I was here, my powers didn't work except in the strongest of vortex fields, and even then, it was for shyfting," Ian said. "Is there a strong field near the animals?"

"Some of the strongest left on Thrae. But no one has been to the preserve, not since Liem was killed," she said. "He used to check in on the game warden and make sure the dome engineers had supplies. Their rations must be getting low by now."

"Give them the coordinates, Gwynn." Dr. Mac appeared behind Rayne. "This battle is our last stand. They need all the troops they can get. Even if they walk on four feet."

"Sister?" Gwynn regarded Sophenna with concern. "You are the Keeper of Thrae. All that has survived is entrusted to you."

Sophenna regarded Ian with regret creasing her face. "So be it," she whispered. "God help us all."

NINE

Gwynn's coordinates brought them to a nature preserve in what on Earth would be central Europe.

Ian's earlier journey on Thrae had brought him to barren lands laid waste by Aeros and ruled with an iron fist by the Primary. He didn't know what they would find in Europe's untouched preserves. According to his mother, this area remained relatively unscathed for decades. But an enormous biodome was eventually needed because of the methane storm that traveled across the planet, devastating every living thing in its path.

Ian shyfted them, and what rations the Northern Colony could spare, to a maintenance shed. The second they solidified, everyone's hands covered their noses in unison at the overwhelming odor of manure. Pitchforks, shovels, and rakes hung on rusty nails along the weathered wooden walls. Ian and Marcus remained in the vortex, replenishing their cores.

Rayne turned the door handle, but when she tried to open it, nothing gave. "I think something's outside, blocking it," she said.

Marcus leaned a shoulder against it, and Ian joined him. They shoved the door wide enough to slip out the narrow opening.

Ian stepped in a large pile of dung. "Oh, blast."

Rayne chuckled. "I'm glad you were the one to find it."

Marcus unfolded the hand-drawn map Gwynn made and studied it while Ian and Rayne got their bearings. The biodome wasn't a single oasis like others he had encountered, but one of three, clustered together.

He wandered toward the center where the domes met, making his way through dense, jungle foliage. The chatter and calls of a variety of bird species sang throughout the dome. This dome was circular in shape, the width of two football fields and at least that high. It was clear enough for natural light to penetrate. They'd arrived on a sunny day, with puffy clouds passing overhead. There was a fine mist in the air and high humidity. Ian lifted his hand and a drop of water from a hovering plant dampened his palm.

Rayne scaled a nearby boulder and stood, facing the structures. "Each dome looks like a different environment. That one," she pointed, "is a prairie, or savannah. I can see termite hills. Oh, a vulture just landed on one."

"We need to stay close," Marcus said. "Remember, these creatures are left undisturbed as much as possible."

The cold tip of a rifle poked the back of Ian's head.

"Who the hell are you?" a man asked in a thick dialect that Ian couldn't quite place.

"Mother-to-us-all sent us," Ian said. He glanced up at Rayne.

"Where's Liem?" the man asked. "He's the one she sends."

"He was killed during one of the last big earthquakes," Rayne said.

The gun drooped in the man's hands. "That's why we haven't heard from them. We were sure Aeros had finished everyone else off."

"He ravaged the Northern Colony," Rayne said. "There aren't many survivors."

"The Primary's penal colony is gone." Ian turned around with painstaking care not to spook him, and he faced the haggard, filthy man.

"Who the hell is the Primary?" he asked with irritation.

"You know him as Johann," Rayne said.

The man had been there a while, Ian surmised by the look of his camouflaged clothes. A sleeve was torn at the shoulder, but an unskilled hand had repaired the other rips. He wore a short, untrimmed gray beard and had dark, penetrating eyes. His gun was an antique by Earth's standards.

"We've brought you rations," Rayne said. "They're in the maintenance shed."

"Good thing. The engineers were looking mighty tasty," he said with a halfhearted smile. He offered a grimy hand. "I'm Claude."

They introduced themselves in turn. "How long have you been here?" Ian asked.

Claude let out a whistle that morphed into a sigh. "It's easy to lose track in these parts," he said. "A few years, I reckon."

"I can't place your dialect," Ian said.

His laugh drowned out his rumbling belly. "Born here, raised in another colony, but when its dome crashed," he said, "I was relocated back here since I had the most experience with animals."

"Are you the only warden?" Rayne asked.

"I'm all these babies have," Claude said with a puffed-out chest.

A snowcapped, furry tuft and a short, black snout appeared from between the leaves. The animal rested its head on Claude's shoulder. It drank them in with black eyes as big as saucers. "Hello, my sweetie." He patted the llama's cheek and leaned in to give it a hug. The curious animal pushed against Claude's back and he stepped out of the way for her to emerge from the bushes. "She's typically the shy one around here. She must like you," he said.

When the entire animal entered the path, Rayne gasped. It had two heads, one at either end.

"A pushmipullyu," Rayne said. Claude gave her a puzzled glance. "From a movie on Earth, called Doctor Doolittle," she added.

"This girl is a tweeruit." Claude patted the animal's cheek and made a purring sound.

"Eve said Aeros and the Primary brought some of the strange creatures to Earth," Marcus said. "Just to mess with our heads."

Rayne's face was radiant while she and Ian stroked the two-headed llama. They lobbed wide smiles at each other across the animal's sloped back.

"I'll introduce you to some of my favorites." Claude wandered down the dirt path with the tweeruit following.

The creature's hooves had a cleft in their keratin, both in the front and at the back. The dewclaws were absent on all four hooves. The rear facing head snorted as it passed Ian. At the guttural, rumbling sounds, Ian pulled Marcus away just as a slimy wad of spit shot in the old general's direction. It landed on a broad leaf and the stem bent from the weight.

Claude's laugh erupted from the head of the line. "She's a cautious girl."

"That's not the word I'd use," Marcus muttered.

The zookeeper was keen on the behaviors of the strange creatures and their hiding places. He often stooped and gently lifted leaves to expose small animals resting inside their dens, or brushed aside clumps of vegetation to point out nests in the wide branches of the overhead tree limbs. Ian and Rayne followed on his heels, captivated by the spectacle of strange beasts.

Rayne stuck her hand between branches and returned with a creature, a cross between a hammerhead shark and a gecko, resting on her open palm. It tilted its wide head back and forth, examing her with each eye, then wrapped it long, pointed tail around her wrist. "What is this?" she asked Claude. At her touch it arched its back, but didn't scurry away. "It's slimy, like a fish."

"That's a chuk," he said. "They're originally from a subterranean environment, and need the extra moisture."

She set it down and it scurried away, disappearing into the thick brush. An animal resembling a potbelly pig, but with a snowy, lion's mane, emerged from the thicket and took off down the path with a high-pitched yap. Ian couldn't make out its eyes from the numerous brown speckles coating its sunburn skin.

"That's an opeck," Claude said. "They're like dogs around here."

"These are all cute and cuddly, but that's not what we've come for," Marcus said.

Claude gave them a discerning glance. "I thought you were just bringing us supplies. Why are you really here?"

Ian removed the envelope from his back pocket and handed it to the game warden. "Mother-to-us-all sent us. She and the Keeper of Thrae have a special request."

Claude ripped open the envelope and unfolded the letter. A second later, it trembled in his hand at the same time his knuckles turned pale. "They ask too much," he said under his breath. He crumpled the note into a tight ball and clamped his fist around it. He stormed off in the direction of the vortex shed.

The others hurried to catch up. Claude pushed aside the dung pile with the edge of his boot until he could open the shed door wide enough to drag the ration boxes outside.

"Let me help," Ian said and squeezed inside, then pushed against the tower of crates. The stack slid out and Claude stumbled back.

Marcus caught him before he landed on his butt. "I don't need your help," the game warden roared with a reddened face. "You can take your worthless asses back to Earth and leave us Thraens alone!"

"But—" Rayne said.

"You're like all the others." Claude paused and wiped the beads of sweat off his brow with his forearm. "You claim to want to protect them, but the historical journals give a very different story."

Confused by the man's reaction, Ian wasn't sure how to respond. "What story?"

"When others from Earth came, they took our animals promising to find them good homes. They guaranteed they would mate with those of their kind and live in the riches that Earth had to offer. But journals were kept." He glared at Ian with a lopsided sneer. "They were hunted and slaughtered along with those creatures born to Earth. Your people feared them."

"We're not Aeros and the Primary," Ian said.

"They weren't the only ones to exploit our creatures," Claude said. "The one called Eve, she filled my head with promises that our beloved animals would find a good home, a better life than what we could give them on our dying planet."

"I don't blame you for feeling betrayed," Ian said. "On Earth, humanity destroys wildlife in the name of progress and self-indulgence, every day. It's a battle that has raged over decades with no clear remedies."

"Despite Ian's tireless efforts," Rayne said.

"Then you understand why I can't honor the mothers of Thrae and fulfill their request." Claude handed Ian the crumpled note.

"I understand," Ian said. "But I need *you* to understand what's behind the request. Thrae is dying and might not survive a week, much less longer," Ian said.

"Like that's news to us," Claude mumbled.

"It took Aeros centuries to do this level of damage on Thrae, but Earth is succumbing at a much faster rate."

"Practice makes perfect," Rayne said.

"What's that got to do with my babies?" Claude jerked his chin at the wrinkled note in Ian's hand. "You're asking to take most of our powerful creatures to your world. I may be old, but I'm not stupid. You're going to use them in battle, aren't you? Aeros used our dragons hundreds of years ago."

"What's he talking about?" Marcus asked.

"Aeros took most of Thrae's dragons to Earth during the Middle Ages," Ian said.

"They weren't just stories?" Marcus settled back on the crate.

"Out of a hundred, only two returned," Claude said. "Unlike other species that were never seen again."

"Oocaw's mate was killed by Aeros," Ian said.

"She's all alone here," Rayne said. "Ian and I have ridden her. She risked her secrets and chose to help us."

"You're asking a dying race to give even more than we already have," Claude said.

"If this battle on Earth isn't won, Aeros and the Primary will continue to plunder and ravage other worlds," Marcus said.

Ian faced Claude. "Give me and the other Heirs a chance to reverse what Aeros has done to Thrae."

Claude stepped back and collapsed onto a crate. "You're an Heir?"

"I'm son of Mother-to-us-all. Brother to Jaered, son of Keeper of Thrae."

"And brother to Patrick, son and Heir of Earth," Rayne said.

Ian pulled down his shirt collar, far enough to expose the Heir's Seal on his upper left breast. Claude fell to one knee and bowed his head. "Sire, I did not know."

Ian tugged on the man's arm, and he stood but kept his gaze lowered in reverence. "I am not here to exploit Thrae," Ian said. "But trust that I ask this sacrifice as a means to save you and all of Thrae."

Claude paused. Deep creases lined his face, as if he was pained by a deep ache. "I will take you to the creatures you seek."

TEN

Too exhausted to keep his eyes open, Patrick collapsed onto his bed, turned his face to the pillow, then sat up as though stung by a wasp. He withdrew a large envelope from beneath his pillow, confused about where it'd come from. He could have sworn he checked every inch of the room, not trusting their Weir support to find all listening devices.

Patrick sat on the edge of the bed and opened the flap. He pulled out a few sheets of paper. They were instructions from his mother, and his role at the bank. At the bottom, she'd signed it, EVE. The impersonal, fact-based note could have been written to anyone. Duty before anything else. Even love.

The next morning, the teenager from the rooftop pool waited at the hotel curb, next to Patrick and Tara's limo. He'd exchanged his poolside white shirt and pants for a limo driver uniform.

"Are you old enough to drive?" Patrick asked.

The teen gave him a crooked-toothed smile. "I am today," he said, and opened the door for them.

A while later, the teenager parked at the downtown curb. Patrick leaned against the passenger door and stared up at the towering Banco do Brasil building in the heart of São Paulo. The boy rushed out and approached the rear passenger door, but hesitated, perusing their surroundings before opening the door.

Jaered's voice appeared in Patrick's earbud. "You're on, Langtree," he said.

Patrick jerked. "Where the hell are you?" he asked.

"Covering your ass," Jaered said.

Patrick exited first, buttoned his suit coat, and extended a hand to Tara. She handed him the briefcase, then emerged and slipped her arm around his bent elbow. They approached the bank with the crisp stride of importance and purpose.

The high ceiling of the financial trade center lobby and old-world charm gave the appearance of the historical interlaced with modern commercial.

Patrick informed the nearest bank employee they needed to meet with the manager, handing her a thick business card from one of his mother's internationally known enterprises. Patrick lifted the briefcase to imply they had come bearing a sizeable deposit. Tara didn't remove her sunglasses but stood still, purse dangling from her wrist, oozing an air of impatience.

The young woman offered them the chairs facing her desk and left with the promise she would track the manager down. They ignored the chairs and took the opportunity to study the bank lobby with its bustling clientele. Patrick had done his homework since discovering the envelope under his pillow. The bank combined elements of commercial holdings and trading on the stock exchange, with government-sanctioned enterprises. Several businessmen and women arrived and exited through the lobby of the skyscraper. A sign near the front door boasted they were the proud sponsors of the Brazilian national volleyball team.

A short man with graying temples, dark complexion, and spider web wrinkles at the corners of his eyes approached them with stifled eagerness. He shook hands with Patrick, then extended his hand to Tara. She rewarded him with a half-smile.

"*Senhorita, eu sou Jorj de Sosa. Como posso ser útil?*" the manager said.

Tara looked at Patrick. "English, please," he said. "My companion does not speak Portuguese."

"Ah, I am quite fluent in many languages," the manager stated with the merest of dialect seeping into his intonation. "How may I assist you today?"

"We represent a private party with substantial international holdings," Patrick said. "You have their business card, but otherwise we will not exchange their name, understood?"

"Of course," the manager said with one hand pressed against his suitcoat pocket. The man's fingertip outlined what Patrick assumed was his mother's business card.

"Patrick Langtree," he said and extended his hand. "It's a pleasure to meet you, Senhor de Sosa." The manager's smile was genuine and his handshake firm. Patrick might not be recognized in his parent's financial world, but his surname opened many doors.

"This unnamed corporation is about to take control of a local corporation," Patrick said.

The manager smiled. "Also, to remain unnamed at this stage, I assume. May I inquire as to the nature of the business at hand?"

"I can share this much." Patrick gave him a sly grin. "Senhor de Sosa, our eminent purchase deals with what's below ground."

"A mining acquisition, most intriguing," the manager said.

"We will be depositing a large amount of capital." Patrick gave him one of the sheets from his mother's envelope. "Good faith money, if you will, just prior to taking control."

The monetary amount listed on the sheet widened Senhor Sosa's eyes. "A wise choice, depositing it with Banco do Brasil," he said with increased exuberance. "We can offer you many options for transferring large funds, set up employee payment plans, and so forth. If I may be so bold to suggest." He took a step closer, lowering his voice. "We can also help you invest some of your capital with our stock exchange."

Patrick sighed. "Our unnamed party chose Banco do Brasil for your . . . historical dealings." From Senhor de Sosa's expression, he wasn't offended. His institution had a reputation for supporting large corporate desires with the government ties to insure it.

He ushered them into the elevator, and Patrick took a position behind the man. The manager removed a passkey and held it to a pad on the elevator panel. Then he pressed an upper floor button.

"Senhor de Sosa, how long have you been with the bank?" Patrick asked.

When he turned toward Patrick and drummed on about his history with the institution, Tara stepped closer to the panel. Patrick shifted to the side to obstruct any security camera view while Tara pressed a clear strip to the button. She linked arms with Patrick and he angled the briefcase lens toward the strip hiding in her lowered palm.

The hidden camera inside the briefcase had recorded everything from the logo on his passkey card to which finger he used to press the button. An almost imperceptible vibration traveled from the briefcase handle up into Patrick's hand as the lens adjusted to get the fingerprint impression. His mother's people were already creating what they needed to infiltrate the bank.

Senhor de Sosa led them into his office and offered them seats. Patrick sat across from the man, but Tara remained standing. She wandered toward the windows.

"What a magnificent view," she said.

The bank manager stepped up next to her. "I was born here," he said. "The first to attend college."

"Your parents must be very proud," Patrick said. "Rising to such a position here at the bank."

When Senhor de Sosa turned toward Patrick, Tara's hand slipped out of his suit pocket with his passkey in her grip.

Tara pressed a button on her sleeve, then swiped the card inside the stiff cuff where the decorative black stripe camouflaged a card reader. She took a step toward Senhor de Sosa but tripped, colliding with him. The manager lost his balance and fell onto the carpet.

"I'm so sorry!" Tara exclaimed.

"It's those heels you insist on wearing, darling." Patrick rushed over and together they helped Senhor de Sosa to his feet. She slipped the card back into his pocket and feigned brushing off his suit jacket. Tara batted her eyes at the manager. His cheeks turned bright crimson, and he patted her hand on his arm.

"Let's get down to business, shall we?" Patrick said.

Tara sighed. "Numbers bore me. I will take my leave." She leaned down and gave Patrick a lingering kiss on his lips. "I want to explore what the stores have to offer," she said with an extended hand.

Patrick pulled his mother's credit card out of his wallet and gave it to her with a raised eyebrow. "Enjoy yourself," he said.

"I'll meet you at the hotel, darling," Tara said.

"There are many fine boutiques nearby," Senhor de Sosa said, and escorted her to the door.

Patrick set the briefcase on the manager's desk, angling the chip side toward the computer.

"Keep stalling," Jaered's voice hissed in Patrick's ear. He glanced over his shoulder. Tara's smile broadened on the bank manager in confirmation.

"You've been so kind," Tara cooed when he opened the door for her. "So helpful."

"I am happy to serve," he said. He stuck a finger in his collar and tugged.

Tara turned up the charm, linking her arms around Senhor de Sosa's arm. "Is there a Senhora de Sosa?" she asked under her breath. Thanks to Patrick's keen hearing, he caught it loud and clear.

"I'm afraid so," the bank manager said with true regret in his voice.

"I need more time," Jaered's voice urged. "His code has twelve digits."

Tara leaned in and swiped the manager's shoulder like brushing off crumbs. Patrick mused it was dandruff. "Of course, that's never stopped me before," she said and nibbled his ear.

"Got it," Jaered said. "Meet me at the curb."

"If you don't leave us to our business meeting, I'll take back that card," Patrick said.

She sighed. "Very well." She gave the manager a wry smile, turned on the ball of her foot, and strolled away.

Patrick grabbed the briefcase off the desk and placed it on his lap a second before the bank manager closed the door and took his place across from Patrick.

Senhor de Sosa took a seat behind his desk and swiped his brow with a handkerchief from his pocket. Patrick smiled. The rest would be basic contract negotiations, which he could do in his sleep. The hard part was over. Now it was up to his mother's technical team to get the necessary data.

Jaered inserted the magazine in the automatic's handle and pushed it into place with a resounding *click*. He loaded a round into the magazine, then grabbed the next one, checked that Tara had loaded it correctly, and repeated the final prep of their ammo.

Tara strapped a sheath to her thigh, out of sight beneath her skirt. She flipped the knife around in one hand with the skill of a weapons expert, and secured it in place. Jaered wasn't sure if it was the exposed thigh, or the way she expertly handled the weapon that triggered the ache in his groin. He turned away before she noticed.

It had been ages since he'd felt anything but anger and angst. Determination drove him forward, fueled by the thirst for blood. His father had slaughtered his wife and unborn child in the most torturous of ways. The opportunity to return the favor was on his doorstep. He closed his eyes, envisioning it, tasting it.

He'd never met or had any contact with the Primary. If everything went according to Eve's plan, his uncle would curse Jaered's name until his dying breath.

Tara tossed her high heels into the open closet and they landed on the carpeted floor with a *thump*. She grabbed the knee-high black boots and sat on the edge of the bed, slipping into them. She stuffed the rest of the ammo in the large suitcases, zipped them, and waited at the ready.

From the corner of his eye, Jaered noticed her scratch her forearm beneath the long sleeve. She and Eve had something going on the side, but he wasn't going to ask. If he was supposed to know, Tara would tell him when the time was right. Not only had Tara been trained well, she was no-nonsense and a woman of few words.

"You need to tell him." Jaered walked to the window and parted the curtains to study the street below.

"Tell who, what?" she asked.

"You were merciless to Patrick in the limo yesterday. You should tell him how you really feel."

"You shouldn't have eavesdropped," she said.

Jaered faced her, and she threw him a disgruntled glare. "You were the one to start something you weren't ready to finish. Don't use me as the excuse for not following through."

She sobered and fiddled with the button on her shirt. "I'm afraid of hurting him."

"Then be honest with him. We might not survive this. Don't give him hope and then pull it away because you're afraid." He checked the time on his watch. Patrick would be returning any minute. He grabbed his jacket from the nearby chair, but paused and stared at her. Thoughts of Kyre engulfed him. Memories of his wife hadn't invaded his emotions for a while. Was it an omen? Would he be joining her soon? "Fear doesn't belong in our hearts any more than it does in our heads," he said. Rayne's time on Thrae had changed her. She'd abandoned her fear for the sake of duty and resembled his deceased wife in more than just looks.

He peered into the hallway, leaving the munitions-filled suitcases on the bed, and he stepped out. At the sound of the opening door, the hotel cleaning crew entered the hall from the room across the way. Tara held the door open for them and they entered, pushing their cart inside. The hotel door locked behind them with a metallic scrape.

Jaered and Tara made their way to the lobby via the stairs, and by the time they stepped to the curb, the limo pulled up. Patrick opened the rear passenger door for her and she slipped in the back. Jaered kept his limo driver cap low over his face. He exchanged places with the teenager and a minute later, they took off down the driveway.

He studied the side and rearview mirrors. It would be several hours before Eve's crew infiltrated the bank and the Primary would learn what they'd done.

From what Jaered could tell, no one had followed them. To date, they hadn't found any surveillance equipment, listening devices, or people tailing them, and he wondered if Eve had been overly cautious. It was possible that the Primary considered Patrick and Tara nothing more than a harmless loose end. Regardless, Jaered remained on the alert. Just because they didn't see evidence of a threat didn't mean one wasn't there.

The privacy window lowered. "It'll be a lengthy jet ride to Belo Horizonte, then a jeep ride to the mine, so get some rest," Jaered said.

Patrick glanced at Tara. "What happened to the whole prying ears concern?"

"The limo was swept before we left the hotel. It's clean," Jaered said.

"When are the rebels infiltrating the bank?" Patrick asked.

"That doesn't concern us," Jaered said.

Tara left Patrick and sat on the seat closest to the pass-through. "A simple 'I don't know' sounds a lot more cordial," she said. "Come on, give it a try."

Her pragmatics lesson left Jaered bewildered, and he turned his attention to the road ahead. "I don't know," he tossed back at her. "Sometime this evening."

She squeezed his shoulder. "There, that didn't hurt, did it?" She returned to the seat next to Patrick and looked out the window.

Jaered kept one eye on the road and the other one on Tara, but she sat in silence and didn't open up to Patrick. He sighed and raised the privacy window.

They arrived at the private hanger on the outskirts of the airport and exited the limo. The jet's engines picked up speed when the stairs lowered. "You two get on board. I'm going to check on our reinforcements."

Patrick and Tara entered the plush interior of Eve's private jet and, from what Jaered could tell through the windows, they sat next to each other on one of the anterior couches.

"How did phase one go?" a deep-throated voice asked from behind.

It was Wyatt, one of Eve's most trusted rebel lieutenants and one of Jaered's friends among their forces. They shook hands. "Now for phase two."

"So, the Duach Heir is holding his own," Wyatt said, slinging his rifle over his shoulder. "His mother will be pleased."

"With Tara along, I'm babysitting lovesick puppies," Jaered said.

Wyatt chuckled. "There's reasons why relationships are discouraged among the ranks."

"Our intel on what we'll find inside the mine is sketchy at best," Jaered said. "Is your squad ready for this?"

"Born ready, sire!" one of Wyatt's soldiers shouted and saluted Jaered.

"He's new," Wyatt said.

"No shit." Jaered gestured for the young man to stand at ease. "There's nothing formal about my operations," he told the soldier, not much older than twenty. "Just focus on what needs to be done."

"Yes, sire!" the young man said, and caught himself in mid salute. He lowered his arm.

The engines revved to a deafening pitch. "You better get on board," Jaered said. Wyatt signaled his waiting squad. A minute later, they entered the private jet, made their way down the center aisle, and took up seats at the rear of the cabin. Wyatt raised the stairs and secured the door.

An airport mechanic pulled the blocks away from the jet's tires and returned to the edge of the tarmac. Jaered shyfted aboard the aircraft and sat on the couch facing Patrick and Tara.

"You cut it close," Patrick said.

"As far as spying eyes are concerned, I'm not on board," Jaered said. His seatbelt *clicked* into place.

The aircraft took off a moment later, and when it reached cruising speed, the passengers huddled together. Jaered stood and gripped the closest seatback to steady himself. "The Duach Heir, Tara, and I will arrive through the front gate of the mining operation. Wyatt, the rest of you will take up your marked positions on the outskirts of the grounds and await our signal." He tapped his watch while everyone checked theirs. An electronic signal vibrated on everyone's wrists, including Jaered's. He handed the rebels maps of the outlying mine, indicating their positions.

"What's this next phase about?" Patrick asked.

Jaered cleared his throat. "We're to infiltrate the Primary's diamond and gold mine in southern Brazil and take control of it."

Patrick's jaw sagged. Tara shut it with her index finger. He glanced at the other rebels. "Not that it's a suicide mission or anything, but don't you think that's a huge job for this measly crew?" Patrick said.

"The mine has a skeleton crew. We're not even sure it's a working vein any longer," Jaered said.

"As far as this team goes, you won't find a better trained and more skilled group among the rebels," Wyatt said.

"No offense, but the last time we infiltrated a piece-of-cake operation, we nearly all got killed." At Wyatt's dark look, Patrick regretted bringing it up. "I'm just saying, I'd feel safer if our backup was in the double digits, that's all."

"If we went in with anything bigger," Jaered said. "The Primary wouldn't remain curious, he'd be—"

"All over our asses," Wyatt said. The others snickered and hid their grins by lowering their faces. "We can take the mine. Just get us inside."

"Then what?" Patrick asked. "Ransom it and get the Primary to tell us what we want? What's to stop him from storming the place with the Pur Army and just waltzing back in?"

"The mine isn't our ultimate goal," Jaered said. "But it'll get us one step closer."

"To what?" Tara asked.

"Discovering which planet the Primary has targeted next," Jaered said. He sat down on the couch facing Patrick and Tara, rested his forearms on his thighs, and met Patrick's stare. "We need to figure out how to get the—"

A racing blur passed between them and down the center aisle. It slammed against the back of the cabin with a resounding *splat!*

Jaered bolted out of his seat and froze in stunned silence. A Weir Sar had attempted to shyft onto the jet at full speed. What used to be a human had materialized as miscellaneous body parts, most of which fused with the back wall of the cabin. Blood leaked from the bits of flesh. It mixed with human skin and muscle tissue in a growing puddle on the carpet at the base of the wall.

The jet jerked and a shout came from the cockpit. "Holy shit!"

Jaered rushed forward and banged open the door. Another shyftor's body had reappeared inside the control panel with gruesome results. The pilots fought the loss of power with white-knuckled strength.

"We're going down!" the pilot yelled.

"Get back and buck—" The copilot's shout was cut short when another shyfting body appeared in his lap. The force of the impact crushed the two men against each other like a fly to a flyswatter, and they died in each other's arms.

"Swerve, goddamn it!" Jaered reached in front of the dead men, grabbing the controls, banking a sharp left before the stunned pilot could react. He swerved away from a crimson cloud appearing in midair. Whoever the shyftor was dropped thirty-six thousand feet to his death. The jet slammed into another shyftor and his remains smeared the jet's windshield. Soft tissue was shoved off to the side by the wiper blades.

Shouts came from the rear of the jet. Intermittent audio could be heard whenever the cockpit door swung open and closed with each jarring motion.

"Keep swerving until we can land," Jaered said.

"Land!" A hysterical guffaw erupted from the pilot. "I've got one sputtering engine left on this bird!"

The aircraft's nose dropped into the clouds. Jaered teetered backward but managed to remain upright. The opaque mist further obstructed his view between the splatter of blood and tissue working its way to the outer rims of the windshield as if being blown by powerful fans at the end of a car wash.

"Strap yourself in!" the pilot shouted.

Jaered pressed against the walls and worked his way to the main cabin. He didn't have to make an announcement. Ashen faces and widened eyes stared at him between swinging oxygen masks.

"I can't draw enough power to shyft," Patrick said.

"We're going too fast," Wyatt yelled over the whine of the remaining engine.

Patrick's face lifted. "The book!"

To Jaered's horror, Patrick unbuckled his seatbelt and rushed to the rear of the jet. He slipped on the pooled blood and fell headlong into the remnants of body parts embedded in the wall. He swiped bloody residue off his face and raised his hand at an upper panel. A crimson glow lit up the wall. A hidden door popped open, and he grabbed something out of the compartment.

The plane dipped at a sharp angle. Jaered fell into the closest seat and buckled in, cinching it tight. Wyatt steadied Patrick and he stumbled down the aisle, clutching an old, weathered book to his chest.

"Are you insane?" Tara waved him on.

"It's the Book of the Weir," Patrick said. "Mother's been hiding it here."

The fuselage buckled and he lost his footing. The book flew down the aisle. Jaered scooped it up and reached out for

Patrick, but his brother's momentum was too great and he fell, landing hard at Tara's feet. Beyond the windows, the jet banked and the ground rushed toward them. The last thing Jaered remembered was Patrick's limp body flying about the cabin.

ELEVEN

Ian willed his feet to keep moving, and he fought not to get caught up in his surroundings. Claude had led them between the intersecting domes via underground tunnels, passing a large control room. Ian stole a peek at the bio-dome engineers in white lab coats, busy at their controls and talking among themselves. In turn, the engineers threw curious stares at Ian. They must have been wondering who Ian was that Claude would kneel before him.

The blinding glare of the energy column that powered the three massive domes gave off enough lumens to light the tunnels without need for additional sources. When they neared the column, Ian's core pulsed with such force that it stole his breath. From Marcus's reaction, he too felt the immense, channeled power of the dying planet.

Ian yearned for more time to explore the strange and unique wildlife and to study the dome ecosystems further.

Regret at not having a chance to ask the engineers about the masterful designs of the amazing zoological structures slowed his steps, but Claude hurried them along at a brisk pace.

The game warden opened a door and they entered an earthen tunnel. From what he could tell, it led them away from the biodomes. They descended deep into a cavernous lower system with dull, motion-controlled lighting. The moisture coming from the wall cooled the air, and the earthen floor proved slippery in the sections where dirt turned into natural stone steps and then back to dirt paths.

"It's like the tunnels beneath the Northern Colony," Rayne said, catching up to Ian.

"Are you sure we can trust this guy?" Marcus mumbled, bringing up the rear. "I can't help but feel he's leading us into a trap."

"It's not anything of the sort," Claude said from the front of the line. He stopped and waited for them to catch up with a scowl plastered on his face.

"Dangerous creatures need to be kept apart from the more docile," Ian said.

"Not any different from humans." Claude turned away and continued. "But what sets us apart from the animal world is that we take beyond our basic needs and waste so much. We kill beyond food consumption," Claude said. "Animals can't help what comes naturally to them."

Claude must have experienced great sorrow when the Australian dome was destroyed, Ian thought. In the aftermath of tremendous loss, he'd found a kinship with the animals entrusted to him. Ian's request must have torn at the warden's soul. Would he hand over the most feared of their beasts when the time came?

Somewhere ahead, the subtle drip of the tunnels transformed into the thunderous rush of an underground river. It reminded Ian of the subterranean waterways connecting the Northern Colony with the southern reaches, and his arm muscles ached at the memory of rowing for days in the raging currents.

Claude stopped at a rocky edge and peered down while Ian and the others came to a stop beside him. Unlike the waterway he'd traversed a few weeks earlier, this river was enormous, spanning more than half a mile across. The amount of water crashing through the natural rock bed was similar to the fierce rivers of the Amazon, Ganges and Yangtze on Earth.

"Oh my god," Rayne said with her face raised toward the ceiling.

A trailing neon glow spread across the ceiling and down the far walls resembling arteries and veins, filling the cavern. Bright green striations were the most abundant while others pulsed bright aqua. Some were the width of Ian's finger, while others were as wide as his torso. It appeared to come from a crevice across the expansive cavern.

It wasn't what Ian saw, but the lack of odor in the air, that piqued his curiosity. "It's not zinc sulfide," Ian said. "But some other natural bioluminescence. What's its energy source?"

"From what we can tell, groundwater seeping through this crystalline river causes it. I'm sorry, I'm not a geologist or a chemist. A couple of the engineers back at the dome could explain it better." Claude crouched and studied the raging river. "With each quake, the river has grown wider, but I had no idea it had eroded the banks. It's washed away the dock and taken the boats with it."

There were a few ripped planks sticking out from the water's edge. Ian joined Claude for a closer look. "We need to get across? There's no other way?" he shouted over the rushing water.

"I'm afraid so," Claude yelled, scooting away when a wave rose above the ridge and threatened to knock them both into the current.

"Can you shyft?" Rayne asked.

"I couldn't the last time I was here, not without a powerful vortex," Ian said. "We could return to the energy column at the domes and try from there." Yet, when he stilled, he swore his core pulsed as strong as ever. He drew energy on his first attempt and his core sizzled. He raised his hand and a core blast swirled above his opened palm.

"I have my powers as well," Marcus said, pressing a fist to his chest. "But how, why? We were both powerless the last time we were here."

Ian turned and watched the glowing veins with each of his energy draws. They pulsed in rhythm to his core, deep in his chest. "It's the crystals in the veins," he said. The greater Ian pulled on the planet's energy, the brighter the striations glowed. "I think they're a conduit for Thrae's core."

Marcus spread his arms and drew upon the natural power. In a matter of seconds, his chest glowed.

"Where were we headed?" Ian asked Claude.

"We were to take the boat downstream about two miles. That's where the animals are kept. But I fear the worse. If the river's gotten this out of control, they might have already perished in the flood waters."

"We have to try," Rayne said. "They may be trapped."

"Describe in as much detail as you can where we're headed," Ian said.

Claude pointed downstream. "It's an open cavern similar to this one, but with a sloped, rock outcropping on the opposite side, much like a pebbly beach. A tall, wood-slatted door rests in the rock wall. The door has rusted brass hinges and a weathered ring pull. But you'll need this." He dug his fingers inside his pocket and withdrew a long, brass key. Ian took it and stepped away.

"Shyfting blind is too dangerous." Marcus grabbed Ian's arm. "I'll go, I'm expendable."

"Wait!" Rayne screamed. They stared at her. "Something's happening!"

Rumbling beneath their feet. The walls and ceiling cracked. Sediment rained upon them, turning into an avalanche of rocks the size of baseballs. The trembling ground knocked them off their feet. They fell hard against the rocky cliff, and were tossed about like Ping-Pong balls.

Rayne tumbled over the cliff's edge and was swept up by the river before she could utter a sound.

Ian scrambled toward the embankment and fell to his chest, reaching for her, but the second his hand submerged, energy drained from his core despite not touching her. He pulled out of the water and the drain effect ceased. "Rayne!"

he roared at the top of his lungs, but there was no sign of her flailing in the current or her head bobbing above water downstream. "Rayne!" he screamed from the depths of his soul.

The rushing water slowed to a gentle flow, as though obeying his very command. Stunned, Ian froze. Strong hands helped him to stand.

"Did you do that?" Claude asked.

"I don't think so," Ian said. "An underground crevice must have opened up and is diverting much of the force upstream." He pulled away from the men and ran to where the ridge ended at a bend in the wall. "Rayne!" But his shouts echoed off the cavern and were lost beyond where he stood.

Rayne swam and then clawed her way out of the river. A racking cough dropped her cheek to the cold stone and she lay limp, gasping for air. Each inhale teased another hacking cough from her, and she rolled onto her side with the water lapping at her legs. She retched river water from her lungs and stomach.

Rayne had no idea how long she lay there, sucking air to mend her ravaged lungs. It was the stink that awakened her senses and she sat up, twisting around to see behind her. A wooden-planked door was attached to rusted brass hinges in the sheer rock wall. What caused her to hold her breath wasn't the door, but the size of it. It rose high above her head, nearly touching the cavern roof. A brass ring hung at the lower third of the door. A padlock as large as Rayne's head kept the door securely closed.

It was then that she noticed the quiet of her surroundings. Rayne stared at the river. Instead of the monstrous, raging force of nature from upstream, it had turned calm. Why? What happened after she'd fallen in? She garnered the courage to approach the door. This had to be where the Thraens kept their monsters. But now that she arrived, without Ian, fear kept her riveted to the rocky shore.

Rayne stood on shaky legs. She rubbed her arms and braced against the cool temperature in the cave. She reached up behind her and wrung out her long, damp hair, then tied it into a knot, tucking the ends into a makeshift bun. "Okay, girl, you can do this."

She approached the massive door with cautious steps and wrapped her hand around the padlock. A forceful tug rewarded her with an orange-tinted palm, which she wiped off on her wet jeans.

A crack between the door and the jamb gave her hope to see beyond, but she couldn't make out anything on the other side. Fresh air flowed out of the crack, and a pungent tropical flower odor tickled her nose. "Hello," she called, at a loss about how to gain entrance. "Is anyone there?" Silence. What had she expected, talking gorillas? "Enough with the blonde jokes. Think." She searched for a sizeable rock to break the padlock, but she couldn't find anything bigger than a golf ball.

The emerald arteries and veins around the door glowed bright and pulsed. Ian appeared between her and the water's edge. In an instant, he was on her, and she pressed her back to the door, aching to throw her arms around him.

Ian leaned his forearms against the door and bent close with his heartbeat ringing in her ears. She felt the warmth of his breath upon her cheek. "I thought I'd lost you," he murmured. "Are you all right?"

"Feeling like a drowned rat, but otherwise okay," she said with more strength then she felt when he was this close. He inhaled deep and sent an aromatic cloud of lavender across her lips. The only kiss he could give her. She breathed in his tenderness, filling her sore lungs with his love, and allowed herself to get lost in the rare moment between them. Ian must have noticed her shivers because he drew energy into his core, filling the narrow space between them with warmth of a comforting fire. It robbed her body of the river's chill and at the same time, magnified the rising heat of emotions. "How did you find me?" she asked, slipping out from under his raised arm.

"I shyfted to the only location I could, downstream from you." He pushed away and turned his attention to the worn padlock.

"I tried. It's locked," she said.

"I have the key," he said. "Ready to meet Thraes biggest and baddest?"

TWELVE

an inserted the key and turned it until it clicked. The padlock swung open. He slipped it off the hinge and pulled the iron ring. It took a couple of forceful tugs, but with a drawn-out *creak*, the massive door gave way and they were met with a burst of fresh air. Closest to the door, the ground had been cleared of any vegetation. Several yards ahead, thick reeds, bushes and trees rose high, lining a narrow dirt path. From the suffused light, Ian judged they stood at one end of a great cavern.

He hesitated. "Maybe I should return for Claude. He knows these animals."

"Do you trust him?" Rayne asked. "I'm mean, *really* trust him?"

Before Ian could answer, Rayne traversed the narrow clearing and stepped onto the dirt path without looking back. He caught up and held out his arm to stop her. "At least give me a chance to study our surroundings." He stilled and tuned into the sounds, sights, and odors. "This end of the cavern is tropical."

"I might not have your eagle sight or hearing, but what I got works just fine," she said. "Do your mojo thing so we can get a move on."

Ian closed his eyes and reached out to the expanse with his mind. He could communicate with the dragon Oocaw on his previous trip. Perhaps she wasn't the only creature he had a connection with on Thrae. *I am the one called Ian, son to Mother-to-us-all. We mean you no harm.* He kept his thoughts open for the next few moments, but there was no response. The chirp of birds echoed off the cavern walls, but otherwise the immediate area remained serene.

"Do you think Claude misled us?" Rayne asked when Ian opened his eyes.

"Given the size of that door and the enormous padlock, I'm guessing this isn't the way to the amusement park," Ian said. "Stay close."

"I call dibs on the front. I'd rather see it coming," she said.

"Drop if you see anything ahead," Ian insisted, not sharing her glib attitude. He tested his powers and felt a twinge of comfort when the heat formed at the center of his outstretched palms. At least he had core blast weaponry this close to the glowing arteries and veins, but he didn't know how far they reached into the cavern, or if he'd eventually lose his powers.

An elongated shadow passed overhead, turning the dim light to momentary darkness. The rushing air of a winged creature startled Ian and Rayne, and they collided. Her power drain sent excruciating pain shooting through his limbs and she fell back onto her butt, breaking the painful connection.

"What the hell was that?" she blurted.

Ian scanned the expanse overhead. Whatever it was, it was gone. "When I was here before, a giant bird attacked me in Oocaw's den. Maybe it was one of those."

Rayne got to her feet. "That wasn't a bird. It had a point at the end of its tail, and I didn't see feathers, or scales like on Oocaw."

"If Oocaw was here, she would have answered my channel," Ian said.

Rayne blew aside a strand of hair. "So much for covering the aft and stern. Who's going to look out for above?"

Ian gestured for her to keep going. The farther they ventured into the cavern, the more his skin prickled across the back of his neck. A creature was stalking them. Leaves off to his left rustled despite the lack of wind, and his keen hearing picked up subtle twig snaps. From the displaced vegetation, Ian surmised the wolfish beast was at least the size of a full-grown man. It appeared to alternate between walking on two legs and all fours. It was intelligent, keeping the same distance between them, yet pausing whenever Rayne and Ian stopped.

A couple of miles or more down the path, the sounds of a waterfall echoed off the cave walls. The vegetation grew sparser, and natural light filled the cavern from a wide opening in the ceiling. A waterfall flowed into the cavern from above and ended in a churning pool at the center of the opening. Ian could make out another massive dome, high above. "I think we're in a giant sinkhole dome," he said.,

An enormous creature the size of a school bus glided down through the open ceiling on outstretched wings. It swooped and banked, circling where Rayne and Ian stood in shadow below. As it came lower, Ian could make out a baboon-like face with curved fangs protruding on either side. It had arms and legs, but with paws instead of hands or feet. Partially retracted claws protruded from the toes. It was the color of wet cement.

Rayne stood still but kept her attention riveted on the creature. "Told you so."

Not only did the creature have wings spanning for several feet on either side, its long tail ended in an arrowhead point. "It's a gargoyle," he whispered.

"I'll leave the introductions to you," she mumbled.

The winged creature turned back in their direction, extended its claws to twice the length, and headed straight for them.

Snarls came from behind. Ian and Rayne ducked at the approaching winged creature. The wolf beast pursuing them emerged from the brush and leapt at Ian. The gargoyle snatched up the wolf and flew off with it, but not before the beast had dug its claws into Ian's back. He lifted off the ground, rising high above the cavern. Shock transformed into agonizing pain and he wailed.

"Ian!" Rayne screamed, tearing through the brush to keep him and the two creatures in her sights.

The wolf thrashed about and its grip on Ian loosened. He pushed the piercing agony aside and tried to get a handhold on the gargoyle's ankle, but his struggles prompted the wolf to sink its teeth into Ian's shoulder.

"Ugh!" Ian roared. The gargoyle's claws sank deep into the beast's chest, and blood squirted across Ian's face. A deathly howl, split Ian's eardrums. The beast went limp. Ian fell.

He landed against a cushioned surface and rolled to a stop. It took a moment for him to regain his senses. Searing spikes of pain spread in all directions, and he pulled himself to sit with a moan. The roar of rushing water came from beneath him.

A mound of fur landed next to Ian. The wolf was the size of a large man. Its huge, dark eyes stared unblinking at him while blood mixed with saliva trickled out of a gaping mouth. Long, curved canine fangs and razor-sharp teeth brought to mind his injured shoulder and he winced, exploring how serious the punctures were with his fingertips.

The winged creature landed silently across from its kill and folded the expansive wings behind like a closed fan. It focused ebony eyes on Ian. He stiffened.

The gargoyle bent down and ripped at the wolf's neck until it all but separated the head from the body. The gargoyle buried its snout against the opened wound and proceeded to slurp.

While it gorged itself on its meal, Ian glanced about. He had been deposited in an enormous nest created from twigs, branches, dead grasses, and shrubs. Through slits in the branches, it appeared to be positioned on top of dead tree trunks extended above the waterfall. Two small gargoyle heads poked above the edge of the nest opposite from where Ian sat.

The offspring hopped onto the raised edge of the nest, their cooing growing louder by the second.

The gargoyle raised its blood-soaked face and tossed a growl at them from over its shoulder. Their cooing softened, but they crept closer, fluttering their small wings.

Ian peered over the edge of the nest into the sink-hole. He searched for Rayne, but there was no sign of her. He willed her to stay put and not bring undue attention to her presence.

You are son to Mother-of-us-all. The gargoyle paused long enough in its meal to meet Ian's gaze.

The creature could channel with him! *Yes,* he replied.

The gargoyle rose to its full height and spread its wings. *I serve Mother and all that roams Thrae,* it channeled.

I am Heir to Earth, brother to Thrae's Heir, Ian replied.

The gargoyle gave Ian a deep bow. *Then I serve you as well, Earth's Heir.*

Ian gestured to the gargoyle's kill, lying between them. *You saved me from this beast. I am in your debt.*

Debt begets recompense. You owe no one. The gargoyle dipped its wing and the offspring hopped over and set about tearing at the beast's flesh with their petite fangs.

Ian wrapped his thoughts around the gargoyle's command of language. Where Oocaw was ancient and worldly, this creature was something quite different. *I am in awe of you. Has Thrae always been your home?*

Father-to-Thrae brought my kind to fight his battles centuries before your time, the gargoyle channeled. *But those on Earth both revered and were repelled by us. My brethren who were not killed in Earth's wars returned to Thrae many, many years ago.* The gargoyle perched on the edge of the nest as its offspring fought over a sliver of muscle. *Those of us that remain reside deeper in the caves below you. Others are scattered among the ruins of our world.*

Where I come from, Ian channeled, *your kind has been remembered for your bravery and sacrifice. Earth has immortalized you as statues on buildings, throughout the lands you defended,* Ian left out the comic books and cartoon characters that didn't do these amazing creatures justice. The gargoyle didn't respond. *What do I call you?*

Those on Earth called me Jestueax, she channeled.

Jestueax, I have come seeking warriors for another great battle on Earth. Can you help me? Ian channeled.

The gargoyle's attention dropped to its offspring. *Most of my kind were killed on Earth. I am but one of few, left to Thrae.*

Is that why you sought refuge in this enclosure? Ian asked.

Keeper of Thrae protects and seeks only to preserve, Jestueax channeled with raised chest. The gargoyle ruffled its wings, sending a gust of wind in Ian's direction. *I am far from a prisoner . . . nor any man's pet.*

Keeper of Thrae loves and cares for all, Ian responded with lowered face. *She does not bind man or creature. She wishes for you to decide for yourself. This I have promised her.*

Jestueax's wings relaxed. It cocked its head and appeared to be studying Ian. *You are Heir? You remind me of Father.*

I am not the one you know as Father, Ian channeled. It was the first time he'd been compared to Aeros. *I do not torture, coerce, or enslave. I strive to lead, together with my brothers, the Heirs, at my side. We unite under a single goal, to rid this universe of Father's wrath.*

Jestueax approached with padding steps. *You are but one of three? The Three Heirs are united, as prophesized?*

The triangle of power is complete. We prepare for battle, Ian channeled. He pulled down his shirt to expose his Heir's Seal. *Will you join our fight for the salvation of Thrae, and Earth?*

There are few left to my world, Jestueax replied.

Mother-to-us-all and Keeper of Thrae profess you to be a great leader of all beasts, Ian channeled. He stood and steadied himself on the thicker branches. *I seek introductions to your world, and will impose nothing else upon you, if you wish.*

Jestueax extended a single wing toward Ian and bowed. *I choose to follow the Three Heirs.* It lifted its baboon face and stretched toward Ian. The smell of blood, dripping from its fangs, turned his stomach and he struggled to remain impartial. *But beware, young Heir. Be cautious of what you seek.*

THIRTEEN

Patrick couldn't quite make out the voices in the distance. His head swirled with every breath as he lay still, bound to something stiff beneath him. He attempted to clear his throat, but all he could muster was a feeble cough. The taste of blood was strong, and he used the tip of his tongue to press against a tooth. One of his molars was loose.

A gentle hand rested on his forehead. "Patrick?" It was Tara. She sounded far away, and her voice weak.

He fought to open his lids but regretted it when the sun's glare turned his pounding headache to a jackhammer. He squinted through the canopy overhead, but was concerned when he couldn't lift his arm to cover his eyes. "What the . . ."

Tara's face hovered over him. "Wait, we want to be sure you didn't injure your spine. We've been waiting for you to wake up." She kissed his forehead and stroked his cheek.

"What happened?" Patrick asked, but it came out in a croak.

"The Primary sent a suicide squad to attack us. Plane went down. You're the last to wake up," Jaered said from beyond Patrick's head. "Check him out, and let's get going."

Tara squeezed Patrick's toes. He nodded to confirm he felt it, and wondered where his shoes had gone. She followed her triage training and one body part after another was checked. To his relief, she announced he was good to go. Jaered reached down with his opened switch blade and cut the bindings. Tara helped Patrick to a sitting position.

They'd strapped him to a section of the tail. The rest of the jet lay side up on the ground, about twenty yards at the end of a wide path the airline dug on its skidded landing. What was left of the cockpit faced Patrick. An uprooted tree had embedded itself in the windshield.

Tara punched Patrick in the arm, hard. "Ow," he said, although it didn't throb any worse than most of his body. "What was that for?"

"Why did you go after the book?" she wailed. "It wasn't worth your life. And then you pulled your stupid hero crap and flung yourself over me. You're not expendable," Tara said.

Jaered flung a backpack over his shoulder. "There isn't a word in the English language that describes your level of stupidity."

"Where's the book?" Patrick asked. "Did it survive?" Jaered patted his pack. Patrick rose on wobbly legs and pressed fingertips to the back of his head. Dried blood stuck to his hair in clumps where it ached the most. "What about the others?"

"You can guess about the pilot, but the guy did a hell of a job bringing us down like he did," Jaered said. Honest admiration seeped into his voice. "The copilot was toast before we nosedived. Lost one of the squad when the tail separated. "A young recruit," Jaered said with a twinge of remorse. "I never caught his name."

"How far away are we?" Patrick asked.

"About two miles to the nearest road," Wyatt said, emerging from the brush. "The vegetation isn't as thick in these parts but it still took a machete to clear a path." His gaze lingered on Patrick. "You good to go?"

Patrick nodded. "Lead the way."

Tara grabbed the other backpack, but Patrick snatched it from her and slipped his arms into the straps. "I'm okay, really." Being upright and on his feet got his blood flowing and downgraded the pounding in his head to a dull ache.

"Sar or not, you were just in a plane crash," Tara said.

"I wasn't the only one." Patrick hurried to catch up with Jaered and the others.

They walked a mile or more in silence before Patrick's thoughts cleared and his shortterm memories returned. "How could they have hoped to infiltrate the jet? At the speed we were going, it would have been impossible to shyft onboard safely."

"The Primary didn't send them to commandeer the jet," Jaered said.

"He sent them to disable it, and hopefully to take out some of us in the process," Tara said.

Jaered paused and signaled Wyatt to hold up. They waited a few yards ahead and passed around a canteen. He took a swig from his canteen and offered it to Tara. She declined and handed it to Patrick.

He took a mouthful and swished it around, rinsing the blood from his teeth, then swallowed. "Why wait until we were in the air? He obviously knew we were in São Paulo. Why didn't he attack us there?" Patrick asked.

"It wasn't until we took off that we gave our hand away." Jaered stowed the canteen in the outside pocket of the pack.

"The jet's flight plan," Tara said.

Jaered slung the pack over his shoulder. "Now he knows what we're after."

"What's to stop him from sending his Pur troops to protect his mine?" Patrick asked, but Jaered didn't answer.

It took another hour for them to make it to the road and close to another hour to flag down a produce truck going their way. The five squad members didn't take any chances and turned their guns on the unsuspecting driver, who didn't hesitate to pull over.

Wyatt took the wheel and Jaered sat in the passenger seat in the front cab. Patrick, Tara, the driver, and the rest of the squad found crates of lettuce and ears of corn to sit on in the back. The refrigeration dissipated the sweltering heat of their trek to the road, but sent shivers through Patrick a few miles later. He rubbed his arms and leaned against the pack.

"You might still be in shock," Tara said, eyeing him closely.

"Look who's playing the hero," Patrick said and gave her a half-grin. "It's the Freon, not shock."

She grew pensive. "I was trained for this, Patrick. I can't turn it off, even if I wanted to."

"Does that include your emotion?" he asked, but immediately regretted it. He grasped her hand and squeezed it.

"I'm the one who's expendable, not you," she whispered.

"Don't say that," he said.

She pressed a gentle hand to his cheek and peered into his eyes. What he saw wasn't a woman in love, but a warrior. "It's the truth. Come to grips with that, and we might have a fighting chance, you and I. Not as lovers, but as co-patriots."

"What if I want both?" he asked.

Tara laid her head on his shoulder and wrapped her arm around his. "We rarely get what we want in this world."

Her words cut deep. What future would they have, even if they both survived this? He dozed off and lost all track of time until the truck slowed and the brakes hissed as it came to a stop. Tara had fallen asleep in his arms, but at the jarring motion of the tires she bolted upright, wide awake in an instant.

"Where are we?" she asked.

Patrick shrugged and stood, stretching his sore limbs and flexing his neck. Every inch of him screamed for something to ease the aftereffects of his body falling to earth, but no one had offered anything and he wasn't going to appear the wimp and ask. He'd had a restless nap with Tara's words infiltrating his dreams. Patrick was the Duach Heir. If he was going to come across as half the leader Jaered was, it was about time he adopted that mindset and stopped letting his human emotions get the best of him.

Sounds of footsteps walking along the length of the truck pricked Patrick's ears. From what he could tell, no one else heard it above the refrigeration fans circulating in the cramped space. Patrick grabbed a handgun from Tara's holster, put a finger to his lips and got the others' attention with a feeble attempt at a whistle.

Patrick eased himself to the rear of the produce compartment just as the doors were unlatched and thrown open.

The tip of a gun was thrust in Jaered's face. "Put that away," he snapped at Patrick. "We're as close as we're going to get without walking into a trap." Jaered stepped to the side and held the back door wide open. The truck driver ushered everyone out quickly, perhaps concerned that the precious cool air would escape before he reached his destination.

"From this point on, we're on foot," Jaered said, stowing two handguns in the holsters under his jacket and withdrawing a rifle out of Wyatt's duffle bag. The others armed themselves with enough ammo for a small war.

Tara held up a loaded magazine for Patrick to watch what she was doing, then shoved it with a resounding *click* into the empty handle of his gun. Patrick stuck it in his belt, underneath his thousand-dollar suit jacket, which had seen better days. Jaered marveled at how far his protégé brother had come in such a short time. "What's the plan?" Patrick asked.

Jaered unfolded a map, and everyone gathered around. "For obvious reasons, we're scrapping the plan to go in the front door. From this point on, we're Squad One." He indicated Tara and Patrick. "The rest of you are Squad Two." Wyatt nodded. "Squad One will take the west entrance and work our way down to the mine. Squad Two will use the exhaust system to breech the building, and cover the elevator for us."

"We're going inside the mine?" Patrick asked.

"The Primary has converted most of his financial holdings into gold and diamonds over the past few years." Jaered folded the map. "He stores the bulk of his reserves underground."

"So, we need to find a way to get it out," Patrick said.

"Something like that," Jaered said, loading a round into his rifle.

When both squads drew within half a mile of the mine, they waited for darkness, and then separated. Jaered kept low the last few yards and crouched next to the wire fence. By the time Tara and Patrick joined him, he was busy cutting links for an opening. Patrick grabbed an extra set of wire cutters from his pack and assisted Jaered with the fence. "Remember our hand-to-hand combat training," Jaered said.

"Lose the pack if we're confronted," Tara said. "Your core blasts will trump handguns anytime, but their red glow will give us away."

"Drop everything and punch like hell. Got it," Patrick said.

They finished creating the opening and Jaered went first, tugging on the wire flap for the others to pass through. He pushed it back just enough for it to appear untouched, unless a passing guard came within a couple of yards.

The fact they hadn't found resistance was more disturbing than comforting. Jaered hoped for the best and counted on the Primary's men still combing the wreckage, trying to figure out who might've survived before descending on the mine.

A subdued flash from the opposite side of the compound stopped Jaered in his tracks, and the others held up behind him. Squad Two was in position.

Jaered took a second to peruse their surroundings. On paper, the mine was a small, privately owned company, operating for about twelve years. Eve knew better. The Primary had maintained it as private property and left the fact it was a working mine off the books for decades. When the government took notice of the mineral rights, the working mine seemed to spring up overnight. The Primary declined any attempts to negotiate a quick sale and managed to guarantee retention of his mining rights indefinitely.

From the hustle of machinery and glaring floodlights, the mine had the appearance of operating 24/7. The absence of loading trucks confirmed Eve's suspicion; whatever the workers were uncovering remained in the mine. Jaered couldn't fathom how much wealth the Primary hoarded.

"Help me catch up with what you already know," Patrick said. "Most of the Primary's finances are in gold and diamonds, not in a bank. If that's the case, why the dog and pony act at the bank earlier?"

"We needed access to his financial records to confirm that the bulk of his money wasn't there," Jaered said. "It's got to be here." He jerked his chin at the corrugated metal warehouse that served as the door to the underground mine.

"In this century, why the tangible wealth?" Patrick asked. "It would be easier, and immediate, to electronically transfer funds anywhere across the world."

"The Primary isn't keeping his wealth on Earth," Jaered said, and paused to let that sink in.

"He's using it to buy his way into the next planet," Tara said.

"Planetary minerals, such as gold and diamonds, are a universal door opener," Jaered said. "Have been for thousands of years."

"He doesn't have to start from scratch. He'll establish himself as a wealthy man and solidify his position in a strange world from the get-go. It won't take him long to create a new, massive flock of worshippers." Patrick raked his fingers through his hair. "The guy knows what he's doing."

"He's had thousands of years on Earth to get it right." Jaered held up his rifle and peered through the scope to get a closer look at the warehouse entrance. "We have until dawn to bring it crashing down."

FOURTEEN

Rayne lost sight of Ian when the gargoyle took them above the sinkhole. The vein in her neck throbbed as she scanned the nearby rock walls for any possible access to the ecosystem above, but towering, sheer cliffs prevented animals from scaling the walls and potentially escaping topside.

The waterfall made it difficult to hear much of anything, but at a snapping twig, Rayne cocked her head to the side. She ducked low and covered her mouth in the crook of her arm to muffle her gasping breaths, not yet recovered from the mad dash to keep Ian in her sights. She closed her eyes and did everything in her power to settle her beating heart. She was the stranger in this strange land. Should another walking wolf turn its attention to Rayne, she'd be dinner.

The slow prod of steps came from down the path and she carefully separated the tall grass for a better look. The two figures turned, and Rayne dropped her arm in relief. "Marcus," she hushed.

Marcus and Claude joined her. "You should have waited for us," Claude hissed. "You have no idea how dangerous it is in here."

"Where's Ian?" Marcus asked.

Rayne pointed at the opening to the sinkhole. "A gargoyle flew off with him." Marcus chuckled. "That wasn't a joke," she said.

"They're called kymera. Very ancient and rare," Claude said. "Her nest is at the peak of the waterfall."

"There was another beast, a wolf that I swear could walk on two legs," Rayne said.

"Don't tell me you've got werewolves around here." Marcus lifted his head and looked around.

"They're fenris," Claude said and withdrew the dart gun from his holster. "I haven't seen one in some time. Their leaders are quite intelligent, but most are feral animals. Expert killers, especially in a pack."

"It attacked Ian. That's when the gargoyle grabbed them both," she said. "Is there another way up to its nest?"

"There's a door to the dome, but it can only be accessed from the upper terrain," Claude said.

"Can the fenris climb?" Rayne asked.

"I doubt it," Claude said.

Rayne took off for the dangling vines growing toward the cavern floor.

"I'm too old for this crap," Marcus said.

Despite the thunderous crashing of the waterfall, the next sound stopped the blood in Rayne's veins.

Snarls. The brush rustled and collapsed about thirty yards behind them. "Run!" Marcus yelled. The snarls morphed into growls that grew closer by the second.

Marcus collided with Rayne and moaned when her power drain was triggered, but they stayed on their feet and kept going. Claude reached the closest vine and leapt up, grabbing it high above his head. He wrapped his legs around it and hand over hand, he made his way higher and higher.

Marcus gripped one. The old general's training kicked in and he made his way up the makeshift rope.

A few yards farther and Rayne reached a vine low enough for her to grasp. She wasn't as athletic as the men, and her hands slipped on the vine with its leaves coated in moisture from the waterfall. She managed to rise just out of the fenris's reach. Enraged roars came from below. The fenris were unable to scale the vines with their paws. Claws scraped across the vine and set it swinging, taking Rayne with it. She managed to hold on and inched her way toward the sinkhole opening.

The dark corridor was rank from mildew. A muted *drip, drip* came from above. A steady stream of water ran down the handcarved steps and pooled in whatever crevices it found on its way to the floor of the staircase.

The muscles in Rayne's arms and hands threatened to wane, but she clung on tighter than ever when daylight blanketed her face. The men grabbed the vine from above and pulled, lifting her to safety. She soon emerged above ground. The brilliant glare wasn't all natural. Much of its intensity came from the energy dome overhead.

Marcus stood, and grabbed his lower back with a moan. "I'm going to kill the boy, if he isn't dead already."

"He's not," Rayne said, kneeling on the ground with limp arms. Her hands were numb. "I'd know if he was."

Marcus gave her a curious stare. "What do you mean?"

Rayne couldn't tell Marcus what she didn't understand. Ever since Ian parashyfted her back to Earth, she'd felt a strange new connection. The first time she'd noticed it was weeks earlier, when Jaered brought her to Thrae. She had hoped to ask Ian's mother about it, but there hadn't been a chance.

Her chest throbbed. She'd been overwhelmed with intense heartburn since returning to the dying planet, like something had awakened inside her. That could only be true if she, too, had a core, but that was impossible. Her father had genetically engineered her to be the first female Weir Sar, but he went to his grave believing he had failed. Rayne wasn't so sure.

Marcus and Claude closed the trapdoor and they covered it with handfuls of dead grass. The gargoyle's nest was enormous, perched above the small river and supported with a checkerboard of fallen tree trunks. Movement came from the corner of Rayne's eye. The gargoyle's pointed tail waved above the rolled edge of the nest.

Chirps came from behind. Rayne stole a peek from over her shoulder. Two miniature gargoyles hopped toward her with flapping wings. The one in front took flight, but only for a second before it face-planted against the ground. The second one tripped over its sibling and they tumbled in unison with wings wrapped around each other until they came to a rest at the back of Rayne's ankles. She bit her lip to stifle a cry at the sight of dried blood covering their snouts.

One of them hopped to its feet caked in dust, and sneezed. The other rolled on its back and kicked at its sibling with a high-pitched chirp. They were no taller than a foot, but with wing spans twice as long. They were the color of putty with bright-pink tongues that whipped in and out like snakes.

A looming shadow engulfed Rayne and a deafening roar dropped her to her knees. She cowered with her hands covering her ears.

"Stop!" Ian shouted. "She won't harm them. She's a friend." He placed himself between Rayne and the gargoyle with raised palms.

A moment of silence passed between Ian and the gargoyle.

"No, she only knows of you from Earth's history and statues," Ian said.

It dawned on Rayne that they were channeling. A sigh of relief deflated her chest. Marcus and Claude stood frozen nearby.

"It's okay, Rayne, you can get up," Ian said without turning around.

She stood and faced the winged animal. It was almost twice as tall as Ian and had broad shoulders with an hourglass waist. The legs resembled a lion's hind legs. She stared at the retracting claws until they all but disappeared inside the gargoyle's paw.

"She was only protecting her babies," Ian assured everyone. "She meant no harm."

"Uh, huh," Marcus said, not peeling his eyes from her.

"Her name is Jestueax. She has sworn allegiance to the Heirs and is willing to introduce us to the other great beasts of Thrae," Ian said.

"She has a name?" Claude whispered. He approached with cautious steps. "I've never seen her this close." Jestueax lowered her head and stared at Claude face to face.

Ian took a step toward Claude. "She has recognized all that you've done to care for the most feared beasts of Thrae. You have her undying gratitude. She wishes for you to care for her offspring until our return."

Emotion crept into Claude's expression and he slowly nodded. "Tell her I will guard them with my life."

"She understands everything, although she is unable to form the sounds," Ian said.

"May I touch you?" Claude asked. "It is our custom to greet through touch."

Jestueax unfurled one of her wings and wrapped it around Claude like a blanket, pulling him close. The old game warden's lower lip quivered.

Once Ian relayed the necessary care for Jestueax's offspring, he climbed upon her back. Claude fell to one knee and helped the squawking babies up so they could perch on his shoulders.

"I'll be back once we find Oocaw," Ian said. "Then we'll set out to connect with the other animals."

"It's a big planet," Marcus said.

Ian held onto Jestueax's folds at the back of her neck. "I've been to her den. It's a good place to start." The gargoyle hopped from one paw to another in an impromptu dance. "The dragon's den is halfway around the world. I'm going to need the dome's energy if I hope to shyft us both there."

"The energy column is not far. Jestueax can fly you there," Claude said. One of the gargoyle babies nipped at the snowy tuft of hair sticking out of the warden's ear. If it pained him, he didn't let on.

"Ian, be careful. We still don't know if Aeros followed us to Thrae," Rayne said.

He gave her a reassuring smile. "Likewise."

Jestueax extended its wings and flapped. It dredged up the surrounding dirt and covered them in a fine layer of dust.

The gargoyle lifted into the air and with a tremendous roar, it shot straight for the dome's ceiling. A second before smashing into the force field, the gargoyle dipped and dove for the sinkhole opening. Rayne reached the edge in time to see Ian flying over the trees below, headed for the far reaches of the cavern.

FIFTEEN

Marcus tossed Rayne a concerned glance that gave her pause. "What is it?" she asked.

"The only way back down, is the way we came up," Marcus said.

"If we're lucky, the fenris were discouraged and left." But from Claude's expression, the game warden wasn't convinced.

"Regardless, they'll pick up our scent the second that door's open," Marcus said.

"Can't you shyft us?" Rayne asked.

"I lost my core power as soon as we put some distance between us the green crystals. There's not enough to shyft you." He averted his gaze.

Her drain would rob him of what little he had. Marcus could get himself to safety, maybe even Claude. But not her. "Go, get help," she said.

"We're not leaving you," Marcus said. "End of story."

The gargoyle pups whipped their tails at each other from behind Claude. He cringed when one of the blows missed and connected with the back of his head. Rayne pressed her shoulder against Claude's and one of the pups hopped onto her. It dug its claws in but to her relief, they weren't near as long as its mother's.

"You know the area and the animals better than anyone," Rayne said. "What do you suggest?"

Claude thought for a moment. "I hate to put untrained engineers at risk with any of these beasts, but I suppose this calls for an exception." He removed a walkie-talkie from his belt and turned a dial. Static spit from the speaker. He brought it to his mouth while depressing the button on the side. "Control room, come in."

"Control room here," floated out.

"Three of us," he paused at the gargoyle pup's yawn, "plus a couple of tagalongs, need reinforcements in dome four. Over." Claude lowered the walkie-talkie as far as his shoulder.

"Unless this is a life-or-death emergency, you'll have to wait," the voice said. "Big Red is headed our way, and dome three has sprung a leak."

"Affirmative," Claude said, and rotated the dial. He returned the walkie-talkie to his belt. "Looks like we're on our own."

"What's Big Red?" Marcus asked.

"The methane cloud," Rayne said.

"It's the largest storm front we have on Thrae and it traverses the globe, suffocating everything in its path," Claude said. "If dome three is compromised, so are the plants and animals within it."

"We've got to get back and try to help," Rayne said. "Think, there must be a way."

"Preferably that won't get us mauled by those rabid dogs," Marcus said.

Claude stared at the gargoyle pup resting on Rayne's shoulder. It'd fallen asleep with its snout pressed under one wing and its tail wrapped around her upper arm. "We swore to protect them," she said. "Whatever the plan, they're part of it."

"Agreed," Claude said. When he glanced over his shoulder, the pup's snout found the warden's ear and he shivered from the tickle. "I have an idea, but you won't like it." He walked toward the nest and disappeared around the other side.

A moment later, a rancid smell wafted toward them. Rayne's stomach lurched. Claude emerged, smeared in gargoyle dung. She had no idea what it consisted of, and didn't want to know.

"Oh, hell no," Marcus muttered.

The rest of the sinkhole cavern stretched for miles and Ian enjoyed his birds-eye view. The environment was lit by veins of the planet crystals with intermittent openings, exposing the sky and dome overhead. Wherever the natural light bled into the cavern, the vegetation changed from one ecosystem to another.

Jestueax's flight was a ballet of pumps and glides. Unlike Oocaw's dragon scales, Jestueax's wing joints at her shoulders made it easy to hang on and Ian's legs were the perfect length, enabling him to press his feet against her wings. Without the aid of an instruction manual or the need to channel, Ian discovered whenever he applied more pressure to one foot over the other, he could steer Jestueax, similar to a bareback rider on a horse.

You are a magnificent beast, Jestueax, Ian channeled.

I am the creation of all that hailed before me, Jestueax replied. *Nothing more, nothing less.*

Ian smiled at how humble Jestueax's thoughts sounded, but from the sudden warmth billowing from the animal's flank, he knew she felt pride.

The light in the cavern grew brighter, despite no opening in sight. Ian sat upright, peering over Jestueax's shoulder. A tremendous column of vertical energy shone ahead. The gargoyle skimmed over the tops of trees, banking a hard left, and then right, while Ian felt the tugs and pulls of flimsy branches against his boots.

As they neared, Jestueax reared back, and Ian hung on tight. She approached a clearing in front of the column while reaching out with her paws. They touched ground, and Jestueax landed with a jolt that buried Ian's face at the back of her neck. She dipped one of her shoulders and Ian slid off her wing. She folded them behind her and stood in wait, several feet from the column.

Are there any animals that live in this part of the cave? Ian asked.

The energy disturbs all living things, large and small, Jestueax channeled. She lowered her eyes, in reverence, or to avoid being blinded by the column's light was anyone's guess.

It was then that Ian understood why the clearing was so wide. Not only did the column emit energy, it also absorbed it. Nothing could grow within several feet. *Have you ever touched it?* Ian asked. Jestueax shook her head.

Ian approached the column and reached inside, up to his wrist. His core absorbed power, filling to full capacity within seconds, and his chest sizzled with renewed strength.

How does it . . . Jestueax paused.

How could Ian describe it in a way the animal might understand? *It feels like the air during a lightning storm,* he channeled. Jestueax didn't respond and Ian wondered if the animal was remembering its time on Earth, centuries earlier. *Are you ready?* Ian asked. The gargoyle stepped toward the column with cautious steps. *You need to be touching me for this to work,* Ian channeled.

I may be centuries old, but my memory is as strong as ever, the gargoyle responded.

Ian hid his grin as Jestueax rested one of her wings across his shoulders. He stuck his hand inside the column and drew upon the energy. The tingling ignited his core and spread to Ian's limbs. The gargoyle shuddered.

Ian shyfted them halfway around the world.

They appeared deep in Oocaw's den. Ian had chosen the spot where Rayne had left scratches in the rock wall weeks earlier. If Oocaw was sleeping or feeding, this was deep enough in the cave not to shyft on top of her and potentially meld together.

Ian cocked an ear in the direction of the cave entrance. If she was home, nothing gave her presence away.

Jestueax wandered about, alternating between sniffing and scowling. *Why is it so offensive?*

Her cave is a horizontal branch of a volcanic plume, Ian responded, then realized it might have been too scientific an answer for Jestueax to understand. *She draws her power from the volcano's energy, deep in the planet.*

Jestueax sneezed and wiped her snout with the edge of her wing. She headed in the direction of fresher air.

Ian caught up and fell in step with her brisk walk. *We need to be cautious,* Ian channeled.

Then the introductions are yours to make, Jestueax replied.

They'd walked about a quarter of a mile until a subtle vibration stopped Ian in his tracks. The ground beneath his feet rumbled at the same time a loud, drawn-out *craaack* came from overhead. The earthquake grew in intensity and the surface of the cave walls crumbled. Ian crouched and raised his arm to shield his eyes.

A huge stalactite jarred loose and fell toward them.

Jestueax swept Ian up in her wing and twisted them out of harm's way. *I suggest we keep going,* the gargoyle channeled.

This way, Ian urged. They hurried in the direction of the cave entrance, but Ian's steps slowed as the path grew steeper. Jestueax extended her wing and ushered Ian along, using her claws to dig into the dirt path for a surer grip.

Ian didn't recall the pronounced incline of the path from his earlier visit. He feared the volcanic activity from below was reshaping the volcano's chimney. If so, they were in graver danger than he realized.

The heat at Ian's back grew fierce. "We need to move!" he shouted, relying on his tone to convey what his thoughts didn't.

Jestueax encased Ian in one of her wings and took flight, taxing the other to keep them airborne. The beast's grunts echoed off the cave walls, drowning out the volcanic rumbles.

Ian drew upon his core at the same time sulfuric acid burned his lungs, but the tingling cold of his attempt to shyft never came. His thoughts turned darker than the surrounding ash.

SIXTEEN

Jaered wanted to crawl out of his skin. A mere fifty yards separated them from the entrance to the mine building, but it was wide open in all directions, not offering coverage for them to advance any farther.

The decision to approach under the cover of darkness had been trumped by the fact there was an absence of vehicle traffic. The mine appeared to run on a graveyard shift and Jaered hadn't seen more than five men walking around. If the Primary didn't know they had survived the plane crash, he would soon.

At the sound of a distant engine, Jaered stole a peek above the crate. A weathered truck with a rising aluminum frame approached with grinding gears. The frame was covered in a camouflaged print tarp. From the truck's jiggle and flailing jerk at each pothole in the road, Jaered guessed it was empty, or near empty.

A few minutes later, the electronic gate opened to admit the vehicle into the mine's inner compound. Jaered raised his scope when it stopped, and the driver handed the guard a paper. From what Jaered could tell, the driver was the sole occupant. Jaered slung his rifle over his shoulder and gestured for Patrick and Tara to get ready.

They waited for the truck to pass their hiding spot behind some stacked, rectangular metal crates. Jaered made a dash toward the truck and jumped onto the passenger side of the bed. He clung to the tarp ropes and gripped the side with the toes of his boots.

Tara appeared next to him and worked her way up another rope, one hand above the other, until she pulled herself high enough to support her weight on the upper edge of the truck bed.

At a thick, rising cloud of dust floating out the rear, Jaered noticed dragging boots that swung in and out of sight from beneath. Patrick had a lot to learn about being stealthy, Jaered thought, and rolled his eyes. He let go of one of the ropes, traversing the other until he reached the upper side of the truck alongside Tara. He stole a glance in the rearview passenger mirror, but in the wee hours of the night, the truck's tires kicked up enough dust to conceal their hitchhiking.

The vehicle slowed and lights grew brighter. It pulled to a stop next to the warehouse building and the driver got out. Footsteps came from the opposite side. Metal scrapes and squeaky hinges preceded a *clang* when the back hatch dropped open. Scrapes rang out from inside the cab when the driver dragged something out the back, then walked away from the truck.

Jaered held a finger to his lips and Tara nodded, not moving. They waited another couple of minutes and when it was obvious no one returned, they lowered themselves to the ground and crouched low.

Patrick was caked in dirt and his face scrunched like he was fighting a sneeze.

Jaered tugged on his arm, indicating he could let go of the undercarriage. Patrick gave into his sneeze. A wisp of dirt mixed with mucous smeared Jaered's hand. Patrick dropped with a muted thud and Jaered and Tara pulled him out from under the truck.

"Breathe in through your mouth and out your nose," Tara whispered. "Pinch your nose if you're about to sneeze again."

Jaered rose higher and peeked under the tarp. The back of the truck carried the same long metal crates they'd used as cover for half the night.

"What's inside them?" Tara asked.

"I suspect they're empty," Jaered said.

They ducked at approaching footsteps. The driver's side door opened and closed. The engine turned over.

"Now or never," Tara said.

Jaered rolled under the truck and came to a stop against the corrugated metal siding of the warehouse. Tara did the same. Patrick landed on top of her. They lay still until the truck backed up and turned away from the building.

During their long vigil, Jaered had tuned into the guards' rotations, and he estimated they had two minutes to make it inside. He took off for the rear of the building with Tara and Patrick following.

To his dismay, there wasn't a rear entrance. Tara gave him a raised eyebrow.

Patrick crouched next to the rear wall. He ran his hand across the surface, then paused. He stuck a finger in a hole about knee high where a stray bullet, or something similar, had pierced' the back wall. Patrick withdrew his finger when Jaered crouched lower. The hole gave him an inside view.

Jaered squinted. There were two men standing with clipboards next to the elevator shaft. Their hard hats had printed words on the side, but because of how the men were positioned, Jaered couldn't read what their hats said.

The center of the building was lit with floodlights aimed into the elevator shaft. A caged elevator sat at the opening. The rest of the building was in shadows. A couple of heavy equipment lifts and an open bed two-ton truck were parked off to the side. An upstairs office sat at the top of a metal staircase. The office lights were on and the door open. Lack of movement or loud voices made it impossible to tell how many people might be inside.

Music blared. The two men in hard hats, talked amongst themselves and occasionally made notations on their clipboards. Otherwise, all was serene. Whenever the men spoke, Jaered couldn't make out what they were saying. The dialect wasn't the typical cadence of Portuguese.

"Well?" Patrick whispered.

Jaered pushed away from the hole and sat on the ground. Tara stooped low to peruse the interior for herself. "Now that

I got my bearings, I can shyft us inside the building. But from this angle, I can't see into the mine," he said.

"The elevator shaft is the only way down," Tara mumbled with her face pressed against the wall. She pulled away from the peephole. "The second we operate that elevator, we give ourselves away."

Patrick threw them a sly grin. "Distractions are my specialty."

Tara grabbed his chin and planted a wet kiss on his forehead. It glistened in the moonlight. "That's my hero."

Patrick held up a lighter. "Just point me in the direction of a trash can."

But their adolescent behavior gave Jaered a better idea.

Hoots and shouts came from the front of the warehouse. From his peephole, Jaered watched the two hard hats lower their clipboards and hurry in the direction of the voices.

A shadow filled the office doorway and the man walked to the railing. Jaered pulled back when he recognized Falcon, the Primary's lieutenant. Jaered's thoughts raced. The man would recognize Patrick and Tara. Their cover would be blown.

He had to warn them, but it was too late when their voices came from the open doorway. Patrick and Tara stepped into the warehouse with purpose.

"This is private property," one of the hard hats said. "You're trespassing."

"We're here on business," Patrick said.

Tara raised her chin. "The Primary sent us."

A lump lodged in Jaered's throat as Falcon silently descended the stairs with a bemused expression. Jaered willed them to look up, but they broke into their skit, unaware of the danger.

Falcon leapt over the staircase railing and landed in a crouch. He approached Patrick in no time and grabbed him by the arm.

Recognition lifted Tara's expression, and she glanced in Jaered's direction with a look of sheer panic. She rushed toward Patrick, but the closest hard hat jerked her back, not letting go. "What the hell!" she yelled. Jaered couldn't tell if the fear in her voice was real or contrived.

"I swear you two are like a bad penny," floated down from upstairs. "Where's the Heir, or has he abandoned you, too?" The Primary stepped out of the office and glared at them both.

Falcon grabbed Patrick. "By all means, have a closer look. He grabbed Patrick's belt and lifted him. Patrick struggled, trying to grasp the edge of the elevator cage dangling overhead, but it swung out of the way.

Jaered pushed away from his peephole to shyft, but couldn't draw the energy quick enough. Falcon let go, dropping Patrick into the mine shaft.

Tara's scream drowned out the background music. Jaered pressed an ear to the hole, but try as he might, he couldn't hear anything from the depths of the elevator.

She transformed into a feral cat and scratched at the hard hat's face and neck. Bloody streaks ran from his cheek to his shoulder, but he didn't let go.

The Primary's gaze turned murderous. "I've lived for centuries!" he said, tugging on his long sleeve. "Yet you treat me like these foolish humans."

"Murderer!" Tara screamed. She managed to slip out of the hard hat's grasp and she took off up the stairs, headed for the Primary.

She almost reached him when he lifted his hand. Tara rose from the staircase, suspended in midair, clawing at her throat. The Primary brought his fingers together, and her screams turned to gargling and choking.

Jaered's pulse pounded in his ears. She was too close to the Primary. It was impossible to shyft inside and rescue her, without potentially taking the Primary with them.

A second later, the Primary flicked his hand and Tara crumbled onto the metal stairs, gasping for air.

He crouched over her. "The powerless human was expendable, but you . . ." He grabbed her arm and pulled her to stand, but she was too weak. He stroked her cheek. "You, my dear, will tell me everything I want to know."

"Should I take her below?" Falcon asked.

"No, I want to make an example of her when the time comes." The Primary shyfted Tara away in an emerald cloud. Falcon peered into the mine shaft, then shyfted.

Jaered leaned his shoulder against the outside wall and slid to the ground in utter defeat.

SEVENTEEN

A tingling sensation spread from the center of Jaered's chest to his hand, and he scooted away from the sparkling, crimson image. Patrick solidified beside him.

"What the . . ." Jaered grabbed his brother by the shoulders to make sure he wasn't a mirage. "How did you—"

"I shyfted before I crash-landed. I floated a couple feet from the ground, ready to catch Tara in case they sent her down after me. When nothing happened, I took a quick look around the mine before shyfting back." Patrick peered into the peephole. "Where's Tara?"

"The Primary took her," Jaered said.

"No!" Patrick scrambled to his feet, but Jaered grabbed him and pressed a hand to his mouth. "Where?" Patrick shouted, but his voice came out muffled from beneath Jaered's muzzle.

"I don't know," Jaered said.

"We've got to find her," Patrick hissed between clenched teeth.

"If we complete our mission, he'll give us whatever we want. That includes Tara," Jaered said. He hoped he came off more convincing than he felt. "You need to shyft me into the mine. The longer this takes, the more time he has with her."

Patrick stared at Jaered, weighing his options. He grabbed Jaered's shoulder in a painful vice and shyfted them. They appeared standing on the elevator platform deep inside the mine. Jaered looked up the shaft. If Patrick hadn't kept his wits while falling, his brother would have been dead for sure.

"This way," Patrick said with forced civility. He led Jaered down a narrow tunnel lit with a string of dim lights. A few flickered, threatening to die, but then found renewed life and shone as bright as ever.

The lower chambers were a spider web of interconnecting rooms, each bigger than the next. It was eerily quiet. Jaered had no trouble picking up on Patrick's heartbeat. For all his outward control, the guy's pulse pounded in his chest. Jaered willed his brother to keep his cool and wanted to believe they would get Tara back.

For that to happen, they needed one gigantic carrot to dangle in front of the Primary. Something he desired more than revenge. When it was clear they were alone, Jaered broke the silence. "He doesn't know about you."

Patrick stilled. "What are you talking about?"

"The Primary called you a powerless human," Jaered said. "He still doesn't know you're the third Heir."

"If he has his way with Tara, that might not be true much longer," Patrick said.

The truth behind Patrick's words fueled their steps and they paused at a door where the vortex energy felt the strongest. A subtle glow leaked into the corridor from beneath. Jaered wrapped his fingers around the handle and shoved the door open.

They stepped into a massive room with a wide, sparkling vortex at its center. It reminded Jaered of the energy columns on Thrae.

The room was filled floor to ceiling with stacked rectangular metal boxes, identical to the ones he'd seen in the delivery truck. Jaered estimated there had to be hundreds or more of the coffin-sized containers.

Patrick approached the nearest box and lifted the lid. It held gold bars. "I'm guessing we found the Primary's piggy bank," he said.

Jaered opened a container. It was half filled with rough stones. He picked one up and held it to the light coming from the vortex. "I think these are uncut diamonds."

Patrick wandered closer to the vortex, but stopped and pressed a fist to his chest. "Wow, that really tickles," he said.

Jaered thrust his hand into the energy field. His core ignited and the afterburn took his breath away. "It's got to be one of the most powerful vortexes on Earth."

"My mother may command a shipping fleet, but this . . . this is something different altogether," Patrick said.

His comment hit home and Jaered stared at the energy field with fresh eyes. "This is how he transports it." The revelation of what they'd uncovered, where they were, gave Jaered an adrenaline shot of hope. He rushed among the boxes, opening one after another. Each one was either filled to the top with gold bars, or partially packed with precious gems. Besides the uncut diamonds, he discovered rubies, emeralds, and sapphires. There were minerals he couldn't identify, and others that his nose couldn't miss, like sulfur and the pungent garlic of arsenic. Eve's intel had come through in aces. Jaered wondered who her mole was to be privy to this kind of intel.

Patrick didn't share Jaered's enthusiasm. He sat on the edge of a crate with a stooped back. "Now that we found it, how does it help to get Tara back?" he asked.

"We use it to find the real prize," Jaered said. "Where he's taking it."

"The vortex doesn't have a circuit board we can hack into." Patrick picked up an emerald off the ground. "How are we supposed to figure it out?"

Jaered sobered. Even if the Primary hadn't kept his stash a secret, the vortex field was huge and the Primary's powers were endless. He wouldn't require help to transport it. Jaered's moment of elation drained between blinks. "I have no idea."

"I do," Patrick said. "But we have to act fast if we're to get Tara back in one piece." He tossed the emerald into the air and caught it, closing his fingers around it. "And I guarantee, you're not going to like it."

Strong hands shoved Tara from behind, and she tasted dirt when she landed on the floor of her cell. The door slammed behind her with a resounding *Clang!* A metal scrape locked her inside. She rose on all fours with a sharp inhale, but it morphed into a sob and she collapsed onto her side. Tara curled up into a ball, consumed at the loss of Patrick to the man she'd served and revered for half her life.

"Mara," she whispered. A feeble attempt to summon her sister, who'd been with her in spirit since the estate fire took the body, but not the soul. "Mara, please take care of him until I join you both."

Tara stared at the ceiling of the earthen cell. Her sister's apparition didn't have to appear for her to know Mara was still with her. All Tara had to do was look in a mirror.

The cell was about the size of the walk-in freezer at Eve's training center. A metal chair leaned on its side against the far wall. The absence of a cot, mixed with the odor of blood in the room, left little doubt this was the Primary's torture chamber.

Tara stood and peered out into a tunnel lit by a dim light at the far end. She was in an underground cell block.

How long would it take for them to find her here? She chastised herself for not using her head when she was whisked away, but she'd been too distraught and half-strangled to notice details.

She closed her eyes and drew upon her meditation training. In through the mouth, out through the nose. Her breathing mantra relaxed her in mind and body, and she kept at it for the next several minutes with her palms pressed together in front of her.

Memories flowed and mingled. The warehouse mine, the Primary at the top of the stairs. She never laid eyes on Jaered, but trusted that he was there, watching from their peephole. At the large shyftor tossing Patrick over the rail, Tara's stance wavered, but she regained control of the images and swept her emotions to the side. There had been something that sat at the back of her mind. A stitch in the events that was frayed, and didn't belong.

Tara focused on images and details her emotions kept behind an invisible door. The smell of the room with its leaking oil and diesel in puddles where equipment sat here and there. A flicker of lights from the upstairs balcony, and the scuffle of the Primary's steps across the metal scaffold.

She cleared her mind, tumbling into a void of nothingness that engulfed her, and she tuned out her senses, focused on nothing but her memories.

An eternity later, the itch revealed itself. Tara opened her eyes with a start. It wasn't what she'd seen, felt, or heard. It was the absence of something that caused a sliver of hope. While falling to his death, Patrick hadn't screamed.

A door opened and closed in the distance. Tara rose on tiptoes and peered out the barred opening in her cell door.

It was Heinrick, the Primary's assistant, carrying a tray covered in a loose cloth. It had been years since she'd seen the wiry, mid-aged man, but would never forget his sharp nose and large ears that protruded between long strands of graying hair. He was shorter than Tara remembered, but his dark, piercing eyes had always left her cautious.

His gait slowed, and she dropped out of sight, standing at the ready to jump him. His footsteps stopped on the other side of her door. "Move to the back of the cell," he commanded. Although he couldn't see where she stood through the thick planks, Heinrick was familiar with Tara's training. He was no fool.

She shuffled her steps loud enough for him to hear her comply, and she leaned against the back wall of the cell. Keys clinked against each other, and the cell door opened wide enough for Heinrick to enter. He paused.

"Those bloody idiots, what did they do with the table?" Heinrick muttered. He shifted the tray to one hand and waved his other. A small wooden table appeared in the middle of the room and he set his tray on it.

"Where's the Primary?" Tara asked. "Or doesn't he have the stomach for this?"

"I serve my master in many capacities," Heinrick said with his shoulders rising in pride. He stretched his hand toward the metal chair. It flew toward him, froze in midair, righted itself with a turn of Heinrick's wrist, then rested on the dirt floor. "To answer your first question, the Primary will be along shortly. I am here to prep you."

He removed the cloth, like a magician exposing a trick. It revealed a fluid-filled syringe.

"What's that?" Tara asked, but glanced toward the empty corridor, confused why Heinrick came alone without backup. The keys jingled at his waist as he folded the cloth and placed it next to the tray. Tara had no intention of being his next meal. She took a step toward him as every muscle tensed at the ready.

"I don't suggest making a—" Heinrick paused and stared ahead. "What do the Americans call it? Making a break for it?" He sighed. "So many languages, colloquiums, metaphors, and idioms to keep straight nowadays. They change faster than my underwear."

At his attempt to make a joke, Tara hesitated. The man had never uttered a word. He and the Primary communicated with looks and gestures. It never occurred to Tara until that second that perhaps they could channel.

Heinrick lifted the syringe and pressed the plunger with his thumb. A squirt burst from the tip of the needle. He returned it to the tray and regarded her with a keen eye. "Now, are we going to do this the easy way, or the painful way?"

"I still don't know what this is," Tara said.

"The injection acts as a kind of truth serum," Heinrick said. "You will tell me everything you know about Eve and her rebels, and why you and the Pur Heir's manager were snooping around the Primary's personal affairs." He clasped his hands. "And the Primary is quite eager to learn the young master's whereabouts."

Tara wanted to believe she could withstand physical torture, but mind-altering drugs were something else altogether. Regardless of what little she knew about Eve's operations, it was what she knew about Patrick that scared her the most. "That sounds like the easy way," Tara said. "What's behind door number two?"

Heinrick pursed his lips together and the knuckles on his clasped hands grew pale. "I will demonstrate why the Primary finds me . . . useful."

DIM THE LIGHTS

Behind Heinrick, a spot in the hallway grew opaque, filled with hundreds of sparks lighting the air. The wiry man didn't turn around, but gave Tara a wicked grin. "My master has arrived, and look at me, behind schedule." He grabbed the syringe off the tray, and took a step toward her.

EIGHTEEN

Sulfur burned Ian's lungs and he gasped for air. He sat up with a start, sucking in the bounty surrounding him. He turned to his side and gave into a racking cough to purge the last of the acid fumes he'd inhaled in the volcanic tunnel.

You shouldn't have come, young Heir, entered Ian's thoughts. He looked up and stared into one of the dragon's eyes, a huge onyx boulder with a golden iris.

Earth is in dire need of the wisest and most ancient, such as yourself, great Oocaw, Ian channeled.

I would have thought you beyond flattery, youngling. Oocaw pushed up from the cave floor like a rising mountain, and whipped her head about, shaking off sleep.

Ian got to his feet. Jestueax sat off to the side, near the rocky ledge. The gargoyle appeared to be dozing with its snout tucked under one wing and its chest rising and falling with subtle regularity. It all but blended into the rock wall.

Oocaw caught Ian's concern and snorted a flame of irritation. *You have brought a stranger without invitation, young Heir. I am not pleased.*

Yet, you did not harm, Ian replied. *Are you keeping it for a snack, or out of good manners?* One of Jestueax's eyelids raised at half mast, found Ian with a beady stare, then closed. Ian wondered if the animal could channel with both of them, and eavesdropped on the conversation.

Why are you here? Oocaw channeled. *Thrae is beyond your reach and certainly not of your concern. Aren't you needed on Earth?*

All are my concern, Ian replied. *What injures one, bleeds the other.*

The dragon settled onto her belly and scratched behind her brow with the tip of her wing. Ian ducked before he was beheaded by the wing's swipe. He approached and climbed onto the dragon's back, using the edges of her scales to reach the natural saddle at the base of her neck. It wasn't too long ago that he had ridden her across the land, discovering firsthand the devastating damage his father had wreaked upon Thrae.

Ian stretched his arms on either side of the dragon's neck, as far as he could reach, and pressed his cheek against her. *I need your help,* he channeled.

Thrae needs it more, Oocaw replied.

I believe we can save both Thrae and Earth, Ian channeled. *If we unite all creatures under our common enemy.*

The young have such short memories. I am the last of my kind on Thrae . . . and Earth. Oocaw scraped the rock with one claw. Ian shivered.

Would you rather stay and watch your beloved planet succumb to your greatest enemy, or spend your last breath defending it? Ian insisted.

Where is it noble to sleep while our planet burns? Jestueax fluttered her wings and rose to her full height, until her chest extended like a balloon.

You dare question me? Oocaw raised her head and sent a stream of flames beyond the cave's entrance, missing the gargoyle by mere inches.

It is not a question, Jestueax channeled. *It is a challenge. Fight alongside the great beasts of Thrae, or stay in your cave and slumber yourself into oblivion.*

Oocaw spun around knocking Ian off his perch. He tumbled down the dragon's side, landing hard against the rocky ledge.

The dragon's tail whipped through the air, headed straight for Jestueax. The gargoyle flapped its wings in a leisurely fashion and lifted off the ledge, avoiding the spikes on the tail and its razor-sharp edge with little effort.

The gargoyle dipped, avoiding Oocaw's flames. She darted at Oocaw, whipping her tail. It landed with a *smack* against Oocaw's snout. The dragon's cry rang down the valley in echoing protest.

Stop! Ian implored, unsure if his desperate channel got through or not. "Your battle is not with each other!" he shouted as the two beasts took to the air beyond the cliff and parlayed in a battle dance of cunning and wits. Wings flapped, claws thrust, and tails sliced the sky. Jestueax was the more agile of the two, but Oocaw's size and flames proved formidable as they snapped, snarled and tried to get advantage over the other. Ian's quest would be a shamble, and the risk he'd taken to return to Thrae fruitless, if these two great beasts should kill each other.

Ian planted his feet against the ledge and summoned a tremendous energy blast, coming close to draining what power he had left. It spun in a sparkling emerald, growing wider and wider with each energy draw. It wasn't until he grew lightheaded and feared he'd pass out from the power drain, that he flung the core blast between the two beasts. It exploded as a firework against the night's sky.

Startled, the two beasts jerked backward. In unison, they turned their attention to Ian while flapping their wings.

Ian teetered from the energy drain but managed to stay upright. "Now, if you two are done with your ridiculous power play," he said, "I vote we put everyone's energy to better use."

The warring beasts stared at each other in midair. Jestueax was the first to concede, turning and landing on the cliff ledge next to Ian.

Oocaw glided through the sky, turning in concentric circles like an ice skater creating a path of figure eights. Ian and Jestueax waited for the dragon in silence, and wondered if it was a demonstration of superiority, to regain its pride, or stubbornness that kept it airborne for a few more minutes.

Ian was ready to return to the sinkhole and leave the dragon behind when Oocaw swerved toward the cave. With outstretched talons, it gripped the rocky ledge with such force that boulders cracked off and tumbled down the slope.

I will return to Earth and fight alongside the Heirs, Oocaw channeled. *But you must understand that my reluctance to join your crusade has nothing to do with cowardice, indifference, or neglect.* The dragon growled at Jestueax, then marched deeper into the tunnel without looking back. Ian and Jestueax followed at a safe distance.

They traveled about half a mile when Oocaw stopped and nuzzled a pile of rocks. They rolled away, exposing a nest of tree branches and dried grass. Although the nest was not as large as Jestueax's it, too, was skillfully crafted. At the center rested a large oval rock with striations circling it.

Ian stood, speechless. He headed toward it, but caught himself. "May I?" Oocaw lowered her head onto the tunnel floor and snorted a puff of gray smoke. Ian climbed over the edge of the nest and gently touched the dragon egg. "How?" Ian asked. "You are the last."

I cannot tell you what I don't understand, Oocaw channeled. *But it is so, nonetheless.*

I, too, am a mother, Jestueax channeled, and gave the dragon a deep bow. *It appears we are kindred spirits in heart and soul after all.*

Ian pushed aside what he knew about amphibians and reptile reproduction, and settled against the nest with jockeying emotions. The full extent of what he asked of them, and their sacrifice in joining him, struck. If they didn't win this battle, these majestic beasts would be lost forever.

The stench wasn't Rayne's biggest obstacle. It was keeping the gargoyle pups calm. Claude had them tucked inside his jacket and for the first mile or so, they hadn't made a peep. But the animals must have sensed something, because they became agitated and chirped at the top of their lungs. Claude pressed his arms to his sides, perhaps to give them a reassuring hug, but they continued to squirm and chirp.

"What's wrong?" Marcus hushed from the rear of the line. He lifted the rifle, and his shadow over Rayne's shoulder rose like a whip ready to strike.

"Perhaps they're hungry, or thirsty," Claude said.

"We're a little short on baby bottles," Marcus said. "And patience."

"I'd hoped the dung would calm them and keep our scent from attracting the fenris," Claude said.

"One out of two," Marcus hissed.

"Shhh!" Rayne said. A rustle came from their flank. Everyone stilled, but a second later, Marcus nudged Rayne with the edge of the barrel. She nodded. He'd heard it, too.

"Make that zero out of two. How much farther to the energy column?" Marcus asked. He'd said it so softly, Rayne could barely make it out.

Claude held up two fingers. No way could they out-run the beasts with two miles to go. Farther up the path, a gigantic tree rose at the center of the sinkhole. It offered thick branches, but from this distance, none of them appeared close enough to the ground for the men to reach.

The gargoyle pups quieted, and Rayne stole a sigh of relief. Whatever danger they'd sensed, may have passed. A heartbeat later, the pups let out a shrill cry and flapped their wings, bulging Claude's jacket in all directions.

"Run!" Rayne headed for the tree. They took off down the path. Marcus had the longer legs, but Rayne had the youth, and they soon passed Claude where the path widened. Marcus grabbed the game warden's jacket and half-dragged him to keep up.

Snarls and growls grew fiercer as the fenris bridged the gap. The trio reached the tree and Claude bent down with clasped hands. Rayne pressed her boot against his foothold and was tossed high enough that she could wrap her arms around the lowest branch. The emerald arteries covering the cave ceiling glowed brighter. Marcus shyfted Claude and himself on top of the branch. Claude grabbed Rayne, hoisting her up and out of reach of slashing claws below.

The wolves leapt at the branch as others joined the pack. It would be impossible to evade them now. They were trapped in the tree. The two closest wolves dropped their heads back and released a deafening howl.

"That's not good," Claude said, slipping on the tree branch with his dung-covered boots. He dropped and straddled the limb. The gargoyle pups chirped but must have sensed they were safe because their cries morphed into whines.

"There's something worse than this?" Marcus asked.

Claude scooted toward the tree's massive trunk. "Those howls. They're summoning the pack leader."

"Marcus, shyft Claude to the third dome, before Big Red arrives," Rayne said.

He shook his head. "No way am I leaving you here."

"Claude needs to help the engineers with the animals," she said. "I'll climb higher and hide in the branches. As soon as you can, come back for me."

Marcus peered up the tree. Claude stared at the animals below. "She has a point," the game warden said.

"Go," Rayne insisted. "I'll be okay."

Marcus worked his way along the branch and grabbed Claude's arm. "I will return, I promise."

"If not, you'll be answering to Ian." She gave him a pained smile. They vanished. A deep breath filled her lungs with gargoyle dung as much as needed oxygen. She climbed, but as she made her way higher, her foot touched on a flimsy branch. It snapped and Rayne fell.

NINETEEN

Gunshots rang down the elevator shaft as loud as church bells in a tower. Jaered and Patrick hurried to the base of the shaft, but the commotion soon turned silent.

"Since I can't find your bloody corpses up here, are you down there?"

Jaered leaned against the elevator cage in relief. It was Wyatt. The squad leader had taken the warehouse, even without a signal.

"The Primary kidnapped Tara," Patrick shouted.

"Do you have any explosives on you?" Jaered called up.

"How much you need?" floated down.

Jaered stared at Patrick, weighing their options. He hadn't come up with a less risky plan, not if they were to get the answers they needed, and keep the Primary's attention off Tara until they could rescue her. "Enough to blow this shaft beyond repair," Jaered shouted. "With or without powers."

A drawn-out silence hung in the air. "Got it," Wyatt said. "We'll take it from here."

"I can do it," Jaered said. "Just send it down with a detonation remote." Patrick pressed the button on the control panel and with a grinding whine, the elevator cage ascended. "They can get word to your mother. She might have an idea where the Primary would take Tara," Jaered said.

"You and I both know the chances of that are slim to none," Patrick said. He headed for the vortex room. "Just hurry."

A couple of minutes later, the elevator cage *whirred* and returned with enough explosives to collapse the shaft. Jaered didn't trust his or Patrick's powers not to bring the mine down on top of them. Jaered set up the C-4 against the elevator beams several feet from the base and inserted the blasting caps. He sent the elevator topside with written instructions. Wyatt and his squad were to take off and contact Eve about Tara. Jaered couldn't tell them where he and Patrick were headed. He had no idea.

Jaered ran to the vortex room clutching the remote. Patrick had left a message for the Primary spelled out in the uncut diamond rocks at the base of the vortex.

Patrick was out of sight, but had left one of the metal container's lids propped open. Jaered counted on his brother's plan working, otherwise the storage containers would be their coffins.

He lay down on top of the padding, slammed his fist against the lid, and it shut. Jaered cursed at the top of his lungs. Patrick had misjudged the space and the lid rested a couple of inches from Jaered's nose. The remote smashed against his chest and his finger depressed the button before he was ready.

Tara's thoughts clouded and swirled. The chill of the metal chair spread to her veins and she swore ice chunks formed in her blood stream. It took a couple of breaths for them to reach her brain where a spike drove deep and threatened to split her head in two.

Heinrick's drug took full effect and she whimpered, losing her battle to the mind-altering substance. Voices came and went like an ebbed tide, and she struggled to make out their words.

"You gave her too much," the Primary said. His face drew close with a concerned expression, but his voice was more of a scolding parent.

"She resisted the first dose. I had to give her more," Heinrick said. He stood at a distance, or perhaps it was Tara's imagination because she swore his hand was on her shoulder.

A deafening bee buzzed next to Tara's ear. The Primary pulled out his cell, checking the screen. His growl, low and throaty, grew into a threatening storm.

"What is it, sire?" Heinrick asked.

"I'll be back." The Primary wandered out into the hall. Tara closed her eyes, unable to resist the weights tugging on her lids. "Get the answers I need, Heinrick," were the Primary's parting words. At a bright flash, he was gone.

Heinrick leaned in and his stale breath blew across her nose. "Rest assured, my dear. No matter what it takes."

TWENTY

The explosion rattled the metal storage containers in the vortex room. A spattering of rock and clumps of dirt landed on the container lid like hail against a tin roof. The lid popped open, then slammed shut with such force it rung Jaered's ears. A cloud of silt rushed inside and he choked.

Jaered gave thanks for his explosives training, and for not collapsing the mine on top of them. He focused on slowing his racing pulse to calm his breathing, willing Patrick to be doing the same wherever he hid.

At an itch, deep within his chest, Jaered held his breath. The vortex field sizzled as the magnetic molecules reacted to the Primary's powerful shyft.

Footsteps came to a halt and the Primary's roar filled the cavern. His uncle must have seen the message Patrick left. EVE.

The Primary's footsteps grew frantic, distancing themselves from the cavern at a mad dash down the tunnel.

A few minutes later, angry steps returned. "Ugh!" came from the entrance at the same time a massive pull of energy swept across the room. A creak of metal scraping metal came as one of the columns of stacked crates must have crashed to the dirt floor. A clatter of gold bars told Jaered at least one or more crates had burst open. Steps crunched toward Jaered's container, but paused. Creaks came in rapid succession as the Primary opened one container after another. Had he sensed Patrick and Jaered hiding close by, or was he checking that his wealth hadn't been disturbed?

Jaered clutched the remote in his hand as the Primary's frantic search reached the surrounding crates. At a buzz, the Primary's commotion came to a halt and his voice sliced into the calm. "I'm headed off world."

A moment later, Jaered's core ignited as the vortex field sucked a tremendous amount of energy, not just from the center of Earth, but from the room itself. The vortex energy swelled. Blinding light shone into Jaered's container at the slit near the unlatched lid.

The surrounding containers creaked from the increased pressure. The vibrating uncut diamonds etched pits into Jaered's back. At the exact moment Jaered couldn't take the crush in his chest, the Primary parashyfted.

Shivers racked Jaered's body and he opened his mouth, sucking stale air mixed with dirt. The tickle up his nose wouldn't be contained and he scrunched his face, managing to keep the sneeze from giving his position away. The parashyft energized his core, but he didn't dare move.

The Primary didn't waste any time, and from the energy draw, parashyfted back to Earth in a bright flash. Jaered waited a few minutes longer, then pushed the lid high enough to turn his head and peer out the opening. Once the fading sparks of the Primary's parashyft dispersed, it was pitch black. At lingering silence, Jaered rolled out of the container, landing on a dirt floor.

"Patrick?" he hushed, but was met by a foreboding calm. "Patrick!" Jaered called louder.

A moan came from the opposite side of the piled containers. "Get me out of here," Patrick said.

The collapsed tower of containers had landed on Patrick's hiding spot. Jaered tried to push them off, but they were too heavy. He pressed his hands against them and shyfted them to the center of the vortex clearing.

A muted creak, and Patrick's lid rose higher, casting the surrounding space in a gentle glow. The dull light came from his brother's torso. His core had absorbed some of the parashyft energy, much like a battery. "What the hell was that?"

"Your first parashyft." Jaered patted his shoulder. His heated breaths blew tufts of air ahead of him and he rubbed his upper arms. Were they were in a gigantic meat locker? Jaered helped Patrick out of the storage container.

Jaered stumbled about the pitch-black room, bruising his knees and shins, feeling his way toward the outer walls. His fingers found something hard and cold to the touch. He ran his palm over it. It was a wall of ice.

The room appeared, lit by a fiery, rhythmic dance. A small scarlet core blast swirled in Patrick's open palm. He held it high. Jaered studied their surroundings, committing every detail to memory.

"Fresh air, this way," Patrick said. He wormed his way between the stacked crates and headed down an ice tunnel that branched away from the huge cavern. They walked for several yards until they came to a narrow opening in the ice.

"Parashyft home, or explore further?" Patrick asked.

Jaered contemplated their options. "Let's get outside and see what we're up against."

Patrick snuffed out the core blast and turned sideways, squeezing his way through the horizontal crack about two feet wide. Jaered followed. Despite the tight fit, he managed to make it outside. It was night with a full moon casting muted shadows behind them.

Frigid gusts of wind whipped past, threatening to knock them off a narrow rock ledge and their panoramic view. Patrick whistled. They stood on the edge of a mountain with a large town sitting at its base. Hundreds, maybe thousands of lights twinkled below.

"Where are we?" Patrick asked.

"Let's find out." Jaered perused their surroundings and dropped to the closest foothold.

The wind swept across the icy mountain surface. More than once the men were forced to hug the surface or risk being knocked off the mountain face. They frequently paused to draw energy into their cores and warm themselves to avoid frostbite. The amateur rock climbers often slipped, and Patrick fell once, but Jaered managed to catch him.

It took close to an hour to reach the base of the mountain. They wandered into a large village. The stretched fur pelts and yapping sled dogs resembled those of the Inuit in Earth's North America. Patrick stopped at the next team they came across and pet the lead dog. It paused in its yelps and leaned into his touch. The rest of the team followed, calming as though of one mind.

A short-statured figure stepped out of a wooden structure and headed for the animals. He wore a bulky coat of fur patchwork, and his head was covered in a hood with a thick fur trim. The figure came to a halt at discovering Jaered and Patrick. "Who are you?" the gravelly, deep voice asked in English, clouded in a French-Canadian dialect.

"A storm struck and our party got separated. We've stumbled into your village," Jaered said. "We don't know where we are."

The man eyed their simple, thin clothes and scowled. "By the looks of it, you stumbled off course several hundred miles or more."

"We need to speak with the leader of your tribe," Patrick said.

A hearty laugh revealed stained, chipped teeth. "I don't know where you hail from, friend, but we haven't been thought of as a tribe for centuries." He ushered Patrick and Jaered inside. "Come on before you turn into icicles."

He held open the wooden door. It led to a small mud room. He stomped his boots on the floorboards to rid them of the sediment and continued into a single, massive room, supported around the center with wide, hand-carved posts. A fire sparked and crackled in a potbelly stove at the center. Thin strands of smoke leaked from where the chimney was bolted together, adding to the haze in the air. Jaered's stomach lurched at the smell of grilled meat. Several slices of fish hung from hooks. They smoked what they caught.

A man crouched next to the stove and stoked the fire with an iron rod. Another placed raw meat skewers directly on the surface of the stove. The juices sizzled and spit.

A gathering of women and men ranging in age from young teens to the elderly sat together repairing fur pelts and fabric clothing with large needles and thick thread. A middle-aged couple stood next to a sink with modern plumbing, skinning what must have been the fresh catch of the day.

The carefree conversation ceased, and a sea of eyes bore down on Jaered and Patrick.

Their escort flashed a relaxed smile. "They asked to speak to the leader of our tribe." A pregnant silence, the small crowd burst out laughing. Only the youngest of them glanced about, ignorant of the joke.

"Come, sit," their escort said. He gestured to log stumps beside the fire. One of the women grabbed a couple of large pelts and placed them across their shoulders. From the size of the hide, Jaered wondered if it was caribou. The man extended his hand. "I'm Yuka."

Jaered and Patrick introduced themselves with a firm grip. "Are you American?" Yuka asked.

"I'm from California," Patrick said.

"Even farther than that," Jaered said when Patrick's response didn't earn a raised eyebrow. This alternate Earth appeared to offer similar geographic markers.

"Welcome to Pangnirtung," Yuka said.

Given the harsh environment of where they'd landed, Jaered didn't know if Pangnirtung was a province, village name, or country. The unknown irritated the hell out of him and he'd been mulling over how to find out where they were without appearing any more like strangers than their clothes already implied.

"What brought you this far north?" Yuka asked.

"We're in search of someone," Jaered said, zeroing in on the mention of *north*. "We believe he's made several trips to this area."

"The only visitors we get are rock climbers," Yuka said. "We'll get a warm meal in you. I'll introduce you to some of the guides."

When Jaered glanced over Yuka's shoulder, one of the women gave him a pensive stare.

Yuka's family scrounged up more appropriate clothes for Jaered and Patrick, and they set out into the village, Yuka introduced them to a few of the area's climbing guides. From the looks of it, Yuka enjoyed making the rounds at his favorite taverns. Several hours later, Jaered and Patrick half-carried, half-dragged Yuka home. Although it was near midnight, the sky wasn't darker than just past sundown.

They had taste-tested many different ales and other home-brewed concoctions, but were no closer to discovering if the Primary simply stashed his wealth in the nearby mountain, or if he had begun to ingratiate himself with these people for some larger purpose.

Once Yuka's wife took over to put him to bed, Jaered and Patrick warmed their hands next to the potbelly stove. The woman who'd eyed Jaered earlier approached them with steaming mugs of strong coffee, and they accepted her hospitality. When Jaered took the mug from her, he said, "You know something about the man we seek," under his breath.

She regarded the rest of the room out of the corner of her eye. "Outside." She left, carrying the coffee pot to the sink.

Jaered and Patrick donned their pelted coats and stepped into the bitter cold with theircoffee mugs. The steam dissipated in the frigid air, and it didn't take long for their beverages to turn lukewarm.

"I think we're on Baffin Island. At least that's what they call it on Earth," Patrick said, wrapping his hands around his coffee mug.

"How'd you figure that out?" Jaered asked.

"I saw a map hanging on the back wall of one of the taverns," Patrick said. "The island is off the coast of Canada."

"Why would the Primary be interested in this region?" Jaered took a sip, scrunched his nose at the undesirable drink, and tossed it out. It blanketed the surface of the rocky ice mound like fudge topping on ice cream.

"The island's history goes as far back as the Vikings and Norse gods," Patrick said. "At least it did, back on Earth."

Jaered gave him a skeptical stare. "How the hell do you know that?"

"I'm a big Thor fan. Norse gods are right up my alley," Patrick said.

"We didn't explore the other fingers of the cave," Jaered said. "It's possible the Primary has been hording wealth here for longer than we realized."

"The one you seek claimed to be a descendent of the Viking god Thor," the woman said. She closed the door behind her. "You're off-worlders, aren't you?" she asked. "Are you gods, too?"

Jaered and Patrick exchanged uneasy glances. "How do you know him?" Patrick asked.

"I was raised in a house filled with superstition and tall tales," she said. "My grandmother spoke of a stranger who would appear after great thunderstorms and lightning that came from inside Mount Asgard." She indicated the mountain towering above the village. "He was revered as a god because of all that he controlled. The ocean tides, plants and animals. It was said that he could strike men down with the flick of his finger, and for a while, the ground was stained red after each visit."

"Why doesn't anyone here remember him?" Jaered asked.

"He has not returned for many generations," she said. "I'm not sure if my grandmother, or her grandmother before her, ever laid eyes on the Norse god. But I'll never forget the stories." She reached up and pushed the hood off her head. Wide streaks of gray blended with strands the color of coal. The elderly woman's eyes grew wide. "Has he returned? The lightning storms have struck Mount Asgard from within, several times, over the last few years. I have seen the flashes, as well as others in the village."

"But the Norse god hasn't come down from the mountain and appeared," Jaered said.

"No, I pray he stays away," she said.

Because if the Primary reveals himself, Jaered thought, the ground might once again run red with blood. He stared up at the mountain looming over the sleepy village. It was one of two, connected in the middle by a slope resembling a saddle. "What is this world called?"

If she was shocked at his question, her expression didn't give it away. "You have traveled to Smara."

"What year is it?" Patrick asked.

"Year?" She bit her lip. "I believe it is two thousand Barren. I can't remember. Time means very little to my village." Jaered fought to control his soaring impatience. They didn't have time to learn the customs and cultures of a new civilization. "How do you communicate?" he asked. "Across this world?"

"Is that what you use?" She'd been watching Patrick fiddling with the cell phone in his hand. A security blanket of sorts.

Jaered grabbed it and held it up for her to see. "We call it a cell phone. Is that term familiar to you?" She took it from Jaered and ran her finger across it. "I don't have one. But many of the visitors have something like it."

Hope ignited Jaered's core. It warmed his spirit along with his limbs. "Where do the visitors stay?" he asked.

"You will have to go farther, into the city. Perhaps near the airport. That's where many of the visitors stay." She returned to the house and disappeared inside.

"We found the Primary's wealth and where he's hiding it," Patrick said. "How does this help us get Tara back?"

"I'm not convinced this is the bulk of his holdings. Chances are he's been spreading it across Smara for years," Jaered said.

"Then he still holds all the cards," Patrick said, scratching his arm. "And Tara is as good as dead."

Patrick's gesture spurred a memory. Tara and Eve whispering before they left. Tara scratching her arm. A ray of hope flushed Jaered's concern. "I think your mother used Tara to bait the Primary."

"Damn her!" Patrick snarled. "The last time she pulled that stunt, the tracker was found and put Tara in even greater danger."

"This time, I think she injected it under her skin," Jaered said. "We're going back to Earth, but not before we get all that the Primary holds dear."

Patrick rubbed his face. "It's the middle of the night."

Jaered held out his hand. A gold bar appeared. "I'm betting this will open a few doors."

TWENTY-ONE

Rayne lay across the tree limb, stunned, and with the wind knocked out of her. For a second she couldn't remember where she was.

Snarls and gnashing fangs brought her back to reality. She straddled the branch and lay her head on it to regain her senses.

The snarls and growls quieted. Rayne lifted her head. An enormous wolf entered the group on all fours, slashing out to either side with a quivering lip and fangs that reached as long as a saber-toothed tiger. As the beast neared, it rose to its back legs and stood a good foot taller than the nearest contender.

Rayne sat stock-still. Sweat blended with the gargoyle dung and dripped down her cheek and under her shirt. Her short nails dug into the bark of the tree.

The fenris leader stopped under the branch where Rayne sat and turned a dark eye on her, then cocked his head. Confusion leapt into the animal's expression and its snout wrinkled, exposing front incisors that made Rayne's legs quiver. It gnashed its teeth and spewed grunts much like a pig. As it walked around the tree, the lesser of the pack backed away.

The beast jumped onto the tree trunk, digging its claws deep into the bark. With a solid hold, the animal leapt higher, landing again with all fours digging into the bark. It repeated the action until its head was even with the branch supporting Rayne. She stood and jumped for the limb above her, snagging a solid handhold. But the gesture didn't discourage the fenris and it leapt onto the branch Rayne had just vacated. It scurried on all fours along the limb, snarling with dripping fangs. Rayne hung on tight, but her branch was too flimsy and she couldn't pull herself up. She lifted her legs, wrapped them around it, and reached out. She pulled back on another hanging limb.

The fenris leader attempted to stand on the lower limb, but slipped and it dropped back to all fours. With a toss of its head, it lunged for Rayne.

She let go of the loose branch. It struck the fenris leader hard enough that the animal lost its balance in midair and fell to the side, missing the lower limb. The beast dropped to the ground below.

Howls and snarls erupted from the crowd. They surrounded their leader but the enormous fenris was not discouraged. It rose on hind legs, enraged, giving off an ear-splitting howl. The rest of the pack held to the edge of the vegetation. This was their leader's prey.

Drool dripped from its fangs. Rayne didn't have to be a mind reader to know what the beast was thinking. She grabbed the branch with both hands and drew upon her years in gymnastics to swing herself up to the next branch. She worked her way higher in a circular pattern while the fenris leader followed her progression from the ground. When it became clear she wasn't going to fall and make herself an easy meal, the animal dug its claws into the tree trunk and reached the lower limb. The wolf sprang from branch to branch and closed the gap between his prey and victory.

He reached a height level with where Rayne stopped to catch her breath, and perched on the opposite side of the tree. The wolf had learned from its first mistake and didn't lunge at her, but kept her in his sights, stalking her in the branches, perhaps hoping she'd make a fatal error and plummet to the ground where the rest of the pack would pin her down until their leader could enjoy the kill.

Rayne slid along the last of the sturdy branches as far as she dared. At the sound of a crack, she stopped and hugged the branch tight. If the fenris lost its patience and joined her, they'd both fall to their deaths and the pack would fight over their carcasses.

At a snarl from behind, Rayne closed her eyes and thought of Ian. "I'm so sorry I pushed you away," she whispered. Tears welled up in her lower lids. Regret weighed heavy in her heart at hurting him that morning on the oil tanker. If she could, she'd take it all back and leave him filled with hope, even when she didn't believe it herself.

A bright flash came from the direction of the energy column. Rayne lifted her head, fearful Claude and Marcus had returned for her, only to be cut down long before they could reach her. She was at a loss how to signal for them to stay away.

A tremendous stream of fire spread across the sink-hole ceiling, setting some of the dangling vines ablaze and spreading blistering heat across the upper cavern.

Howls turned to yelps of pain. Rayne looked down. Jestueax swooped out of reach of the fenris. With extended claws, she ripped at the heads of the pack, using her razor-sharp wings to scatter them.

Oocaw banked and headed for the tree, lowering one wing as if to slice off the top canopy. Ian slid down the dragon's wing and hopped off, landing in the topmost fork of the tree trunk. He raised his hand and an emerald core blast appeared. He flung it at the fenris leader a second too late. The wolf sprang at Rayne. The branch supporting her cracked and the wolf slashed at her as they fell, becoming entwined in the branches.

Jestueax gripped a tree branch and swung full circle, catching Rayne's shirt. The fenris leader landed on the ground with a sickening *thud*. Unmoving, its long purplish tongue protruded from its snout. The rest of the pack scattered except for the bravest few. They hovered over their fallen leader with death cry howls.

The crystal arteries and veins flickered. Ian shyfted to the branch above Jestueax. "Rayne!" he shouted.

"It's about time you showed up," she said in a voice weaker than she meant.

His eyes smiled at her, even when his lips couldn't.

Ian insisted they return to Jestueax's nest to give Rayne a much-needed rest. Once she was safe, he shyfted to the engineers' control room to see if they needed help with the dome repairs or herding the animals. As they had everything under control, Marcus sent him back with the gargoyle pups, which made Jestueax happy.

To Oocaw's chagrin, the pups rolled her egg back and forth until Jestueax saved it from their impromptu game. The gargoyle made a warm spot for it and camouflaged it among the branches in the folds of her nest. It took a couple of growls and wing swipes, but the pups soon got the message they were to leave it alone, and they turned their attention on Rayne. It was clear she wouldn't be getting a nap.

TWENTY-TWO

A bright glare lit up the hallway beyond the torture cell. Tara lifted her head and her drowsy thoughts focused on the Primary's image solidifying before her. She had no idea where he'd disappeared to and why he was gone for so long.

Things were about to heat up.

The Primary paused in the doorway and gave her a scrutinizing stare. "Heinrick?" he said, but silence answered back.

Closer, Tara inwardly urged. Step inside, goddamn it! Were the Primary's powers equal to his brother's? Could he channel with Tara against her will? Her eyelids fluttered and she dropped her head back, no longer resisting the drugs, allowing them to screw with her thoughts.

The Primary took a step back and glanced up and down the dark corridor. "Heinrick!"

Tara dropped her face and muttered to herself.

"Where did he go?" the Primary asked.

The second he stepped through the doorway, Tara activated the jamming device hidden behind her. He stumbled and pressed a fist to his chest at his inability to draw power. Eve rushed in from the cell next door and stuck the needle in his neck. In the space between blinks, the Primary became their prisoner.

The startled look on his face brought a grin to Tara's. She stood off to the side of the chair and gestured for the Primary to take her seat.

Confusion played across his features and he stood without moving until Eve came into view. It took a couple of minutes for his baffled expression to sear with hatred. "You've aged," he hissed.

"Have you looked in a mirror lately?" She walked away.

The Primary reached for Eve but before he could wrap his hands around her neck, the Taser ripped into the side of his neck and he writhed in pain, dropping to his knees at her feet. Tara dropped the discharged gun, and Eve tossed her a fresh one.

Eve leaned her back against the cell wall. "I wouldn't try that again if I were you," she said. "As you can see, there's plenty more where that came from."

The Primary slowly got to his feet. His groan wasn't one of pain, but utter disgust. This time when Tara gestured toward the chair, the Primary obliged. "Where's Heinrick?" he asked. "How'd you find this place?"

"Heinrick's tied up in the cell next door." Eve strolled around the chair like an animal taunting its next meal. "As to how." She held up the tracking device she'd removed from under Tara's skin.

Tara extended her forearm, presenting the wound, still lined in beads of coagulating blood. She pulled down her sleeve and ignored the impulse to scratch it.

Eve stared at the tiny device. "Your biggest weakness is that after all these centuries, you still think old school, Johann."

"She was bait," he grumbled.

"You tried to kidnap Tara in London," Eve said. "That told me you had plans for her. I counted on you trying again."

"*We* counted on it," Tara said.

Eve pushed away from the wall. "I bet you're keeping this location secret from everyone, especially after Jaered infiltrated your bank's torture chamber a few weeks ago."

"And freed all of us," Tara said.

From the Primary's grunt, Eve was right. They wouldn't have unwelcomed guests showing up.

"You have questions for me." Eve stepped in front of the Primary and crossed her arms. "I have a few of my own."

The Primary spit on her shoes. "Go to hell, Evelynn."

"You and Aeros condemned my sisters there long ago." Eve removed her shoe and wiped off his spit on his sleeve. She placed her hand on his shoulder and steadied herself while slipping her shoe back on. "We have much to discuss, Johann, and I'm counting on Heinrick's truth serum to help you along." She got in his face. "Let's start with why you've aligned with your brother?" She straightened up. "Or perhaps we should start with your plans for all that wealth you acquired."

From the amount of sweat beading across his face, the Primary was doing his best to fight the drug cocktail. But to Tara's surprise, he leaned back in the chair with an air of confidence. "You know nothing."

"Diamonds, emeralds, gold. Such an impressive treasure you've accumulated over the centuries. Do your most devout Pur know how you've exploited the very planet they swore to protect?"

"What makes you think I'm not protecting Earth?" the Primary said.

"Aligning with your brother speaks louder than your empty claims," Tara said.

The Primary scoffed and gave Tara a sideways glance. "The Pur don't see me as a traitor, but the same doesn't hold true for you and their defunct Heir."

"You swore to protect Ian," Eve said.

"I swore to protect my Heir apparent!" the Primary bellowed. "Gwynndolyn led me to believe he was mine! Regardless of how Ian came to be, the abomination of it all, I was willing to accept him!" He sobered. "Lies, nothing but lies and betrayal. I was a fool to trust her after all these centuries."

It was the Primary's injured tone that piqued Tara's curiosity. At one time, he had loved Ian's mother.

"We had to stop you both," Eve said. "Gwynn paid the ultimate price when you condemned her to Thrae."

The Primary raised his chin. "Blame Aeros for the living conditions."

"You've abused Earth, as much as Aeros has destroyed Thrae," Eve said. "You were just more cunning and patient than your brother."

"I impassioned my Pur Weir to devote their lives to caring for this planet," the Primary said. "It's the humans who have abused this world, not me. I alone made the difficult choices to save all that I could."

"At the expense of the human race," Tara said.

"To guarantee the most innocent of Earth would survive," the Primary hissed. "It was the only way to free mammals, insects, and aquatic life from human destruction. Pollution was just the beginning. Humanity has destroyed massive ecosystems and driven entire species into extinction before their time."

"Yet, you climbed into bed with your brother," Eve said.

"How's that working out for you?" Tara sneered.

The Primary flicked his hand. "A necessary evil."

"Aeros isn't destroying your beloved surface, he's imploding the entire planet from within. By turning a blind eye to him, you've done more damage to Earth than humans could ever do." Eve gazed down on him with nothing short of pity. "How could you have been so shortsighted, especially after what he pulled on Thrae?" The Primary crossed his arms and didn't respond.

The truth struck a shrill chord at the same time Tara's blood sizzled. "You never returned to Thrae. You had no idea what he'd done to that planet."

"Not until it was too late." The Primary shifted in his seat, turning his back to them, as though he could avoid their standing in judgement over him.

"Don't pretend you're a victim," Eve said. "Ian and Marcus told us how you condemned the non-believers. Those who stood up to you. Not to mention how you persecuted Aeros's followers."

"My prison on Thrae kept Aeros from slaughtering the remaining populace," the Primary said.

Tara leaned close to his ear. "While you got your kicks torturing anyone who defied you and refused to worship you."

Silence hovered in the room and morphed into a stink of frustration. "We both know you can't kill me." The Primary tossed Eve a smug expression.

"What's he talking about?" Tara asked.

"We're connected in ways even we don't understand," the Primary said at Eve's silence. "If Aeros or I should die, so will your precious rebel leader, and her sisters."

"It's never been tested," Eve said.

"Are you brave enough?" A wicked grin appeared on the Primary's face. "Or just that stupid?"

"Stupid is that stunt you pulled on the jet," Tara blurted.

"The loss of a handful of rebels means nothing to me," the Primary said.

"What if the Ancients are connected to more than just each other?" Tara said. Does it apply to offspring? You nearly killed—" But Eve cut her off with a furtive shake of her head.

"You're referring to the Heirs?" The Primary twisted in his seat and peered between the women with keen interest. "They don't pose a threat to us. Only two were born, not three as the Book predicted." He paused, and stiffened. "Who else was on that plane?" he mumbled, more to himself than them.

Could the Primary channel with her? Tara struggled to clear her mind and keep stoic, unmoving. The Primary's face lifted. "There *are* three, not two. He was on that plane with you."

Eve snatched the Taser out of Tara's hand and shot the Primary. She depressed the trigger, increasing the current. The Primary's body convulsed. She didn't let go until his face grew bright red. She handed the Taser to a stunned Tara, then leaned close to the Primary's ear. She whispered something to him and exited the cell.

Tara removed the metal hooks and shut the door, inserted the key into the padlock, and turned it with a resounding *click*. While the jam was turned to full power, they weren't worried the Primary could escape. She found Eve next door, staring down at a bound and gagged Heinrick. He looked at Eve with wild eyes.

"What did you say to him?" Tara asked.

Eve didn't answer while she gazed upon the small, wimp of a man. "There's worse things than dying," she said. "I've had centuries to perfect them." An alarm beeped at Eve's hip and her back straightened. She grabbed Tara, pulling her down, and the two women fell on top of Heinrick while the ground shook beneath their feet.

Rocks and clumps of dirt rained from the ceiling of the cell. They cowered, unable to stay upright as the underground structure gave into nature's force. The walls crumbled, and huge chunks fell in layers. What meager lights they had flickered and then snuffed out, pitching their surroundings in darkness.

What felt like an eternity later, the earth's plates settled, and the trembling planet stilled. Eve moaned, but her voice resonated with aggravation more than pain. Tara pushed a heap of rocks off her. The rebel leader sat up, but panic lifted her features. Tara peered over her shoulder. The wall between the cells had partially collapsed. The Primary was lying on his side, coughing and shaking his head. Tara sensed the subtle draw of energy into his core. The jam was off!

"Find it!" Eve sputtered.

They frantically searched the debris. At the same moment Tara's hand rested on the device, a roar came from the connecting cell. A tremendous surge of energy burst into the room, knocking the women onto their backs. The concussive blast left Tara delirious and the pain behind her eyes blinded her.

She didn't know how long it took for her to recover enough to scramble over the debris and stare at the half-buried chair in the other cell. It was empty. She dropped the jam remote. It'd been crushed in the earthquake.

TWENTY-THREE

S oon after Jaered and Patrick hitchhiked to the small airport, Jaered had disappeared—whether figuratively or for real, Patrick didn't know. He'd been too exhausted and disoriented to try tracking Jaered down. Patrick found the bar and sipped his whisky. The sound of a vacuum startled him awake. He checked the clock on the wall over the bar.

It didn't feel like six o'clock in the morning since the night's sky never darkened beyond deep grays. Being this close to the Arctic Circle threw Patrick's internal clock off. From what he'd observed, the tiny airport operated around the clock at the height of their tourist season.

He'd taken up residence at the far end of the bar, and had come to the conclusion that avid rock climbers were in a league all their own. The four different groups that had wandered in and out of the bar before he'd dozed off, had partied to a variety of drug-induced whimsy.

Patrick stared out the window of the small airport while the unsuspecting Smareans, as he'd come to think of them, enjoyed normal life. Were they relatively untouched by the would-be gods, unaware they existed on the cusp of a war they knew nothing about?

Jaered slumped into a seat across from the bar. Patrick joined him. "It's been five hours. Where the hell have you been?" Patrick grumbled. He noticed the bulge of a handgun inside a shoulder holster beneath Jaered's jacket. Patrick found an odd sense of peace that his brother was carrying.

Jaered helped himself to a generous swig of Patrick's drink. "I've been making the rounds."

"How? We can't shyft here," Patrick said.

"Not true, naïve apprentice," Jaered said. "We can pull core energy from this planet as easily as we can our own." Jaered left Patrick, grabbed a pretzel bowl from the bar counter, then returned. He scooped a handful and fed the pretzels, one-after-another, into his gaping mouth.

Patrick glanced about the small airport bar. A weary waitress sauntered in and set her purse on the counter. "Coffee, thick and black," she said to the bartender.

"Are you going to spill the details, or wait for me to beg, as usual?" Patrick asked.

"When Aeros shyfted me to Earth for the first time as a child, I discovered I could go wherever I wanted, provided I had exact coordinates, or had been in the location before. The same holds true here. I just needed this to test my theory." He held up a pamphlet from the welcome kiosk they'd passed earlier. "If you can envision it, or physically remember it, you can shyft anywhere here," Jaered said.

"But I haven't been anywhere on Smara before," Patrick said.

Jaered rubbed his face. Patrick didn't know if it was from exhaustion or frustration. "Smara is in the image of Earth." He set the pamphlet down on the coffee table between them. The trifold advertised Glacier Bay in western Canada. "It's really quite beautiful at dawn," Jaered said on the heels of a yawn.

It took another couple of seconds for Patrick to connect Jaered's dots. "But there's got to be variations. Not everything between Earth and Smara are exact."

"That's why I slipped into the airport office to use their computer for research. He leaned toward Patrick and lowered his voice. "Oh, and I've hidden the Primary's stash where he'll never think to look."

"A lot of good that does us," Patrick said. "You said it yourself, this can't be all he's brought here."

Jaered finished off the last of Patrick's whiskey. "I love the internet, no matter what planet. That and the tabloids. The more ludicrous the stories, the better. They still have newspaper stands here!" He withdrew a scrap piece of paper from inside the pamphlet folds. It held a list of four names. "I've been researching mountains with internal lightning storm reports."

Patrick's back straightened and adrenaline fueled his weary muscles. "How many?"

"Counting the one here at Mount Asgard, there have been five over the past thirty-plus years," Jaered said. "Let's get some breakfast. We have a long day ahead."

"But, Tara," Patrick said.

"We're onto something big here. Returning to Earth is premature." Jaered stood and placed his hand on Patrick's shoulder. "Trust your mom."

Patrick had yet to win an argument and he was growing impatient. Jaered insisted on securing a motel room near the airport where they could have a base of operations. He'd chosen a two-story structure with every room facing the parking lot and specifically asked for an upstairs room. Jaered paid in cash. Patrick wondered if he'd pawned off some of the Primary's goods before hiding the rest.

Planes lowered at their approach to the runway, less than a mile away. The fixtures in the simple motel room rattled and the odor of jet fuel hung heavy in the moist air.

Jaered drew the thick, heavy curtains across the window. He collapsed onto the bed closest to it, and buried his head under a pile of pillows without a word.

Thoughts of Tara and how the Primary must be torturing her kept Patrick's nerves raw. For a while, he paced at the foot of the beds, but fatigue got the best of him. The second his head hit the motel pillow, he drifted into a restless sleep.

Vivid dreams took hold. The sensation of plunging to his death in the mine shaft gave way to Tara's horrific screams. Patrick's life played out before his eyes. A childhood of emotional neglect, yet wanting for nothing. His wild college years, his first girlfriend, meeting Ian and creating Fade to

Black Productions. Memories picked up speed and ended with Patrick's body smashing onto the iron grate of the elevator cage. His mother, Jaered, Ian and Tara stood next to the elevator, shaking their heads and taking pity on him. Patrick knew better, though. It wasn't pity, it was disappointment. He wasn't the powerful Heir they needed.

Sprawled across the elevator cage, Patrick gasped for air. By the time he sat up, everyone had disappeared and he found himself in the motel room, sitting on his bed. Sunlight seeped in, outlining the curtains in an eclipse glow. The crushing pressure wasn't imagined. It came from his chest, as an invisible weight stole his breath. Patrick pressed his fist to his breast, fighting for every ounce of air. The room spun and he rolled onto his side, facing the outside door.

Footsteps approached along the outside balcony, one set surefooted and determined, the other set, dragging and weak. The two men came to a stop at their room, and their shadows blocked the natural light penetrating the crack at the base of the door. Patrick struggled to speak, but his lungs refused to release the bits of air keeping him alive. He formed Jaered's name in silence. His brother was sound asleep, and unaffected by the debilitating Curse. "Jaered," Patrick managed to say, but it came out a whispered groan. Jaered didn't stir. Patrick rolled onto his back, suffocating.

The door handle jiggled, subtle. At the same time, something heavy slumped on the other side of the door. The Pur Weir's shadow obliterated the last of the sunlight peeking inside their room.

Patrick grabbed one of his pillows. His face contorted from the agony playing out in his chest, and with the last of his strength, he threw the pillow at Jaered with everything he had.

His brother sprang from the bed like an agile cat, and turned on Patrick, enraged. Patrick's gaze flitted between Jaered and the direction of the door.

Jaered grabbed his weapon from under the mound of pillows. He crossed the motel room, holding the gun in both hands, and tilted one ear toward the door. At the scrape of a keycard, Jaered let off two rounds at the base of the door. The crushing pressure lifted in Patrick's chest and he gasped, sucking air into his lungs. Jaered opened fire with a round of shots, creating a dotted circle in the wooden door, then spun around with a forceful kick. The middle of the door gave way and caught the second intruder in the chest. The man yelled. Knocked backward, he tumbled over the balcony railing.

Jaered leapt over the balcony and out of sight. Patrick recovered and ran out the ruined door.

The Pur Weir was sprawled across the hood of someone's Jeep parked in the lot below. Jaered checked for a pulse. Blood spurt from the man's mouth and he choked. From his wheezing, one of Jaered's rounds had collapsed a lung. Another two wounds gushed from the man's legs.

"Who sent you!" Jaered demanded. When he didn't answer, Jaered pressed a thumb in the man's leg wound.

The assassin wailed. "Primary," he rasped.

"Why?" Jaered snarled.

"Find . . . third Heir . . ." he whispered.

Pounding footsteps descended the metal stairs. Patrick hurried over. "Where's he keeping the girl?" he asked.

Even if he knew, he was too weak to speak, Jaered thought. The bleat of approaching police cruisers was drowned out by the jet engines. The motel clerk had a phone to his ear and was partially hidden in the office doorway. He cowered when Jaered locked eyes on him.

A dark car pulled out of the parking lot with squealing tires. It left black slashes of peeled rubber and a stink in the air.

The other motel guests were either gone, sleeping through the commotion, or had the good sense to stay out of sight. Jaered shoved the tip of the gun against the man's brainstem, and pulled the trigger. He grabbed Patrick's arm and jerked him below the Jeep hood. He shyfted.

They reappeared in a bathroom stall at the airport. Jaered turned an ear to the room and when it appeared they were alone, he gestured for Patrick to block the door. Jaered washed the blood off his hands in the sink.

"You killed him, in cold blood," Patrick said.

"I sent a message," Jaered snapped. Crimson flashes blinded Jaered, and he closed his eyes, willing the exhaustion away.

"What did you do to bring the Pur to Smara?" Patrick asked.

"What makes you think this is my fault?" Jaered countered.

"You were gone half the night and left me alone in the airport bar. Research my ass, how the hell did a Pur Weir find us so quickly?"

"Don't be so dim. Use your head." Jaered leaned against the sink counter. "We stood out by asking questions in the Inuit village. They put two and two together." He released a sigh from the depths of his weary soul and the fatigue gave way to a more disturbing truth. "The Primary knows about you."

"So what?" Patrick said.

"As long as he thought there were only two Heirs, Ian and I weren't seen as a viable threat," Jaered said. "The Primary and Aeros have treated us as nuisances, nothing more."

Patrick stilled. "As word got out, so did my secret."

"Or it was Tara." Jaered said, and met Patrick's stare in the mirror. "He targeted her to get what information he could on the rebels. But might have ended up with so much more."

"She wouldn't have broken easily," Patrick said. He leaned a shoulder against the wall and his head drooped.

"The sooner we focus on this end of the mission, the faster we'll get back to Earth and find out what really happened to her," Jaered said. He hoped his tone was more convincing than he felt.

Patrick ran water into the nearby sink. "The Primary's moving all his assets to Smara, including some of his more devout Pur," he reasoned aloud. He splashed water on his face and turned off the faucet.

Jaered handed him a wad of paper towels and pulled the list of mountains out of his pocket. His gut told him this was the key to forcing the Primary's hand. But they were huge mountains, and finding the caverns where the Primary kept his treasures wouldn't be easy, or fast. "If there's displaced Pur here, maybe we can use that to our advantage," Jaered said as an idea took shape. "What would the Pur do if they found out how the Primary has exploited and deceived them all these years?"

"The cult would turn on their leader," Patrick said.

"Instead of using the money to ransom for a cure, we use it to prove just how corrupt the Primary has been, and turn his worshippers against him."

"We don't need to steal the Primary's money," Patrick said.

"We need to steal his worshippers." Jaered headed for the door. "We've got to be smart about this. The Primary's going to throw everything at us, just to cover up his dirty little secret."

PART TWO

There is no greater tragedy than to forfeit one's soul

PART
TWO

TWENTY-FOUR

The Primary shyfted to the pier beside his brother's enormous yacht. The second he solidified, he stepped off the shyft platform, but made a spectacle of himself when a massive wave swept over the dock and knocked him off balance. He stumbled off the raised platform with flailing arms.

"Let me be, you fools!" he shouted at the reaching, helpful hands. The doused men stepped back without a word. They knew how to be invisible when disgruntled gods were present.

Aeros stood on an upper balcony of the castle. Even at that distance, his keen eyesight kicked in and he found an amused expression on Aeros's face.

Enjoying yourself? the Primary channeled. Aeros turned and entered the castle walls.

The Primary considered shyfting to the balcony, but thought better of it. His brother might pull another stunt and he'd already been made to look foolish. Aeros lived to exert his power over everything and everyone. His younger brother was no exception.

A massive storm had descended on the South of France and the seas churned with towering waves that battered the sides of the yacht. Sleet stung the Primary's cheeks. Aeros's message was loud and clear. The Primary wouldn't be staying long.

One of his brother's lieutenants greeted him with a cold stare that mirrored the temperature in the great room. The only warmth in the two-story hall came from a massive stone fireplace at the opposite end of the room. The Primary reached toward it and drew energy into his core, basking in the instant comfort.

The warmth morphed into intense tingling in the Primary's chest and whatever comfort he'd brought with him vanished. The room brightened like a thousand candles were lit at once, but the effect was fleeting and was made gloomy by the elongated shadows that flickered in the fire's glow.

"You usually make me wait longer," the Primary said without turning around.

"I am . . ." Aeros hesitated and a half-grin danced up the side of his face, "entertaining a delectable morsel upstairs."

The Primary hadn't heard any screams. Either the castle offered poor acoustics, a rarity indeed, or his brother's pleasure was strictly sexual. An even greater phenomenon of late. His curiosity was heightened at the prospect of sharing, but his brother hadn't shared anything, not in a very long time.

The wrinkles in Aeros's face deepened. "Why are you here?"

"Eve has gone too far," the Primary said. "She had the audacity to kidnap me! If it hadn't been for one of your irritating earthquakes, I'd still be her prisoner."

"I don't know which is more disturbing. Her getting the better of you, or your whining that she tried at all." He gave the Primary a knowing look. "You've been asking for it."

The Primary crossed his arms, but was forced to widen his stance when a gust of wind whipped through the hall, slamming into him. "Stop this crap," he said. "I have important news!"

Aeros sighed and raised his hands. The storm's fury eased into a gentle breeze, and the cement gray in the high windows lifted to reveal cotton ball clouds floating through an azure sky. "You've become soft, Johann."

"Normal bores you. I find comfort in it," the Primary said. "It lends itself to predictability."

"You've grown dull with age," Aeros said. "I miss how much fun we had. Whispers in emperors' ears, deciding the outcome of a battle with the toss of a dice . . ."

"It was never a game for you." The Primary scoffed. "You fed on screams and blood."

"And you're not happy without a flock kissing your feet," Aeros said.

He clenched his jaw. "Earth was all I ever wanted, until you showed up."

"Spare me the lecture, baby brother. Share your news if you must and be gone," Aeros barked.

"How many Heirs are there?" There was minimal trust between them. Aeros could very well have kept such crucial information from the Primary.

"Two." Aeros peered at him with interest. "Why, what has Evelynn done?"

"Hidden the existence of a third Heir," the Primary snarled. Aeros's jaw bulged and his eyes turned pitch black. It brought a sliver of satisfaction to the Primary that his brother had been conned as well. "You've always underestimated her."

"You dare to confront me with I-told-you-so's!" Aeros raised his hands and his irises turned to flames. The storm returned and gale force winds whipped through the castle with whistling friction. Metal clangs rang about the room when suits of armor crashed to the floor and caved in from the crushing atmospheric pressure.

The armor had withstood battles and the test of time, but nothing could survive Aeros's temper. The ancient, hand-cut stones rattled and the foundation beneath the Primary's feet heaved. He grabbed onto the back of a nearby chair to stay on his feet.

Shrieks and screams came from beyond the great hall as a young woman tumbled down the stone steps. The elongated rips in her flimsy night dress were out-lined in scarlet and her face and silky hair was mottled with blood. Aeros turned in her direction and with a flick of his hand, she flew off the stairs. Her agony ceased the moment she was impaled on the wrought iron chandelier dangling in the entrance hall.

The turmoil ceased. Silence filled the castle. The Primary wondered if others shared the young woman's fate.

"I knew she was up to something." Aeros restarted the fire with mere thought and warmed his hands in its heat. The flames lit his face in a dancing glow. "Evelynn's offspring didn't turn out so human after all."

"You swore he wasn't a threat," the Primary said.

"There was no sign of a core at his birth. Evelynn and her meddling sisters are more resourceful than I gave them credit for," Aeros said. The Primary clenched his fists. The walls rumbled. "Their deception will not go unpunished. Where is he?"

"I don't know," the Primary said. "By the time I discovered his existence, he had slipped through my fingers. I believe he and your bastard son are wreaking havoc with my affairs on Smara."

"Jaered lives to be a thorn in my side with his childish pranks." Aeros stilled. "How did they travel off world without us knowing?"

The Primary's racing thoughts came to a halt. "They're more cunning than we anticipated," he said. "They've stolen from me. I won't ignore the audacity."

"You put too much credence in material goods," Aeros said. "That is your weakness, brother."

"And your arrogance has allowed the sisters to make good on their threat," the Primary said. "If you hadn't given into your lust for power, and just left Earth to me."

Aeros strolled away. "I tire of your whining. Do what you must, but no harm shall come to the sisters. They are mine to punish."

"Punish, but not kill," the Primary insisted.

"We are immortal," Aeros said.

"We are growing old! I barely recognized Eve," the Primary blurted. "Whatever made us immortal is wearing off." When his brother dismissed his concern with a snort, the Primary shyfted in front of him. "Don't be foolish enough to test the waters."

Aeros raised his face to the chandelier and held out his hand. The woman's blood pooled in his palm while her death mask stared at them from above. "Don't waste your breath, brother. It will be motivation, not revenge, that will force my hand." In an instant, Aeros was gone.

The Primary shyfted to the dock, but his brother's yacht was gone. He strolled the grounds, drinking in the aftermath of Aeros's tantrum and the destruction it unleashed on the unsuspecting. Bodies sprawled where they fell. Animals lay where the atmospheric pressure turned their brains to mush. Withered and dead vegetation spread for several yards in every direction. The castle turrets had crumbled and collapsed at the base of the once mighty fortress that withstood centuries of fierce battles and the test of time. Everything succumbed to Aeros' power. The Primary stood among the ruins of what his brother was capable of. If not for his core absorbing the power, he'd be among the casualties.

By the time he returned to the water's edge, he knew what had to be done. He wasn't going to be made a fool of on Smara. His followers on the unsuspecting planet were young, vulnerable and didn't share the Weir history of his doctrine, as those on Thrae or Earth. History had taught him many lessons. The more ruthless and barbaric the consequences, the more motivated the flock.

TWENTY-FIVE

The eerie silence in the library kept Patrick's nerves heightened. He didn't have to convince Jaered about the need to work fast, but they disagreed about how much wealth would be enough to sway the bulk of the Primary's followers. Their arguing had wasted precious time and his nerves were about to snap.

"We don't have the time or the resources to track down three more caches," Patrick said in a tone as tense as he felt.

"If we find that many, we have a chance of not only getting his followers to defect here on Smara, but convincing some of his army on Earth," Jaered said.

"Which will take even more time to spread the word, if we can sway them at all." Patrick lowered his head along with his voice when a few of the library patrons shot him disgruntled glances. He nudged Jaered's shoulder and stormed out of the library's glass doors. When Jaered didn't follow, Patrick was sure he'd be on his own and pondered his next step. A couple of minutes later, Jaered joined him outside on the front steps.

"We've got to stick together," Jaered said.

His brother reeked of frustration, yet Patrick caught an edge of compromise. "One more, and we choose the most logical option. I'm not hiking the Himalayas on a wild goose chase," Patrick said.

Jaered held up the list and pointed to one. "I've been to this area on Earth before and know it the best. It's a valley in the heart of the Andes mountain range."

"If we don't find it in the next five hours, we're heading back to Earth and making the most of what we have," Patrick said.

Jaered crossed his arms, but nodded in agreement.

They slipped behind the library, hunched down behind a cluster of trash cans and shyfted to South America.

The duo made rapid headway by greasing the palms of local storytellers and guides. In a matter of hours, they gathered a slew of information about the Urumbaba Valley and its lore. Some of the stories dated back several generations or more while others were only a handful of years old. They chose to focus on stories within the past twenty years from a boisterous local, then discussed their options over a quick snack.

Patrick took a generous sip of his nectar of life, a Peruvian coffee he'd fallen in love with at first taste. He inhaled the rich aroma and mellowed to it with a relaxed smile.

"Are you going to make love to that, or drink it?" Jaered asked. He scooped the last of his Peruvian hash into his mouth, a combination of tarwi, mashu and quinoa.

"Superstition is a powerful tool," Patrick said.

"Stop gloating. I admitted you were right," Jaered said.

"In what dimension?" he countered. "It wasn't in this one."

"Tell me, self-promoting seer, where do we go from here?" Jaered asked.

"I vote the copper mine." Patrick set his steaming mug down.

"I was sold on one of the iron ore mines," Jaered said. "Regardless, that only narrows it down to a dozen or more."

Patrick flipped through his notes. A memory itched at the base of his thoughts. He found it. "Are there salt mines in the area?"

Jaered dropped his fork and pulled out his cell phone. He alternated between swipes and screen presses. "There's a huge salt mine. Why?"

"Two of the storytellers mentioned the lightning coming from the great preservation of life," Patrick said.

"Salt is a preservative." Jaered leaned back in his chair with a thoughtful stare. "That's as good a place to start as any."

They found a local tour guide center, and Jaered inquired about the mine in Spanish. A few minutes later, he joined Patrick on the sidewalk, but his excitement had lost some of its luster. "It's not a mine, but a salt pan," Jaered said.

"What's the difference?" Patrick asked. Jaered opened the brochure and tilted it toward him. The picture was of hundreds of opaque pools, resembling saucers of milk, with a myriad of shapes from rectangular to oval. They were scattered along a valley and rose like stairs on each side.

"These are exposed," Patrick said. "And too shallow for the size of containers we've seen."

Jaered nodded. "The Primary couldn't hide a large stash of mineral containers in these. I still think we're onto to something, though." He folded the brochure and tucked it into his back pants pocket. "Look at your notes. What was the exact reference to the lightning?"

Patrick pulled the notebook from the pack and found what Jaered referred to. "The waters came alive with liquid lightning."

"What if the pools reflected activity from below?" Jaered asked.

Patrick reread the storyteller's account in silence. "You're thinking there's a mine beneath the salt pan."

"Worth a check," Jaered said. He returned Patrick's notebook to his pack. "Come on. There's a bus that will take us there."

They caught the idling transport with a minute to spare until the scheduled departure. Patrick dropped in the number of coins that coincided with the driver's extended fingers. He chose an empty seat across the aisle from Jaered and gazed out the mud-splattered window. Thirty minutes later, the vehicle made its way along the winding, mountainous dirt road. The gears on the bus ground, and the tires squealed as the old driver with leathery skin alternately accelerated and braked.

A group of young travelers were hunched over their cell phones, trying to get signals instead of taking in the sights beyond their windows. The remaining passengers were dressed in colorful local attire with thick, woven shawls and fringed scarfs on their head.

Machu Picchu rose above the mountain range like a skyscraper, yet the terrain gave way to the Sacred Valley, less green but equally rugged, and more desolate than its better-known neighbor.

Jaered held out his hand, signaling Patrick to allow those behind them to exit first. He stood on the top step of the bus, perusing their surroundings before exiting. "As fast as we're going, the Primary has a stronger command of this planet," Jaered said for the benefit of Patrick's ears only.

"You think he knows what we're up to by now?" Patrick asked.

"We need to assume he does," Jaered said.

"At least his followers are Pur," Patrick said and pressed his fist to his chest. "The Curse will give them away if they come within a few feet of me."

"After the motel incident, he won't be sending Weir Sars after us," Jaered said. "He'll be sending non-Sar followers."

"What makes you so sure?" Patrick asked.

"Because that's what I'd do." Jaered headed for a man holding a sign advertising Salineras de Maras tours. He spoke to the tour guide, gave him enough cash for the two of them, and motioned for Patrick to get on the sleek, modern bus. A direct contrast to the rickety one they'd just vacated.

"Can't we wash up and grab a beer or something?" Patrick asked. He was desperate to rid himself of the dirt road before adding more to it.

Jaered paused with one foot on the bus step. "The tour leaves in five minutes."

"I need a pit stop at least," Patrick said.

"Five minutes," Jaered ordered.

Patrick found a public restroom behind the rest stop. The second he opened the door, the odor of feces and urine nearly knocked him out. There was a single urinal and a chipped porcelain sink. No toilet. The stink came from a brown mound in the base of the urinal. He locked the door.

Patrick swatted at the flies swarming around his head. He unzipped his pants, aimed his stream at the rear of the urinal and it spattered, adding a yellowish tinge to the burnt-orange rust near the drain.

The door handle rattled. "Just a minute," he called over his shoulder. Patrick wiggled the last drop off, tucked himself in and zipped himself back up. He stood at the faucet, staring at the congregating flies near the drain. To his dismay, his only choice was a dangling cloth that was more grimy than dry. He washed his hands without any available soap and partially dried them on his shirt.

Someone pounded on the door. "Coming!" he yelled. Patrick unlocked the deadbolt. The door burst open and he crashed against the sink. The flies swarmed in protest.

Hands wrapped around his throat and the intruder's breath smelled of cheap cigarettes. "There's quite a bounty on your head, gringo," the man snarled.

Patrick's feet lifted off the ground when the robust man pushed him so high he sat on top of the sink. When he couldn't loosen the man's hold on his neck, he tried to get one leg free. But his knees were pinned against the unforgiving porcelain.

The room swayed as Patrick clawed at the man's arms. A dark image rose above the intruder's head and his eyes widened. He dropped to the filthy floor in a heap.

Jaered had clocked him with the handle of his gun. "Leave you alone for one second . . ." he grumbled.

"He couldn't wait to use the toilet," Patrick rasped.

"We can't take the tour," Jaered said, pulling Patrick to his feet. "But while you were doing the waltz with this guy," he kicked the unconscious man in the ribs, "I've been scouting out an alternative.'"

"Go," Patrick croaked, rubbing his bruised neck.

Jaered locked the bathroom door and grabbed Patrick's forearm. He shyfted.

They reappeared about halfway up the valley, standing between two rock outcroppings. Patrick took a minute to finish recovering, and stared, fascinated by the salt pans below. They appeared as a patchwork quilt, ranging in colors of stark white to pinkish tans. A hundred or more covered the lower valley floor but stair-stepped up the side of the mountain, ending about thirty feet below where Jaered had shyfted them.

Jaered scaled the steep slope above them and Patrick followed. His brother slipped into a narrow crevice hidden by a rutting rock outcropping.

The air cooled substantially as they squeezed their way deeper into the crevice. Several yards in, it opened onto a severe slope. Patrick was forced to lean back and shuffle his feet along the rocky floor to avoid falling headfirst into the depths. They soon lost the natural light.

"Wait, I'll use another core blast to light our way," Patrick said.

"Don't, your crimson glow will give us away for sure. Let me try something." Jaered stopped and lowered his gaze. A moment later, his chest gave off a faint glow like a weak flashlight.

"How are you doing that?" Patrick asked.

"I isolate the magnetic field and draw only that power," he said.

Patrick was humbled at what he didn't know about his core powers and how to control them. In the soft glow of Jaered's chest, he envied his brother more than ever.

"Thanks," Patrick said.

"You fall, don't take me with you," Jaered said. He reached out to feel the rock wall. "Neither one of us will be of any use if we break a leg."

Jaered kept his hand on the rock for a moment longer. "What is it?" Patrick asked.

"The salt water doesn't reach this far. I'm not sure if this leads to an underground cavern or not."

"We've come this far, might as well check out where it goes," Patrick said, but they soon came to a halt. A pile of boulders stood in their way. He cupped his face in his hands and tried to peer between rocks as high as the ceiling. "There was a cave-in."

"Feel that?" Jaered held out an open palm next to the pile about shoulder high.

Patrick felt it, too. It was cooler air. When he stuck his face near the slit, it reminded him of walking on the beach. He stood upright. "There's a—"

"Cavern on the other side," Jaered said.

"Under the salt pans on the surface." Patrick stood back and raised his hand while drawing energy from his core. A swirling, crimson ball formed.

TWENTY-SIX

Jaered knocked his hand away and Patrick's core blast snuffed out. "Don't be so eager to knock things down," Jaered said. "Or to give us away." He examined the pile of rocks in search of an opening large enough. A whiff of salty air came from the deep cavern beyond the opening. He used his power to shyft a few boulders. One side of the mound crumbled that offered a wide enough space they could slip inside. Jaered increased the power in his chest and illuminated the cavern nearest them. "Pay dirt," he said.

"You can say that again," Patrick muttered while waving the dusty cloud from his face.

"No, look," Jaered said. The cave was filled with towers of storage containers, many as high as the cavern ceiling.

Patrick scrambled up the boulders and paused next to Jaered. He let off a slobbery whistle. "It's twice as many as the first stash," Patrick said.

Jaered calculated the payload. "I can't shyft this much, not all at once."

"If we divide up the room, I can try to do the other half," Patrick said.

"We have to be careful." Jaered journeyed between the stacked container towers. The rows disappeared in the murky shadows at the opposite end of the cavern. "If we're off, by just a few inches, we'll be shyfting containers on top of each other."

"And bring the whole lot down like dominoes," Patrick said. "Is your hiding spot big enough to hold all of this?"

"No, but Eve will have an idea or two. Let me judge how much there is, and then I'll return to Earth and make a plan with her."

"The sooner the better," Patrick said. "Your five-hour window is about over."

Jaered came to a halt about midway into the cavern and peered at the *drip, drip, drip* coming from overhead. Salt water seeped through the bedrock and formed misshaped stalactites on top of the containers, closing the gap between them and the ceiling, acting like support pillars. If they shyfted the containers to a new location, he worried some of the salt beds on the surface might collapse. "We have to wait until nightfall," Jaered said.

Patrick rubbed the back of his neck. "There's no *we* about this. I did my part and helped you find it. If you parashyft to Earth, you can get some of the rebel shyftors to help you move it."

Jaered clenched his fists at Patrick's priorities. "Double back. We have to collapse the tunnel closer to the entrance before we leave."

Patrick slipped between containers and rushed ahead. A moment later, he must have taken a different turn, because Jaered lost sight of him in the maze. "Patrick!" he called, but was met with silence. "Patrick!" Jaered slowed his steps, and stopped. They weren't so far apart that Patrick wouldn't at least hear him. Alarms went off in his head. Jaered closed his eyes, snuffed out the glow from his core, and focused on sounds.

His keen hearing picked up the muted *thump, thump* of a heartbeat, and then another, and another. They blended together and echoed off the surrounding metal containers, making it impossible to decipher where each one originated from. No matter how much he slowed his own pulse and quieted the beat of his heart, he couldn't separate the intruders' whereabouts.

Jaered shyfted onto one of the storage towers, reappearing hunched over. He banged his head on the rocky ceiling, but didn't utter a sound. It throbbed like hell and when he reached back, a sticky residue coated his fingers. As silent as he could, he dropped to his stomach.

From his vantage point Jaered sensed, rather than heard, the intruders making their way between container towers. They were too silent to be groping around in the pitch black, and he deduced they had the advantage of night vision goggles.

A subtle whiff of chloroform rose on the heated air. If they'd drugged Patrick, no telling how long he'd be out. Escaping the cavern with his brother was looking bleak.

At a metal scrape, Jaered cocked his head. Someone's gun barrel had connected with a container, two rows over and behind where he was perched. The throb at the crown of his skull had turned to a dull ache. The intruders grew closer, and one gave his position away when he sniffed the air. If the Primary had sent a human bloodhound, this cat-and-mouse game would soon be over.

Where was Patrick? Jaered weighed his options. Shyft and leave him behind or stay and subdue an unknown number of enemies, while essentially blindfolded. Jaered clenched his jaw, careful not to grind his teeth and potentially give his position away.

A third option rose from the depths of his desperation. It wasn't ideal, but might buy him the advantage.

He spun around onto his back and brought his knees to his chest. With everything he had, he kicked out the stalactite behind him. His tower heaved and tilted, loosened from the ceiling. At the same time, Jaered conjured a powerful energy surge and aimed it at the tops of the surrounding stalactites.

The rocky ceiling shuddered and with a tremendous thunder clap, it cracked. A widening crevice spread in all directions. A cascade of salt water and rock poured through the crevices, further displacing the towers. The central columns toppled like Patrick's imagined dominoes.

Shouts came from every direction as the intruders were caught in the crumbling towers. Natural sunlight shone through the crevice and Jaered scrambled from one tower perch to another, staying one leap ahead of the falling towers.

Just ahead, Patrick lay on the ground, motionless. Jaered jumped to another tower and rode it as it fell toward his brother, then jumped off when the tower stuck midway against another. With an outstretched hand, he snagged Patrick's leg and shyfted.

They reappeared in a salt pool halfway up the hill, knee-deep in saline. Jaered spit to rid himself of salt water and propped Patrick's torso against the edge of the pool. Several of the salt pools splashed or were already drained at the base of the valley. A few had disappeared with the cave-in. To Jaered's relief, none of the workers were near that section of the pools.

A moment later, a handful of men staggered from the entrance to the cavern on the opposite side of the valley. A couple dragged drenched comrades and dropped them on the ground. Everyone gagged and purged salt water, and by the looks of it, some stomach contents.

A thunderous rumble. Several more salt pools collapsed through the gaping hole in the valley floor. A cloud of silt blew out the cave entrance and the intruders slid or scrambled farther up the opposite hill.

A chunk of the salt pool exploded between Jaered and Patrick. He grabbed Patrick and shyfted them to the bus stop bathroom.

Jaered dragged Patrick to the clogged urinal and turned his nose toward the shit pile. It took to the count of six before Patrick coughed and sucked air into his lungs. Jaered let go, and he slumped to the floor.

"Ugh!" Patrick gagged and threw up. "What the hell?"

"Short on smelling salts," Jaered said. "I had to improvise."

Patrick gagged, but nothing came up the second time. "What happened?"

"We were jumped in the cavern," Jaered said. "They got you with chloroform. I had to bring the ceiling down."

His brother let loose a weak chuckle. "Destruction and chaos follow you like flies to trash."

"I get things done." Jaered stepped over Patrick's assassin, still out cold on the floor, and pulled back the deadbolt. He opened the door a crack and peered outside.

Patrick rifled through the guy's pockets and found a cell phone. When he pressed it, it asked for a password on the screen. He picked up the man's right index finger and tried it. It didn't work. He repeated it with the thumb and middle fingers to no avail.

"Use the other hand," Jaered said. It worked, and the phone opened to the main menu. Patrick gave him a baffled look. Jaered shrugged. "Callouses. He's left-handed."

Patrick searched through the man's call history and phone number list. "There isn't much on here. I don't know if he's antisocial or new to cell phones."

"If he's a Pur disciple, he may be new to technology," Jaered said and closed the door. "The Primary could have brought him here just to help track." He reached down and Patrick handed the phone to him. Jaered read the data. "He's only received two calls, earlier today. Same number."

Patrick got to his feet and spit grit into the stained sink. "Call it," he said, wiping his mouth on his sleeve. "Time to put our money to good use."

Jaered pressed the number.

TWENTY-SEVEN

Ian shyfted Rayne to the Northern Colony and left Marcus to return with Oocaw and the herd of gargoyles. He counted on their migration to Earth masking their intent to evacuate what was left of the Northern Colony. Even if it did, they didn't have much time.

When they appeared in the vortex storage room, Ian let go of Rayne's hand and it took a couple of minutes for the pain to ease. He'd hoped to get used to the effect her power drain had, but no matter how many times they'd shyfted, it was as nerve-agonizing as the first.

"I'm okay," he said at her concerned gaze.

"You're a terrible liar, Ian," she said. "Better stick with the heroics."

While his chest warmed and his core bristled from an energy draw, Ian caught a medicinal whiff and the scent of worn leather lingering in the air. Dr. Mac had been in the vortex ahead of them. Refreshed, Ian stepped out of the vortex field and the emerald glow vanished.

The door opened. "We're here to see the Keeper and Mother," Rayne said to the startled sentry.

He bowed. "Of course, my Sun and Heir, they are in the Keeper's quarters. I will escort you."

"No need," Rayne said. "We know the way."

"Spread word," Ian said. "We're evacuating everyone. Gather in the great cavern. We'll meet you there."

It took a full second for the startled sentry to recover. He took off down the hallway. The motion detection lights blinked on and off, illuminating his path.

Ian and Rayne rushed through the halls in silence, and paused at Sophenna's door. He lifted his fist to knock, but Rayne opened the door a crack and called out. "Sophenna?"

"Rayne?" Gwynn asked. She stood when they entered the front room. From their expressions, Dr. Mac and Ian's mother had been in a heated argument.

Gwynn ushered them inside and shut the door to the hallway. "Why did you return?" she asked.

Dr. Mac stood and grabbed his medical bag from the floor. "Is someone hurt?"

"No," Rayne said. "Everyone's fine."

"We've gathered quite the unruly army," Ian said. "Marcus is organizing them to transport back to Earth. Time for your mass exodus. If we've timed this right, Aeros won't know where to start in all the chaos."

"A couple of the rebel shyftors have already arrived and begun to take Thraens to Earth," Dr. Mac said.

"Aeros found out about Patrick being the third Heir," Gwynn said. "There's no stopping him, not this time."

"We need to hurry," Ian said. "Get to the cavern, now."

"What if we can't—" Gwynn said.

"We save as many as we can, starting with you," Rayne said.

"I'm staying." Sophenna stood in her bedroom doorway. She was as pale as her shawl. "I'll try to reason with him."

"You can't reason with insanity," Dr. Mac said. "I agree with Ian and Rayne. I can use the energy column to parashyft. I'm just a Sar, not a shyftor. If we're lucky, I can bring one, maybe two others with me. But I can get help on Earth. Eve will continue to send reinforcements."

"Go!" Ian said. He grabbed his mother's arm. "Mother, there's someone Eve told me about."

The disgruntled expression on the doctor's face returned. "I'm taking care of it," he said.

Before Ian could say more, Gwynn rushed out of the apartment with Dr. Mac.

Rayne approached Sophenna. "Please, come with us."

Sophenna gazed at her cabinets scattered about the room, filled with memories of a world she'd loved, and was about to lose forever. "I can't leave," she whispered.

"You've given your life to Thrae." Rayne gestured toward the antiques in her cabinets. "These are things. But Thrae will truly be lost if you are not around to keep its memories alive for generations to come."

"Jaered has lost so much already," Ian said. He glanced at Rayne. "Don't force him to lose you, too." Sophenna took a reluctant step into the room. Rayne grabbed her hand and together they headed for the pantry.

Ian shyfted ahead of them and opened the hidden door at the back wall. "Get to the cavern. I'll meet you there."

Rayne didn't want to drag Sophenna through the tunnels, but she feared if she let go of the woman's wrist, the Keeper of Thrae would turn around and return to her museum of memories. She wouldn't let Jaered's mother go down with her ship. This wasn't a time for sacrifices, but to keep a level head for everyone's benefit. If she were honest, she didn't want to face Jaered with the knowledge she hadn't done everything in her power to save his mother's life.

The deeper they hurried through the tunnels, the faster Sophenna's pace. By the time they approached the cavern door, Rayne let go, convinced Sophenna was committed to leave.

Crowds bled into the cavern behind them. Gwynn and Dr. Mac arrived with a young mother and her toddler. Clasping the woman's hand, the doctor disappeared into the column with them without missing a step.

Gwynn took command from a flat rock to address everyone. "Thrae has run out of time. Keep away from the column. Shyftors are coming to help evacuate us." Her words did little to reassure the masses. People kept shoving to be at the front of the gathered group.

"Stop!" Rayne screamed. Tingling in her hands startled her, and she held them up. They glowed as bright as the energy column at the center of the room, and throbbed in unison to its pulse. "What the hell?"

Gwynn stared, mesmerized by the strange phenomenon. A second later, a jockey of emotions flitted across her face.

"Aeros is coming!" someone screamed above the noise of the crowd. It sent the crowd into a frenzy.

Chunks of the cavern ceiling rained at the same time a gunshot echoed about the room. Ian stood next to the column holding a handgun.

"We are forming one line starting here." Ian pointed a couple of feet in front of him. "Women and children first." The crowd complied, a few begrudgingly.

The men at the rear of the line looked scared or disgruntled. Sophenna walked up and grabbed the last man's hand. "We will be saved," she said.

That simple gesture calmed the crowd. Rayne never admired anyone more.

Ian shyfted in front of Rayne. "You got this?"

She nodded and he handed her the gun. Ian left and clasped the hand of a woman with a toddler pressed to her shoulder. "Everyone, create one continuous line. I'm going through first and will keep the shyft connected to Thrae for as long as I can. If you feel a tug, drop the hand of the person in front of you. Trust that I and others will return. We'll repeat this until everyone is through." He locked eyes on Rayne. Stay safe, he mouthed.

She held up her fingers in the sign for love. He stepped into the column and the line followed, one colonist after another disappeared as they stepped into the pulsating energy.

Twenty or more people entered when a young man's arm jerked and fell limp at his side. "It stopped," he cried, his face contorted with panic. He jumped into the column.

"No!" Gwynn screamed. The column convulsed and a tremendous force spit the young man back into the cavern. He hit the ground in a backward slide. The teen stopped when he rammed headfirst into a boulder with a sickening *Crack!* His neck bent to the side on impact. A man let go of the hands next to him and bent down, checking for a pulse. Even before he shook his head, Rayne knew the teen was dead. A woman cried out and bent over him, wailing.

Rayne shivered. "The Heir will return," she shouted. "Help is on the way."

"Please, trust us," Gwynn said. The stunned crowd stood holding on tight to their neighbors, many eyes fixed on the dead youth and grieving mother. No one stirred.

The injustice of it all heightened the simmering burn beneath her ribs, and Rayne pressed a fist to her chest.

Gwynn gave her a curious expression. "What is it?"

"I haven't eaten very much. The stress is giving me heartburn," Rayne said.

"Besides the burn in your chest, have there been other incidences out of the ordinary?" she asked.

"There's been . . . anomalies," Rayne said for Gwynn's ears only. "I don't have to touch Ian to cause an energy drain. It happened a couple of times, whenever we were in the same body of water. And I know, sense, things about him with certainty, as if—"

"You're connected," Gwynn said.

"Ever since I returned to Thrae, the heartburn hasn't gone away. I've learned to tolerate, ignore it."

Gwynn's eyes brightened. Rayne wasn't sure if it was from light reflected off the column, or from excitement. "Your father gave you the genome for a core. But at the time, I never gave it serious thought. Rayne, everything you're describing tells me you have a core, and it's awakening."

"Why now?" Rayne asked. "I wasn't jolted by lightning, or put in a boost like Patrick," Rayne said.

"Thrae's energy is more concentrated than ever. Think of a lightbulb burning brightest before its filament snaps." Gwynn turned pensive. "You told me once, that you've never been able to be around technology."

"My cell phones would drain battery power at an alarming rate," Rayne said. "Computers would crash on me. I came to believe it was because of my power drain."

"Your power drain is triggered when you're in direct contact with a Sar's core. Yet, those incidences happened long before you met Ian, or Jaered, am I right?" Gwynn asked.

The idea that Rayne had a core was too crazy to believe. Yet, her hands brightened and throbbed in beat to the energy column's pulse. A moment later, her hands dulled and the throb eased when Ian stepped out of the energy column and reached for the next person in line. A string of Thraens disappeared into the column. A shyftor, who Rayne recognized as one of Eve's rebels, arrived and grabbed three more people in line. One shyftor after another appeared and disappeared with their own small groups.

The evacuation progressed in a calm and orderly fashion. Rayne sat on the rock and hugged herself. Her thoughts swirled, rejecting that she was the first female in Weir history to possess a core. Yet the symptoms were hard to ignore. There were so many unanswered questions, but she set them aside for the sake of the evacuation. She stood on the rock and took a cursory head count. There were close to fifty people left in the cavern, waiting their turn. "What about Claude and the game preserve?" she asked.

"To my knowledge, Aeros has never targeted what he sees as lower life forms," Gwynn said. "But there's always a first time."

"If he finds the Northern Colony deserted, what do you think he'll do?" Rayne asked.

"He'll be enraged, with no way to purge it," Gwynn said.

She was wrong, Rayne thought. Aeros would drain the rest of the planet's energy and create a cataclysmic chain reaction. Thrae would die within hours, if not sooner. With Thrae gone, how would it affect Earth, its dimensional sister? She watched the shyftors return, one after another. Each one greeted by smiling, grateful Thraens.

The heartburn turned into a sizzling boil. Rayne bent over with a moan. The energy inside the column rose in intensity and shone with a blinding light. A powerful beating heart, it soon doubled in size, driving the remaining Thraens toward the walls.

"Aeros!" Gwynn yelled.

TWENTY-EIGHT

Aeros stepped out of the column with balled fists. The flames of his irises blistered bright red. "You cannot run from me!" he roared. He flung his arm. Several men lifted off their feet, slammed against the cave wall, and crumpled to the ground. Many didn't move.

"Stop!" Sophenna screamed.

Aeros hesitated and stared at her with his chest heaving and his lips parted. She hugged herself and took slow, yet determined steps toward him. The rest of the crowd parted to let her pass, but took off for the door once safely behind her.

"Do what you must to me, Aeros, but these lesser beings are not worth the power it takes to destroy them," Sophenna said.

Her voice was gentle, loving, coaxing. Rayne knew she didn't think of Thraens as lesser beings. Please don't kill her, not here, not now, Rayne pleaded in silence. Don't let those words be the last her beloved Thraens hear from her lips.

Aeros stood his ground as Sophenna came to him, glaring at her with nothing short of hatred. She slowly approached and kept his attention on her while the others in the room didn't hesitate to flee.

"You have loved them above all else," he accused. His tone softened. "Even me."

"My love is reserved for the deserving, Aeros," Sophenna said, coming to a halt in front of him. She touched his cheek with affection and gazed into his eyes. "Long ago, you deserved everything I had to give. But it wasn't enough for you. You have always blamed me for deserting you, but it was you who left me behind. Choosing power and control over my love."

"You're right, my beloved. I'm not here for your pets." He grabbed Sophenna's wrist and turned on Gwynn and Rayne. "You and your bitch sister corrupted her mind and turned her against me!"

"You alone are the cancer to all that exists within your reach," Gwynn said. "Don't waste your breath trying to transfer blame. There's too much blood and destruction on your hands . . . and in your heart."

"Then I shall take what I want, and discard the rest!" Aeros roared. He dragged Sophenna toward the column of energy and before Rayne and Gwynn could close the gap, the pulsating power swallowed them whole. Gwynn screamed.

Ian stepped out of the column a moment later, and paused. "What happened?"

"Aeros kidnapped Sophenna," Rayne said. She tugged on Gwynn's arm. "Where would he have taken her?"

Ian's mother shook her head. "I have no idea."

"What of the others?" Ian asked.

"They scattered when Aeros came," Gwynn said. "We've got to evacuate the rest, now."

"I'll round them up," Ian said.

"We'll help." Rayne took off for the tunnels with Gwynn close on her heels.

At a fork in the tunnel, Ian split from Rayne and Gwynn, calling out to those still hiding.

"What if they went as far as the surface?" Rayne asked.

Gwynn sobered. "The first chance you have, get Ian to shyft you back to Eve and stay out of Aeros and the Primary's reach. Now that you have an awakening core, they will see you as a threat to be eliminated, at any cost. We can't lose you, not when we're this close."

"You still haven't told me what I'm supposed to do, or even when," Rayne said.

Gwynn wrapped her arms around Rayne and held her tight. "I can't prepare you for what I don't know. Trust that when the time comes, you will."

She and Gwynn had spent weeks hiding and evading Aeros. In all that time together, Ian's mother never said it, but Rayne knew she was meant to die to save Thrae and Earth.

The ground beneath Rayne's feet quivered and shimmied. The quake grew as the plates beneath Thrae's crust scraped and shifted. The tunnel walls crumbled and the earthen ceiling cracked. The vibration was a powerful wedge, pulling Gwynn and Rayne apart. The two women fell onto the ground. A chasm formed on the tunnel floor and it raced toward them, widening as it traveled the length of the tunnel.

"Aeros?" Rayne yelled over a deafening rumble coming from the other side of the tunnel wall.

"Thrae!" Gwynn pressed up against the side wall when the chasm threatened to swallow her in its depths. She turned a cheek toward Rayne and her fear was palatable. "Run!" she screamed.

Water burst into the tunnel between them and knocked Rayne onto her back. The rush of water lifted and washed her down the tunnel. She fought the current, groping for a handhold and struggling to rise above the water's surface, but the tunnel was too narrow and the water filled it to the ceiling in a matter of seconds.

A bump at Rayne's hip. She reached out and grasped cloth, hung on tight to Gwynn, unable to do anything but ride the current to the unknown.

Ian found a large group of men huddled in an adjoining tunnel. He shyfted them to the column cavern, but debated waiting for a larger group before transporting them to Earth. Their desperate pleas and terrified expressions were difficult to ignore, and he left with them, concerned he didn't have a way to let the women know.

They reappeared in the field at Eve's safe house—one of many farms and ranches she'd purchased and prepared in case the need to transplant her home-world populace arose. Most were located in America's heartland where working the land was not as profitable as it once had been, and modern generations had lost interest in the manual labor. Ever the savvy businesswoman, Ian wondered if Eve had snatched up the real estate for a song, or had paid generously to reward the landowners for their dedication to hard work and loyalty.

Eve raised herself higher on her toes, perusing the newest group. "Where are my sisters? Rayne?"

Ian gave her a pitiful look. "Aeros kidnapped Sophenna before I returned."

The alarm came and went in Eve's eyes faster than she could blink. "The others?"

"We split up to track down those that scattered," Ian said. "I'm going back for more." Eve nodded. He signaled for two shyftors to follow and stepped into the vortex field.

Ian stepped out of the energy column and was met with a wall of water. It doused him and pinned him against the column. Tingling intensified in his chest. The other two shyftors were coming right behind him. He had to create a force field or they would be crushed for certain.

With a groan, he fought the water's power to raise his hands, then pushed against its force to bring his hands in front of him. He drew energy directly from the column at his back and created an invisible force field, shoving the water back onto itself. The tingling intensified. He took shuffling steps forward, inching his way from the edge of the column, widening the field to give the arriving shyftors room to maneuver.

"Ugh!" he groaned when the water pressure grew too much to handle and he had no choice but to narrow the field.

He sensed the first shyftor arriving behind him, but the startled man had no room to go, wedged between the column and Ian's back. The next shyftor made the mistake of not waiting long enough. Their cells mingled and with a short-lived scream, the two conjoined bodies were swept away.

"Ian!"

Through the wall of water, Ian found Rayne dangling from one of the ledge outcroppings, halfway up the cave wall. The rising water reached as high as her shoes. Whenever the splashes connected with her exposed ankles, her power drain took effect and his force field faltered.

He drew power into his core to shyft. A fraction of a second before he lost physical form, he dropped the force field and appeared on a ledge several feet from where Rayne hung. "Get your ass up to the ledge!" he shouted.

"I can't get a solid hold," she yelled.

"Yes, you can," he roared. "It's that or die!"

She swung her legs and caught the soles of her shoes on the cave wall, but when she tried to pull herself up, her foot slipped and she swung from one hand.

"Do it!" Ian yelled. He took his attention off her to search for his mother in the churning pool, but there was no sign of her. A Thraen washed through the cavern door and was sucked into the swirling pool. He floated by, facedown.

Rayne stomped on the dead man's back and bounced higher, clinging with her elbows to the ledge. She brought her legs up, and to Ian's relief, lay on top of the ledge gulping air.

"Where's my mother?" Ian asked.

"We were separated." Rayne rolled over and sat up on the ledge. "I tried to hold onto her, but when we were swept into the cave, I lost her."

Ian stood and focused on the floating debris swirling around the energy column at the center of the cavern. A dark mass the size of a body came into view and he could barely make out what looked like long, tangled, dark hair. He dove into the water and with powerful strokes, reached her.

He grasped her by the collar and shyfted them to a larger ledge on the opposite side of the cave from Rayne. His mother didn't stir and he pushed her onto her side, pressing a fist against her diaphragm to rid her lungs of water. A trickle ran out of her parted lips.

Ian pulled her onto her back and alternated between compressions and breathing into her mouth. Vivid memories struck of his efforts to revive Mara after the fire, but he pushed that failure aside and inwardly vowed that this time, it would be different. At Rayne's shouts, Ian didn't respond. He counted louder, drowning out everything but saving his mother's life.

He let go of pinching her nose and bent over, listening for any indication she was breathing on her own. Nothing. He resumed the training, alternating compressions on her sternum and blowing into her mouth. "You've lived for thousands of years!" he screamed, pressing so hard he was sure he'd crack her ribs. "But . . . I'm . . . not . . . ready . . . to lose you!"

At a gurgle, Ian hesitated with his hands on her chest. Water escaped from her mouth in a sputtering fountain. She choked and he rolled her onto her side, keeping his hands on her, afraid to let go or she'd slip away from him forever.

"Thank you, Mara," he whispered, imagining Tara's twin kneeling beside him, urging him not to give up. He leaned back onto his heels. "She's okay!" he shouted for Rayne's benefit.

Gwynn turned onto her back and Ian held her hand to his chest. No words passed between them, but what he saw in her eyes ignited his core and warmed his soul.

More rumbling. The surface of the water stuttered. The tender moment was cut short at a scream. *CRACK!* Rayne's ledge separated from the wall and with a tremendous splash, she disappeared beneath the surface. Ian stepped back, preparing to jump in after her.

Gwynn grabbed his leg. "You can't, her drain will kill you both!"

Rayne's head broke the surface. As the column's power weakened, the swirling water turned into a whirlpool, picking up speed in a rotating current. It drained at the base of the energy column. Bodies and other debris were sucked into the cave from the outer tunnels and the pool turned into a floating junk pile as the water level receded, taking everything with it.

Ian snatched a long root out of the water and held it over the water's surface. "Rayne, grab hold!"

She raised her hands above her head and kicked toward the lifeline, but seconds before she came within reach, a drowned man collided with her and she disappeared under the water. By the time she resurfaced, she was beyond Ian and Gwynn's ledge.

Pressure grasped Ian's core, and he pressed a fist to his chest. "Ugh!"

"Oh my god!" Gwynn gasped.

Aeros's face appeared as a giant apparition at the surface of the energy column, and it moved as he spoke. "I will drain this planet, and then Earth. You cannot stop me."

"We can, and we will," Ian shouted.

"Not if you ever want to see Sophenna again," Aeros said with lips magnified and distorted by the water's reflection. His mouth opened wide and, to Ian's horror, Rayne was caught in the faster current near the column. In an instant, she was sucked inside as though Aeros swallowed her whole.

The energy column's pulse returned to normal at the same moment his father's image vanished. The light in the cave dulled as Thrae's core diminished before Ian's eyes.

"He's draining more of the planet's core!" Gwynn cried.

The Heir's Seal, carved into the cave wall centuries earlier, cracked into thousands of rocky slivers and crumbled into the water. Thrae was dying and taking the energy column in the room. Ian felt the power wane in his chest and he pressed a fist against it, praying the protective action could keep it inside.

If he didn't parashyft them now, they might never escape Thrae in time.

TWENTY-NINE

The Primary reread the note, then crumpled it in his fist. "How dare she!" he bellowed. "I should strike you down as an example I will not be trifled with!"

Heinrick dropped to his knees and hung his head. "I am only their reluctant messenger sire!"

Winds whipped through the rooms of the old abbey. Not the most comfortable of quarters, but it was a temporary residence none-the-less. Forced into seclusion since his traumatic experience at the hands of Eve, and being left by his vengeful brother to fend for himself, the Primary found solace in a location from his youth. Neither his brother, nor Eve, knew of his history at the abbey and that brought him a much-needed curtain of safety.

"What did you tell them? Surely they tortured you for information!" he roared.

"No sire, they kept me bound and gagged," Heinrick said. "Hours later, the rebel leader," he turned to the side and spat on the floor, "stuck the note, the one you hold, into my pocket with instructions to bring it to you, and no one else."

The Primary studied his lieutenant closely. Why had Eve released the man unharmed? He might have been made a fool once, but he was not about to fall for her cunning a second time. "Search him!" he commanded.

His elite guards stepped in and patted Heinrick down. A moment later, Falcon announced there was nothing.

The Primary grunted. "Thoroughly."

Falcon and Komodo pulled off Heinrick's clothing, and without hesitation, checked every crevice of the man's body. His most trusted guards stepped away with sly expressions on their faces, leaving Heinrick sniveling and defaced. "Of course, there is always his stomach," the Primary said. Falcon withdrew a serrated hunting knife, its blade glistened in the light streaming from the window.

"I implore you, sire! The note, it is all I was given!" Heinrick wailed.

Falcon closed in and his arm pulled back to ram the blade into Heinrick's gut, but the Primary raised his hand, stopping his lieutenant at the last possible moment. Disappointment flickered across Falcon's face.

The Primary approached Heinrick and held him to his bosom. The wiry man broke down, sobbing into his shoulder. "I serve only you, Master!"

"I know," the Primary said. "You have been faithful and a cherished servant beyond recent memories." Without letting go of Heinrick with one arm, he reached out with the other. Falcon handed him the blade. The Primary thrust the blade deep into Heinrick's diaphragm. "But I know there's been a traitor in my inner circle. I believe it's you." He tilted it upward, under the ribs, piercing the man's heart. A final gasp, and Heinrick went limp.

The Primary let go and the executed man collapsed at his feet. He handed Falcon the dripping blade. He bent down, wiped it off on Heinrick's shirt, and returned it to the sheath strapped under his arm.

"I've made a mess of my clothes," the Primary said absently. "I will require a bath and rest. This has been too much for me." He stared at Heinrick's corpse, expecting his right-hand man to rise and stand at the ready, as always.

"Sire, what made you suspect him?" Falcon asked.

He blinked and thought about it. Why did he murder his old confidant with such callousness? "He allowed himself to get captured and that put me at risk," the Primary said. He wandered out of the room, but called out. "Let this be a lesson to you all. I will not tolerate weakness, in any form."

The Primary found no comfort in his steamy bath, even when the young Weir peasant stroked him until he succumbed to her touch and gave into it with a cloud of release. The moment of weakness further enraged him, and he sent her running from the room with his vile rants.

Fresh clothes warmed near the fire soothed his tense muscles. He tossed his bloody garments into the crackling fireplace. They smoldered, but the fire wasn't to be extinguished. The flames took hold of the natural fibers, consuming them while the Primary fell into a numb stare.

He didn't know how long he stood there in the fire's trance, but a knock on the door stole his more pleasant memories. "What?" he yelled.

"The note, sire. There is a deadline to the request. Will you be responding?" Falcon asked through the iron-hinged door.

The Primary sighed. He found himself at a disturbing crossroads. He hadn't faced such a difficult decision in hundreds of years.

Align with Eve, and take a stand against his megalomaniac brother, or fall victim with everyone else to Aeros's tyranny. The Primary believed he could outrun Aeros and stay one planet ahead of him, but Eve had cut him off at the knees by stealing a tremendous chunk of his wealth.

A part of him wanted to slaughter the sisters and their bastard offspring, swatting the pests into oblivion with a wave of his hand. But if anything cautioned him, in the thousands of years he'd lived, it was superstition. He'd never proven the sisters were seers, able to prophesize the future. However, he'd never disproven it. Between Eve and Aeros, the Book of the Weir was never in the Primary's possession long enough for him to make up his mind.

"Leave Heinrick's body on the steps of Notre Dame with a message," the Primary said.

"What message, sire?" Falcon asked.

"It'll come to me," the Primary said.

The Primary found Eve waiting at the base of the organ. She couldn't resist his message any more than he could resist her offer. Even growing up as children of the same village on Thrae, they had been sparring partners.

"Poor Heinrick," Eve said with her gaze fixed on the massive, rising pipes seemingly growing from the organ. "You really should control your temper."

The Primary ground his teeth. "After centuries of betrayal and lies, it's impossible to find quality help these days."

She gave him a sly smile from over her shoulder. "He wasn't one of mine, Johann."

From her mischievous tone and confident stance, any doubt he'd carried was vanquished. He'd killed a loyal servant for nothing. "I want my money," he said.

"We're here for much more than that." Eve sat on the organ bench and smoothed out her skirt. The sun was at the perfect angle, drenching her in a bath of indigo and crimson as it shone through the stained-glass windows overhead. "He's quite mad. You know that, don't you? Otherwise, this is a huge waste of time for me."

"I've spent much of my lifespan avoiding him for good reason," the Primary said.

"If we don't stop him here on Earth, you won't find peace for long on Smara," she said. The Primary fought for his face to remain stoic, but his nostrils flared. Eve gave him a weak smile. "You must have sensed the numerous parashyfts over the last several hours."

"My brother was bound to take out his wrath on Thrae. I expected you and the Heirs to evacuate as many as you could," the Primary said.

Eve touched one of the keys on the organ and depressed it with such a light pressure, it didn't make a sound. "All I needed was a few parashyfts to go unnoticed in all that turmoil. Even your core can't tell which dimension they come from, correct?"

A cloud of bright sparks took the shape of a man at the end of the balcony. The Primary recognized Sophenna's son once his image solidified.

"I would inform your lieutenant, Falcon, I believe he's called, not to take the shot," Eve said.

"We agreed to meet without backup, Eve. You are the one who clearly violated it," the Primary said.

"As I said, stand your man down, Johann," she said in a stern voice. "Jaered is not here to pose a threat to you. He brings vital information."

"Which is," the Primary said.

She ran her finger across the ivory keys. "In spite of your best efforts to stop them, the Heirs have uncovered much of your wealth in a very short period of time."

The Primary kept his attention on Jaered, but lifted his hand, shoulder high. The signal for Falcon to stand down. "Am I to assume it is no longer where they found it?"

"So many questions must be bouncing about in that head of yours. Is it still on Smara? If not, which dimension has it been transferred to? Could it be scattered amongst Thrae, Earth, and Smara? Or perhaps Jaered chose an alternative universe that's unknown, even to you."

Heat rose in the Primary's core, threatening to go nova and destroy not only Eve and the bastard Heir, but the centuries-old structure itself. "What do you want in exchange for what is already mine," he snarled.

"I've never understood your reasoning, Johann," Eve said. "What good is a treasure, if there are no worlds left where you can spend it?"

"It would be madness to betray Aeros." He gave her a steeled glare. "He's the only thing in this universe that I fear."

"Give me your troops," Eve said. "And the treasure will be returned to you."

Amazed that she could be so ignorant and cunning at the same time, his laugh burst deep. "If my troops don't stand with him, he will know I betrayed him."

"I see your point," she said, and brought a finger to her lips. "I have a different proposition. One that can be well hidden from him and not expose your culpability."

He peered at her with curiosity. Unable to trust her, yet intrigued. "That would be?"

"Remove the Curse between Duach and Pur," she said.

The Primary never admired her more yet hated her with a greater passion than in that moment. "Even if your rebels fight side by side, it won't give you an advantage against my brother. In the end, you will lose, you must know that."

"Your Curse did more damage to the Weir than any persecution or torture could. When you prevented communication between factions, you gave Aeros the power to control not only Earth, but you." She stood and faced him, not as an equal but as a chastising parent. "Stop the Curse, Johann. Once united in body and spirit, my rebels will wield hope as their battle cry. And I need all that I can muster."

"Hope can be a double-edged sword," he said. "What gives you strength, can also take it away. My Pur guards cannot approach because of your Duach Heir, who I anticipated would be near enough to set off the Curse. This meeting may not have been so civil, or so without bloodshed, if the Curse hadn't held them at bay."

"Reverse the Curse, Johann, and you will get what you hold most dear," she said.

Earth was not long for the universe and there was no returning to Thrae. If he wanted to sit this battle out between his brother and the damn sisters, he needed his treasure for a fresh start on Smara. The Primary crossed his arms. "I can't reverse it. But it is possible to turn it off."

"How?" she asked, a little too eager. She had everything riding on uniting her meager rebels.

"You are right in your assumptions, Eve. The Weir are more powerful when united." He ran his finger across the keyboard, the ivory cool to his touch. "Harness what gives life to Earth, and you connect everything. Everyone."

THIRTY

Jaered handed the Primary a scrap of paper with longitudinal and latitudinal coordinates.

"What the hell is this?" the Primary asked.

"The location of where I hid your treasure. I transported it from Mount Asgard and took it there." Jaered bit down on his back molars. Every nerve of his being was against this move, but Eve insisted.

The Primary's eyes flared. "My spies told me another location was missing!" He took a step toward Jaered. "I want it all!"

Eve positioned herself between them. "You will get it, Johann," she said. "But not all at once."

"What's that supposed to mean?" he hissed.

"Consider it an insurance policy," she said. "If any harm comes to the three Heirs by your hand, you will never find the rest of your missing treasure."

"I don't have to kill them," the Primary said. "If you pursue this futile battle, my brother will do it for me."

"Then apparently you are motivated to help us beyond your ridiculous riddles." When the Primary turned his back to Eve, her shoulders relaxed, and she raised her chin. Jaered didn't share her apparent optimism. She was goading the Primary into action. What action he chose would remain to be seen. "You can't hide your head in the sand, Johann. I won't let you idly stand by and wait this out on the sidelines. Not like you've done for the previous thousands of years."

"You will come to regret toying with me, Evelynn." An emerald cloud lit up the, shadows. The Primary shyfted.

"Let's go where it's safer," Eve said. "For all his posturing, I wouldn't put it past Johann to still sic his elite guards on us." Jaered shyfted them to the safe house farm in Ohio.

Relief was palatable on Patrick's face when he opened the door. Once Eve checked on how the displaced Thraens were settling in, she ushered Jaered and Patrick outside. Concern etched deep grooves in her forehead and at the corners of her eyes. Ian, Rayne, and Eve's other sisters hadn't evacuated Thrae. No one knew why.

"What the hell did we pay him for?" Jaered yelled the moment they were out of earshot of the farmhouse. "After everything we went through, he gave us gibberish."

"Was it?" Patrick asked his mother. "Gibberish?"

Eve didn't answer while Jaered and Patrick trailed after her between rows of cornstalks. "Johann didn't give me a recipe, but he did give me a clue." She came to a halt. "The basis of the Curse centers on the Earth's core energy and how it is expunged," she said. "When you consider what little we know about the Curse phenomenon, it makes sense."

"Pur power comes from the energies at the surface of the planet," Patrick said.

"And Duach power comes from the internal energies of Earth," Eve said.

Jaered swung at the nearest stalk. The heavy husks at the top brought it crashing to the ground, bending the stalk in half. "How can we possibly unite the two energy sources under one output?"

"We can't," Eve said. "Not while the Earth's core is strong enough to disperse energy equally, as it has for billions of years."

Jaered quieted. "That's why we don't have the phenomenon on Thrae. There the core energy is absorbed and splintered into columns across the planet."

"The column energy was eventually harvested to power the protective domes," Eve said. "What made Thrae weak—"

"United the Weir," Jaered said.

"So, if I understand all this scientific mumbo jumbo," Patrick raked his fingers through his hair, "while Earth's core energy is stable, we can't eliminate the Curse."

"After all this, we aren't any closer to getting the upper hand," Jaered said.

Patrick grew pensive. "We put our heads together. Find a way to use the Curse to our advantage."

"A legion divided, for any reason, is weaker when it cannot fight as one," Jaered said.

"What legion?" Patrick shot back. "We're still a ragtag team. We might not be scattered across two planets any longer, but we're still scattered across Earth."

"Stop your bickering," Eve said. "I need to think." She left them, walking ahead with a drooped head and slow steps. She held out one hand running her fingers along the cornstalks.

"Now what?" Patrick asked.

"I have to go home. My core's been aching for the past hour or more. Something's changed. I fear for Thrae." He cut through the rows until he reached the powerful vortex in the middle of the field. Patrick followed. Jaered turned on him. "Don't even think it."

Patrick stood his ground. "I'm coming, too. If you're right, something may have happened to the others."

"You need to stay here and protect her." Jaered pointed in the direction Eve had gone. "If we lose her, everything we've worked for is for nothing." At Patrick's pained expression, Jaered backed up into the vortex. "As long as the Curse keeps you and Ian at a distance, you can't help."

"We make a good team, don't we?" Patrick asked.

"You're growing on me," Jaered said. He shyfted.

Jaered parashyfted to the cavern in the Northern Colony. He stepped out, knee-deep in water.

The light emitted from the column was dim and cast shadows in the once brilliant space. His core knew the truth. His beloved planet was on its last breath.

Bodies of those not evacuated in time floated in the shallow water, like bobbing apples of death. He counted fifteen or more. None of them were the loved ones he sought.

Jaered didn't have time to investigate what might have happened. Thrae didn't have time.

He waded out the door and turned a keen ear to the tunnel. The moans and groans of Thrae's shifting plates made it difficult to hear anything else, but he called out in hopes the survivors were within earshot. He didn't know if the planet was gearing up for a tremendous earthquake, or settling itself in a grinding fit.

Silence filled the tunnels. Only the ghosts in the cavern knew why.

His mother, Aunt Gwynn, Ian, and Rayne could be anywhere. Jaered drew energy into his core and shyfted to his mother's quarters. It was a struggle to draw enough, even this close to the column. The second he solidified, he knew they weren't there. Whatever caused the flood had risen as high as her apartment. Many of her cherished curio cabinets had toppled over, their contents scattered in puddles as heaps of trash.

If they'd evacuated to Earth, they would have contacted someone. They had to still be on Thrae. He envisioned his stubborn mother, insisting on staying, no matter what. As Thrae had withered away, so too had his mother these past few years. What he cherished the most, Thrae and his mother, were connected to the bitter end.

Jaered paused and peered at the damage, struggling to put the puzzle pieces together. The earthen walls separating the tunnels from the river passages had given way. Was it an earthquake, or by Aeros's hand?

Fear spurred him to the door. He swung it open and called out. "Anyone here!" The eerie silence of a graveyard hung in the air.

He cautioned himself to stay calm. They might have gone to the animal preserve. Jaered left the apartment and combed the tunnels on his return to the energy column cavern. He would need all the power he could draw to shyft halfway around Thrae.

By the time he entered the muddy cave, the water had receded and barely reached his ankles. He stepped over the bodies, guilt-stricken at his failure as their Heir and protector.

He approached the dim, pulsating column with the intent of shyfting, but he held up at a strong pull to his core. Was the column alive? But that was impossible. It was a conduit of energy. You were either passing through, or were outside of it.

Where had the water gone? He peered down at his feet. The contents of the room were draining into the base of the column. Had a crack opened in the rock floor? Jaered crouched and ran his hand along the muck until it disappeared inside the energy field. He lost feeling in his hand when it ignited his core and numbed him, from his chest to his extremities.

He stared into the pulsating energy and was met with a mental image staring back at him. Why did it seem alive?

Instead of envisioning a location to shyft to, Jaered emptied his thoughts and entered the column with an open mind.

The intensity of light and the tug of power in his core kept him conscious. Yet, he lost track of time, and the sensation of tangible, surrounding space. The energy compressed him from all directions like a comforting squeeze by a giant's hand.

"Is it you, Thrae?" he asked, but wasn't sure his voice carried or if it remained as thought.

He waited for any indication that he'd been heard, but the sensation of being one with the energy was all he perceived.

Jaered concentrated on shyfting, but the tickle of energy took its time to intensify. Thrae wasn't ready for him to go. He closed his eyes as tears streamed down his face. "I'm sorry I failed you," he confessed to the sheer essence left of his once vital, thriving world, compelled to purge what his heart could no longer keep contained. "I'm *so, so* sorry."

The light brightened, burning through his shut lids. The sensation of being compressed intensified until he was sure he'd be smothered before it'd let go. The light dimmed and he opened his eyes to discover the natural light of a blue sky penetrating the column.

Reluctance to let go of Thrae kept him riveted where he stood, but concern for the others drove him to act. Jaered stepped out to find himself in the sinkhole preserve. He turned around and pressed both palms to the pulsating column. Its power tickled his hands. He leaned his forehead against the energy field in a final farewell to his beloved planet.

At a squawk, Jaered pulled away. A flock of gryphons soared overhead. Oocaw met him with a stream of fire that singed the hair on his arm. "It's good to see you, old friend," Jaered said. Oocaw shook her head and thick pools of saliva landed on the rocks around Jaered and across his boots. "What are you doing in this ecosystem?" he asked.

"Jaered!" Gwynn approached from a thicket of bamboo reeds. She wrapped her arms around him. She buried her face into his shoulder and her chest heaved.

He bent close. "What's happened?" She swiped at a tear on her cheek and didn't answer. He gripped her shoulders so tight she winced. "Where's my mother?"

"Aeros took her," Ian said, stepping onto the path.

"Where?" Jaered said.

"We don't know. But it's off world. I . . ." Gwynn brought her clasped hands to her chest. "It feels her absence. Thrae is grieving."

"The energy output from the columns is dimmer than ever," Ian said. "At first I thought it was Aeros's doing."

"It's not a loss of energy," Gwynn said. "It's emotional—"

"Without her, Thrae is giving up." Jaered had stepped out of the energy column filled with despair. "Where's Rayne?" he asked.

Ian and Gwynn exchanged an uneasy glance. "We don't know," Ian said. "She was caught in a whirlpool and just, disappeared into the energy column."

"She never came out," Gwynn said. "That's when Ian shyfted us here. It's the only other conduit that would be powerful enough to draw her out."

"But we can't find her," Ian said.

Jaered shook his head. "That doesn't make any sense. She can't shyft. She doesn't have a core."

"I believe Rayne has had one all along," Gwynn said. "One that took her entire life to awaken, perhaps because she drains it as soon as it ignites. If I'm right, she could have inadvertently shyfted."

"But if not here, where?" Ian said.

Gwynn bit her lower lip. "I have no idea."

THIRTY-ONE

Rayne opened her eyes and found herself in a tropical jungle. The chatter of birds transformed into a melody of song while the buzz of dragonflies come from nearby. She sat up and was welcomed by a soft breeze kissing her cheeks. She shivered. Drenched, she wiggled her toes. Water squished inside her tennis shoes.

The last thing she remembered, she was in the whirlpool inside the cave, gulping bits of air and water as she fought the current. Aeros's voice still rang in her ears, drowning out Ian's shouts.

The ground was a cushion of thick moss and short-cropped grass that felt papery to the touch. She stood and bent over to wring out her hair. Moisture hung in the air while angry and shrill voices carried from farther down the path. They were out of place in the tranquil surroundings. Rayne set out down the path, but her waterlogged shoes squeaked, and she crouched to remove them.

She left a trail of muddy footprints with each step, but she soon reached the voices and peered between tall cattails along a gentle stream.

Rayne clenched her teeth to stifle a gasp. At the base of a grassy knoll, Sophenna sat on a boulder with her face raised to Aeros. He was seething and bent over her with clenched fists.

"I need to return to Thrae," Sophenna said. "You can't keep me here!"

"I can do with you as I wish," Aeros said. "This paradise is your home now!"

Sophenna glanced about. "This isn't real, Aeros. You and I . . ." She waved between them. "This is not real. It hasn't been for eons."

"You will love me. We will exist for all eternity in paradise, and if anyone so much as threatens this, I will destroy them with a wave of my hand!" He spun around and sent a core blast at the vegetation near Rayne. It burst into flames.

Her cheek blistered, but she didn't dare move with Aeros facing her as the flames reflected in his dark eyes. "Now look what you made me do," he said gently. "We can't have paradise burning. That will not do, not at all." He waved his hand and a mound of water rose out of the stream, dousing the flames.

Damp soot splashed on Rayne's hair, but she remained motionless.

"I had to separate you from your vile sisters. They're the ones who turned you against me," Aeros said. "Once I destroy Thrae, you will see how blind your devotion was to that desolate planet. This place has everything your heart desires.

You'll find happiness here." He walked over and touched a lavender peony the size of a dinner plate.

"Even if you take everyone and everything away from me, Aeros, I still can't love you."

His fingers wrapped around the flower with a tight fist, crushing it. Its petals rained onto the ground like tears. "You're wrong, Sophenna. As long as they live . . . that bastard son of ours, lives . . . you don't know what you want." He walked to the edge of the stream and Rayne swore he stared right at her. She found herself holding her breath and willing her heart to stop beating.

"You will stay here until I wipe everything else out of this universe. We will start with a clean slate of my choosing. You will love me, Sophenna. I will not spend eternity alone." A bright flash. Aeros was gone.

Sophenna slipped from the rock onto the ground and bent over with her face buried in her hands.

Rayne waited. When it was clear he'd left Sophenna alone, she slipped out of the bushes. It wasn't until she crossed the stream, wading in the shallow water and splashing about, that Sophenna looked up. "Rayne!" she exclaimed. She glanced around in fear. "How?"

"I don't know," Rayne said and sat next to Sophenna. They hugged each other in a tight embrace.

"Oh, my child, I'm so relieved you are safe. But you shouldn't be here. It's far too dangerous."

"Where are we?" Rayne asked.

"I don't know," Sophenna said. She turned her face skyward. "Does that resemble Earth's sky? It's been so long since I've seen that shade of blue on Thrae."

"It could be," Rayne said. There was something odd about the color. "Did he shyft you here?"

"When he dragged me into the energy column, we ended up here." Sophenna grabbed Rayne's hand and brought it to her chest with a heavy sigh. "We've got to hide you."

Rayne stood and pulled Sophenna up with her. "No more hiding. We're leaving and I'm taking you to Eve. It's the only way for you to stay safe."

Sophenna gave her a subtle shake of a head. "Perhaps I should stay. I can pretend, give him what he desires most. If I do that, he may spare everyone . . . everything."

"No one should tolerate abuse," Rayne said, regretting the lecture voice she'd used.

Sophenna wiped her cheeks and held her head high. "Let's find a way out of here."

"I followed a path," Rayne said. "Let's try and back-track. It might lead to a vortex," Rayne said. She paused and pressed a fist to her chest. The heartburn had returned sizzling greater than ever. "I think I shyfted here."

Rayne retraced her muddy footprints and they stood near the path where she appeared earlier. "I don't know how I managed to come here, rather than somewhere else." She studied their surroundings. "I've never been here before. It's not like I had exact coordinates."

"Or a picture," Sophenna said. "Jaered could shyft anywhere he could envision in his mind."

"But I've never been to the tropics, a jungle, or any place similar to this. I've seen pictures in books, though." Something she remembered Aeros saying stopped her cold.

"What?" Sophenna asked.

"Earlier, didn't Aeros say . . . I have created paradise for you," Rayne said.

"Something like that," Sophenna said.

Rayne peered at the sky overhead. Was that color of blue, *normal?* It had a tinge of indigo and other shades in subtle stripes, resembling a faint rainbow, but this one stretched across the entire sky. She touched the leaves on the rubber tree closest to her. They weren't waxy and heavy in her hand. Rayne examined other plants. Everything was a replica of living things. The moisture in the air wasn't coming from the climate—it was artificial. Aeros's paradise had been created.

"Have you seen any animals since you arrived?" Rayne asked. "Bugs? I can hear birds, but have you seen any in the trees or taking flight?"

Alarm widened Sophenna's eyes. "We're not on Earth, are we?" From her tone, it wasn't a question she wanted answered.

THIRTY-TWO

Ian and Jaered searched in vain for Sophenna and Rayne, but time was their enemy and they were forced to abandon their search for the sake of all others.

Jaered evacuated the protesting engineers while Marcus returned to Earth and brought back additional shyftors. Thrae was hanging on by the slimmest of threads. It was time to flee the dying planet. They hung onto the belief that Aeros would not keep his captors on Thrae.

Thrae's Heir stood on the cliff overlooking the sink-hole. Volcanic activity had grown exponentially across Thrae since his mother was kidnapped. Ash clouds darkened the sky beyond the dome. Big Red was no longer their greatest threat. The energy feeding the game preserve domes still held, hopefully long enough for them to transplant the creatures to Earth.

Jestueax was in her nest feeding strips of muscle and fat to her pups, fattening them up for their parashyft to Earth.

Under different circumstances their chirps and her cooing would've brought peace to Jaered's mind, but he stared down into the depths of the cavern in a troubled daze. He'd always believed that his mother stayed on Thrae because of her love for the planet. It took her being kidnapped for him to understand how much the planet needed her.

Marcus's voice bellowed far below, barking orders to the last of the evacuating gargoyles.

Melancholy took a firm hold and Jaered closed his eyes, giving rise to memories long buried. A life on Thrae with Kyre, the woman who fed his soul and nourished his core, consumed his thoughts. For a blessed moment, he was transported to happier times and imagined them standing on the cliff, their arms wrapped around each other's waist. Kyre rested her head on his shoulder, and he inhaled the scent of her soap while his hand caressed her bulging belly. A smile touched his lips when their unborn child kicked at his touch in playful innocence.

The ground shook beneath Jaered's feet and stirred him back to the present. A part of him was thankful Kyre didn't live to see the extent of his failure to save their world.

What was left of Thrae's life drained fast. The shyfting mass exodus took what energy the planet had left, and the dome overhead buzzed, threatening to snuff out.

Eve's reinforcements were busy evacuating the remaining beasts in the adjoining ecosystems with Claude at the helm.

"It's the unknown that kills you," Ian said, approaching from around the gargoyle nest. He stepped up next to Jaered with Oocaw's egg cradled in his arms. "We'll save what we can."

"We'll save them all," Jaered said. "I won't rest until every last creature has a future filled with hope." He rubbed his face, but it did little to rejuvenate him. He gnashed his teeth to stave the anger pluming in his gut. "I failed Thrae—"

"You saved as much of Thrae as you could," Ian said. "If I had only known in time, I could have—"

"You've been there ever since your eyes were opened," Jaered said. "Fault doesn't lie with you. If I hadn't been so arrogant, I would have recruited you sooner."

"And Patrick," Ian said. "We are stronger, together."

"He really came through on Smara," Jaered said. "I was ready to put down every last bastard the Primary threw at us. It was Patrick who kept a level head. Negotiated with the displaced Weir. Used the Primary's treasure to buy them off and spread the word. Even if the Primary survives the battle on Earth, he won't be buying his way into Smara."

"Patrick's the consummate businessman," Ian said with a weak grin. "His mother might not have awakened his core until years later, but she taught him some valuable lessons in the meantime."

The distant flashes in the sinkhole had slowed like a dying storm. "They're almost done on this end."

"I'll drop this egg off to Oocaw and go to the other domes. See if I can't help finish up there," Ian said.

"I'll come with you," Jaered said.

"We have plenty of shyftors for the few who are left." Ian lowered his voice. "Stay . . . as long as you need."

The second Ian shyfted, Jaered gave into the dammed emotions. He opened his core to the planet's despair and as one, they wept. Moist air grew heavy and rose from the sinkhole as the atmospheric pressure grew intense. A lowlying cloud formed at the dome's peak. Droplets splattered the ground and dampened Jaered's hair and clothing. He found comfort in the sliver of connection that remained with his beloved homeland.

He stood transfixed while the rain mixed with his tears, unable to find the strength to say goodbye.

THIRTY-THREE

The ache in Rayne's chest turned to searing pain and she
fell to her knees. "Ugh!"

Sophenna grabbed her arm and pulled her to her feet.
"Aeros! You must hide!" She half-pulled, half-dragged Rayne
from the path and deposited her in a clump of bushes. "Stay
still," she whispered.

Jaered's mother crossed the stream and leaned against the
boulder where Aeros had left her. His image solidified next to
the water.

Aeros had exchanged his street clothes for a brocaded
tunic, its cream tones stark against the various greens of the
vegetation and the rich colors of the surrounding blooms. He
turned as though surveying all that he created. "You are safe,
whether I'm here or not," Aeros said. "There are no creatures
to harm you, or to compete for food."

"This is not natural," Sophenna said. "Where are we?"

"We are in paradise," he said.

"Paradise isn't made of paper leaves," Sophenna countered.

"Weir cannot control the unnatural." Aeros crouched and scooped a handful of stream water. He spread his fingers apart and the clear fluid returned to the gurgling creek. When he held his hand over the water, it rose to touch his palm, then suspended in place.

Sophenna pushed away from the rock and approached Aeros. "Please take me back. At least allow me to say goodbye to Thrae."

The suspended water funnel fell and mixed with the stream. Aeros rubbed his damp hand on his tunic and stood. "Thrae is no more."

A lump stuck in Rayne's throat, and she fought the urge to scream. An entire planet, Jaered's birthplace, gone. How would it affect Jaered's core, to lose that connection? She squeezed her lids tight to abate the threatening tears. Did he survive?

Sophenna whimpered and her knees gave out, but Aeros caught her and carried her to the grassy knoll. He propped her against the boulder and brushed her hair from her face while she wept. "You see how futile it is to resist me."

"Jaered," she whispered.

He pressed a fist to his chest. "So many parashyfts, not enough time. They believe they can find refuge there. But they are mistaken. I have weakened Earth's core more than their instruments reveal. They will not have long."

"Aeros, don't. What about our prophecy? If you pursue this madness, and Eve and Gwynn are slaughtered, you will be condemning not only me, but you and your brother as well."

"You've kept Johann in line with your superstitions and claims, but I am not your puppet!" He slammed his fist against the boulder behind her and it exploded. Sophenna was thrown against Aeros and he embraced her as if she'd sought a hug. "Now see what you've made me do?" he murmured. He picked bits of rock out of her hair, then stood, and gazed upon her. "I have taken your home. Once I remove all those that you love, you will have nothing left, but me." He was gone.

Sophenna rocked on her knees with clasped hands pressed to the chin. "Gone . . . all gone."

Rayne pushed through the brush and approached her with dragging steps, unable to find the words. She knelt and gathered Jaered's mother in her arms, holding her tight until she was too exhausted to weep any longer. Sophenna lay on the grass staring ahead. When she closed her eyes, Rayne slipped out of her grasp and searched the surroundings, determined more than ever to find a way to escape Aeros's prison.

The muted rainbow sky never changed brightness. She questioned if the passage of time did not exist. The chirping birds grated on Rayne's nerves and she stopped in the middle of the path that led to nowhere. She screamed without abandon until she'd spent every ounce of air in her lungs, but no matter how loud or long she kept it up, it couldn't reverse what Aeros had obliterated from the universe.

"I don't believe I can trick him to shyft me out of here," Sophenna said. Rayne turned to find her pale with dark circles under her puffy eyes, but her eyes shone bright. "He believes he's protecting me by keeping me a prisoner here." Sophenna placed her hand on Rayne's chest. "You do have a core, but it's quite weak."

"There must be a way I can draw enough power for us to escape," Rayne said.

Sophenna shook her head. "If we're not on a planet, your core won't have anything to connect to."

"Assuming he told the truth," Rayne said. "Would he lie to you?"

Sophenna nodded. "To keep me a willing prisoner."

Time for a prison break, Rayne thought. She hurried down the path, convinced they were on a planet. Her heartburn hadn't gone away. If anything it had grown worse.

"Where are you going?" Sophenna yelled.

"To find out how big this prison really is," Rayne shouted. She ran down the path for a mile or more, but soon slowed and eventually stopped with her hands on her knees, catching her breath. Sophenna caught up to her a moment later.

"Oh my god. You were right," she said looking at something from over Rayne's back.

It was then that Rayne knew where they were. They were in a dome, similar to the ones on Thrae, but this one was enormous, even by Thrae's standards. A thick outer wall stood at the dome's base and rose twenty feet into the air. The women stepped off the path and pushed their way through the brush. From what Rayne could tell when she touched the wall, it was made of concrete.

"I think we're on Earth," Rayne said with racing thoughts. "But how is this being powered? Earth's core energy is still healthy. It hasn't splintered into columns, not like on Thrae."

"Aeros said he'd weakened Earth's core, more than anyone could tell. What if we're inside a dome powered by Earth's first splinter?" Sophenna said.

Rayne leaned against the wall. All this time, she and Ian believed Earth had resisted Aeros's wrath. If an energy column splintered from the core, was the damage reversible? "How could he have camouflaged this from Eve? The rest of the world?" Rayne asked.

"Some sort of energy camouflage. The dome's sky isn't like those on Thrae." At the mention of her homeland, Sophenna's excitement drooped.

"Aeros lied to us about where we are." Rayne clasped her hand. "He could have lied about Thrae, too."

She gave Rayne a tight-lipped smile. "Time to test that newborn core of yours."

They headed back the way they'd come. If this dome functioned like all the others on Thrae, the energy source would be hidden somewhere in the interior. Optimism drove their steps and energized their souls. Rayne pulled ahead, eager to power up her core and see what she was capable of.

"It might be near the grassy knoll," Sophenna said in a breathy voice.

"It would make the most sense." Rayne slowed her pace for Sophenna to catch up. "Since that's where he comes and goes."

"And it's near the spot where you appeared," Sophenna said. The dome was gigantic and they discovered that Aeros had very little imagination. There were scant differences between his vegetation as if he'd never truly paid attention to the worlds around him. They found the knoll and the crumbled boulder several minutes later.

"I'll stay up here," Rayne said. "I should be able to tell if I'm getting close by the changes in my core."

"I'll search for an opening to an underground tunnel," Sophenna said. She hugged Rayne. "Be careful," she whispered, then pulled away and headed for the backside of the knoll.

Rayne walked the area, taking slow steps and keeping to an imaginary line. She'd been at it for several minutes, but with no discernable changes to her heartburn. The squawks and chirps no longer grated on her nerves. She had to believe they were right, and that her feet were firmly planted on Earth.

The other ray of hope, what kept her going while bending blades of artificial grass beneath her shoes, was faith. If they were on Earth, they had people who loved them nearby.

At the base of the knoll, Rayne hesitated. Her core churned. She took several steps to the side, and her core quieted. A few steps in the direction she'd come, and the heartburn ignited. There was no doubt. An energy column was in the immediate area. When she approached a small clearing, her core ignited and the sizzle blistered her chest. Rayne opened her mouth and swore that a puff of heat escaped.

At the same time, a blinding flash came from the top of the knoll. Rayne wasn't sure she'd found the energy column, or if Aeros's arrival had triggered her core's reaction. She took off, gaining distance between her and the hill, heading for a thicket of trees.

Rayne dove, landing hard on the ground behind a clump of thick bushes. She winced and shook out her hand. It was numb from taking the brunt of her fall. Shallow scratches covered her arms from her swan dive through the branches, but she focused on stilling the beat of her heart.

Aeros stomped to the crest of the knoll and peered down at the landscape below. "Sophenna!" he bellowed. "Where are you?"

Rayne's heart pounded in her ears and she didn't move. Silence swept over the area as the birds quenched their song.

"You cannot hide from me!" Aeros shouted. "Not here. Not anywhere."

"I was hungry." The voice came from behind Aeros. He turned and faced Sophenna holding several apples. Sophenna held one up to Aeros. "Do you want one?"

His shoulders relaxed and he accepted the offering. "I will bring you food. I don't know if what grows here is palatable."

She lowered her face. "Anything is better than what I had on Thrae."

"You will never starve. I promise," Aeros said. He cupped her cheek in his hand and stroked it with his thumb.

Sophenna leaned into his gesture. "Can I trust you Aeros? Promise me you will always tell me the truth."

"Trust works both ways, my love." He stepped away. "Never forget that." He shyfted in a bright flash.

Sophenna dropped the apples and a few rolled down the knoll, coming to a stop near Rayne's hiding spot. "Rayne?" she whispered. "Where are you?"

She emerged from the thicket. "I think the energy column is somewhere down here."

"I found an opening, come on!" Sophenna led her to an underground entrance, hidden by vines. "I didn't go inside, but from what I can tell, the tunnel leads deep under the knoll."

While peering inside, Rayne's core ignited with a searing flame. "Aeros! He's here," she rasped. Sophenna stepped between Rayne and the approaching Aeros.

He knocked Sophenna to the ground. "For someone who'd lost their entire planet, you looked rather chipper a minute ago," he said. "Now, who is our little interloper?" Rayne spun around, and his mouth gaped open. "You!"

Sophenna rose behind Aeros and clubbed him with a rock. Stunned, he turned on her. "You dare to defy me!"

Jaered's mother looked at Rayne. "Run!"

Rayne took off down the tunnel. Aeros roared. The tunnel walls rumbled and collapsed behind her. Rock rained from overhead and she held up an arm to divert them, but never looked back. A large stone landed at her heels and she stumbled, terrified if she fell she'd be crushed. She regained her momentum, focused on the blinding light ahead. Unable to breathe from the dust, she didn't hesitate and ran headlong into the pulsating energy.

THIRTY-FOUR

Rayne landed on all fours on top of a pile of debris. The tingling in her chest eased sooner than her trembling muscles. She fell back onto her heels, confused about where she'd shyfted to.

The surrounding woods had been ravaged by a powerful storm. She'd shyfted on top of a collapsed building. The nearby pyramid frame once held a beautiful stained glass, but now was bent and mangled. The colorful shards of glass lay scattered among the ruins.

Rayne had shyfted to the northern vortex building. Ian's mansion ruins were a half-mile down a path littered with fallen trees and broken branches. She rose on shaky legs and her heart leapt at the damage the massive earthquake had wrought the day they'd parashyfted to Thrae. She tried not to think about the loss of lives or what was left of the city where she'd loved an illusionist from afar, and the memories of her early days with Ian. A life she'll never get back.

A gust nearly lifted her from the ground, urging her to move and not wallow in her grief. Rayne followed the path toward the mansion ruins, trying to figure out how to contact Ian, Eve, Patrick, or Tara. She had no idea if Jaered was still alive, and held onto the belief that Aeros had lied about everything.

Thrae hadn't imploded, she reasoned. It was holding on, even if by a thread, and Jaered would find a way to save his planet. Sophenna's sacrifice haunted Rayne's every step. Would Aeros kill her, knowing he might never have her, after she betrayed him?

Exhaustion took hold and Rayne's steps slowed as darkness descended on what was left of the Northern California coastline. Most of the inner compound wall had survived the earthquake along with some of the stone animals keeping guard upon their posts every few feet between. A section of the wall had crumbled, and Rayne climbed over the pile of bricks, feeling her way in the dark.

The night's sky was an ebony blanket, thick cloud cover obliterating the stars. Rayne's chest heaved. She missed Milo's meals, Ian's card tricks and sleight-of-hand illusions after dinner. Their strolls around the lake and the comfort she found whenever he was near, seemed a lifetime ago.

Rayne scaled what was left of the front porch and paused at the sound of snoring. It wasn't subtle, but loud enough to bring what remained of the mansion walls down.

"Who's there?" a male voice called out. "I've got a gun and know how to use it!"

"Milo," Rayne said. "It's me."

He stepped into the doorway. Recognition lifted his features and he dropped his flashlight. It clattered down the ruined steps. "You're alive!" He looked around. "How the hell did you get here?"

"I . . ." she hesitated. "I shyfted."

He stared at her like he waited for a punchline. "Seems we have some catching up to do." He ushered her into the ruins. "I'd throw my arms around you if I could," he said. "We all thought you were a goner." He pulled a towel off his shoulder and swiped at a makeshift bench he'd made with scraps of wood in the entryway. Dust flew about and he waved it off."

The snoring grew louder. It came from the great room. A huge mound rose and lowered.

Milo shrugged when Rayne turned back. "Hope you don't mind sharing a bedroom with a dragon. Ian's got me babysitting an egg." Rayne stood in a trance. The old caretaker opened a cooler and handed her half a sandwich. The bottled water rejuvenated her and she guzzled most of it down in a drawn-out gulp. Milo used the last of it to wash some of the grime off her face. "We need to contact the others. I have important news," she said.

Milo fumbled next to the cooler and held up a burner cell. He pressed a button and handed it to Rayne.

Eve answered on the second ring. "Milo?"

"It's Rayne," she blurted. "I'm with Milo at the mansion." Silence. Rayne didn't know if Eve was suspicious of the caller, or in shock.

"Stay where you are. I'm sending help." Eve's voice croaked. "Child, I'm so relieved you made it."

Rayne handed the phone to Milo and he stashed it under his bench. Claws scraped the floor. The noise came from the rear of the mansion. Saxon leapt out of the dark and landed hard on Rayne's lap, giving her a slobbering welcome with a motor for a tail. She wrapped her arms around him and buried her face in his fur. The flood erupted and she sobbed, feeling weak in Milo's eyes.

"Let it out," Milo said gently. The bear of a man sniffled and wiped his nose with the back of his hand. "I'm bound to join you any minute."

A cloud of emerald sparks formed at the center of the entryway and lit up the wall where Rayne sat. Ian rushed over and came to a skidding halt on his knees at her feet.

"Is she—?" he asked Milo.

"She's been through hell," Milo barked. "Give her a minute."

Ian rested his hands on either side of her and leaned close. "I love you," he said with such emotion that her core ignited and she gasped.

Rayne didn't lift her buried face from Saxon's coat, but felt the heat of his breath on her ear. "Sophenna. I abandoned her, to save myself," she murmured. She hugged Saxon tighter than ever. The wolf laid its head on her shoulder and snuggled against her. She wondered if Ian had channeled with the wolf, because it was the next best thing to being in his arms.

Milo wouldn't let Ian shyft her away until he heard her story. When she came to the part about her core allowing her to shyft, the old caretaker slumped back and would have toppled off his bench if there hadn't been a wall behind him.

"I've lived to see it all," he said.

"Do you think you can shyft back to Aeros's dome?" Ian asked.

"I think so." When Rayne stood, she was shocked at how weak she felt. "But only if the vortex is strong enough. I don't know if I can take anyone else. I drain the power as fast as I can draw it into my core."

"Earth's core has already splintered once. If we don't attack him now, others will form soon." He regarded Milo. "You should—"

Milo waved them off. "Get her to Eve, don't worry about me and Mount Gecko."

A heated snort came from the direction of the great room. A minute later, Ian grinned. "Oocaw considers you a toothpick," he said.

Milo took a couple of steps toward the curled-up dragon. "You better behave or that egg is going to be one hell of an omelet."

Her exposed eye opened and the inside of her nostrils glowed like hot coals. She gave the old caretaker a dark stare.

"I'll leave the two of you to your battle of wit," Ian said. He stepped into the center of the entryway, inhaled deep and reached for Rayne. "Ready?" he asked.

She approached and tried to draw energy into her core, hoping it would lessen his discomfort, but her core sputtered in her chest. She took his hand. With a wince, Ian shyfted.

They appeared on a yacht amidst a roiling storm at sea. Tara rushed up and threw her arms around Rayne. Patrick and Eve stood off to the side, drenched from the rain, but didn't budge until Tara pushed back and stared at her. "Let's get inside."

They filed into an opulent, expansive living room. It took both of Patrick's hands to shut the sliding glass door against the storm. Gwynn hurried up the steps and handed everyone towels, then kissed Rayne on her forehead. "You are incredible," she said.

Rayne told her story, from the moment she disappeared on Thrae to when she called Eve using Milo's burner. No one spoke, stunned at the news Aeros had not only splintered Earth's core, but that he'd harnessed it for a massive dome.

"Sophenna is alive," Gwynn said. "That's the best news, yet."

"Aeros will be furious. She doesn't have much time," Rayne said. She glanced about the room. "Where's Jaered?" Their lack of response sent chills up her exposed arms.

"He stayed on Thrae," Ian said. "He was convinced if he left, the planet was doomed. If his mother doesn't return soon, it will implode for sure."

"That's suicide!" Rayne yelled.

"He felt his connection slipping away," Gwynn said. "His core was dying along with the planet. If he stayed, he had a chance to keep himself, and his world, alive."

"We need to get Sophenna to Thrae before we lose . . ." Rayne hesitated at Ian's downcast gaze.

"Them both," he said.

"You have no idea where it is?" Patrick asked.

Tara scooted to the edge of her seat. "Even what hemisphere you were in?"

"The surrounding walls were too high and we couldn't see the sky," she said.

"The rebels and beasts are scattered across Earth. We don't have enough shyftors to launch a blitz attack. We need time to coordinate the assault," Patrick said.

Ian's jaw bulged. "You can't shyft back alone, or you are as good as dead."

Rayne's chuckle bordered on hysteria. She needed to pull it together if she was going to help Jaered and his mother survive the night. "Other than channeling, I don't suppose you have a way to read minds," she said.

Eve looked at Gwynn. "It's a long shot," Gwynn said. "But we've got to try."

Gwynn and Eve sat in the dark room across the table from each other, holding hands. They hadn't spoken since Ian put them in a deep trance, but were fully conscious of each other. The sisters hadn't drawn upon their seer insight in centuries, and had never attempted it without Sophenna.

The expanse of time and space was vast. They searched the globe, starting at the Arctic Circle and working their way south, traveling on the magnetic rays of the aurora borealis as it deposited its energy in specs of dust from one pole to the next. The latitudinal journeys turned to longitudinal treks while they scanned Earth like a magnifying glass sweeping across a spinning globe.

They called out to their sister, searching for her life-line, using nothing but their minds, cognizant they were weaker as two when not three. Ice caps turned to snow-capped peaks. Mountains bled into pastures. Pastures gave way to deserts ending in tropical regions. They found no sign of her. Cities large and small came and went.

All that was left were the vast oceans. They skimmed the surface, skipping over islands and dipping into reefs. They came upon a glow deep in the Atlantic, a concentrated point of energy, burning bright below the surface.

Gwynn and Eve pulled back and broke the connection. They opened their eyes and stared at each other. What they had sought was found, but the reality they brought back with them was too shocking to acknowledge out loud.

"Mother?" Patrick asked. He put a cautious hand on her shoulder.

"We know," Gwynn said, just above a whisper.

"What is it?" Ian asked.

"Where is it?" Rayne insisted.

Eve pushed away from the table. "It's in the depths of the Bermuda Triangle."

Ian hypnotized Rayne, hoping it would enhance her recall of Aeros's dome. She spent the rest of the night recounting as much detail about the knoll as she could to a skilled artist. The man's patience was boundless whenever she instructed him to change colors, lines, and shapes of the stream curvature, the odd vegetation, down to the skipping stones in the middle of the creek bed. She had him add the charred plants next to her hiding spot, but doubt crept in and she shuddered. Would he have repaired them, wanting to keep his paradise unblemished? Or would he have kept them as a warning to Sophenna not to betray him again?

So much rested on her getting the details right. Exhaustion came and went many times over.

Rayne wrapped her hands around her coffee mug. There was a bond between siblings. Between Weir Sars and their cores, and in turn, their cores and the planets powering them. Rayne pressed a fist to her chest. She'd never understood, not fully, until her own core had awakened. Would she, too, know of Thrae's death at the time it happened? Or would it be Jaered's death that would forever shatter her core? She stared at the steam rising from the mug, unable to look Ian in the eye.

He leaned in and blew a strand of hair off her face. "I'm worried about him, too."

The artist motioned for her to return, but Rayne hesitated. "We will save everyone," she said.

"And the planets will thrive once again," Ian said.

The conviction in his voice and the strength flowing from his eyes gave her the boost she needed. They had to succeed, or would die trying.

THIRTY-FIVE

The late summer heat was absent in the heart of the Kamchatka Peninsula. One of the most remote areas of Russia, this region of eastern Russia is closer to Los Angeles than it is to Moscow.

Eve chose their final battleground with care. Ian approved. The energy in his core sizzled with pulsating precision thanks to the spectacular, hyperactive geothermal land and its nearly two hundred volcanos. The Pur, Duach, and rebel Weir Sars will be at their most powerful. In retrospect, so will Aeros and the Primary.

The sun sank below the horizon, pulling an ever-widening shade on the sky. Saxon stood out among the troops, his snowy fur ruffling in the wind. Ian stood on the rising cliff, presiding over the arriving Pur amidst their emerald clouds. The Pur shyftors, still weary from evacuating Thrae, arrived with rebels and members of the Pur army who'd recognized the Primary's traitorous actions, after being given tangible proof of his corruption.

"Word spread fast," Marcus said, appearing next to Ian and widening his stance to avoid tumbling off the lava bed's rocky ledge when a gust of wind slammed into them from behind.

"Not fast enough," Ian said.

"We've made a major dent in the Primary's army." Marcus nodded at his former lieutenant pushing through the gathering crowd below them.

The man paused and saluted Marcus. The old general returned the greeting. "There's more coming, sir," he shouted.

"Good work, Lieutenant," Marcus said, sounding every bit the general of Ian's youth.

Ian hid his smile. Marcus had regained the trust of some of his army and it brought additional warmth to Ian's blistering core. No matter the outcome of this battle, Marcus and his soldiers would be regarded as heroes amongst the Pur.

The last of the emerald clouds dispersed and Ian stared at the nearly thousand Pur waiting for his command. He'd spent his life avoiding this role, rejecting what it meant to be their Heir apparent. Yet everything he'd been taught, shown, and lived had prepared him for this moment. Ian stood frozen in place struggling with his childhood belief he wasn't the savior they made him out to be. Jestueax circled them like a winged predator. The gargoyle landed behind Ian and Marcus, then fluttered her wings before folding them behind her. She snorted and the heat from her breath warmed the back of Ian's neck.

Marcus cleared his throat from behind a fist. When Ian didn't respond, the old general turned sideways and saluted him. "Your army is ready for your address, sire!"

Ian slowly nodded and took a step forward. "Many of you have understood the importance of this day for most of your life." He met the gaze of a few Thraen rebels in the crowd. "Many of you are new to this fight, and it's only through perseverance, tremendous loss of life, and sacrifice of an entire planet, that your eyes have been opened." It wasn't difficult to identify the doubters. Their expressions or downcast gazes spoke the truth. "But understand this. The Duach who are gathering over the ridge behind me are not your enemies. Just as us, they were lied to, manipulated, and raised to hate. Not because of our differences, but because when we are united, we are the true threat to our enemies." The rebels raised their fists into the air and shouted.

"Keep it up, boy," Marcus muttered.

"Aeros and the Primary wish to plunder Earth and suck the very essence out of it so they might live for all eternity." Ian spread his arms wide. "Make no mistake. Earth is not the first planet they have sought to destroy. The men standing at your shoulder have already lost their world of Thrae to these megalomaniacs. If you need further proof, open your minds and your ears. Listen to their stories of devastation, torture, and death at the hands of these would-be gods."

"But they are gods!" The shout came from several rows back. Those closest turned dark glares in the man's direction, but not all reeked of warning.

"How can we hope to defeat the undefeatable?" came from the edge of the crowd.

"It's nothing but your fear that make them gods," Ian shouted. "Our courage and combined strength is all we need to destroy them once and for all." Right on cue, a tremendous roar filled the darkening sky. Oocaw rose above the ridge and flew into the sky. The dragon let out a steady stream of fire, lighting their faces in an orange glow. She swooped low enough for Ian to lock eyes with Patrick, riding on the crick of her neck, but not close enough to trigger the Curse. This was their show of unity, but if Eve's theory on cancelling the Curse didn't pan out, it would be short-lived.

"I am but one of three Heirs. Each of us commanding our legions," Ian shouted. "As you can see, we have formidable weapons of our own." Ian turned and leapt onto Jestueax's back and they took to the sky, gliding low over the heads of his Pur army. As he passed, fists shot into the air and battle cries rose behind him. The rest of the gargoyles emerged from the surrounding brush and an ominous cloud cloaked the sky. Patrick turned Oocaw around and they disappeared on the other side of the ridge to rejoin his Duach troops. A few of the gargoyle herd followed the dragon. The rest flew in tight formation behind Jesteaux. Ian sat rigid upon her back and raised both fists over his head. His troops thunderous battle cry turned deafening.

They didn't have long to wait. As Eve predicted, the power it took to shyft their troops to one location was an irresistible welcome mat. Aeros's army appeared in crimson waves at the top of the ridge, between the two rebel armies. A few moments later, emerald clouds told Ian the last of the Primary's most loyal had joined the fight.

Enemy troops swooped down the hillsides like ants emerging from an ant hill, sending core blasts in all directions. Aeros appeared last, standing in snowy robes. A stark, glowing god at the top of the ridge. He didn't lift a hand, but stood gazing upon the ensuing battle with an amused grin.

Ian shouted and turned Jestueax toward them. He sent emerald core blasts, one after another into the heart of Aeros's troops while Jestueax banked and swooped to avoid their returned fire. A sizzling blast nearly collided with Ian's shoulder, but Jestueax banked and snuffed it out with the edge of her wing. Ian gripped her tight to stay mounted.

Many of the Pur Sars shyfted to meet their enemy head-on with a powerless Pur in tow. They appeared in green puffs amidst Aeros's Duach Core Blasters, triggering the Curse while their companions used firearms and swords to strike down the Cursed. The Primary's Pur Sars rushed in and their hand-to-hand combat swelled to a frenzy as the powerful were either killed or rendered useless.

Jestueax and her fellow gargoyles kept the Core Blasters at bay, but modern firearms and, to Ian's horror, archers, drove their winged compatriots to take cover.

The odor of spilt blood filled Ian's nostrils and quickened the beat of his heart. Ian used his keen night vision on the ebony hillside, but it became impossible to get a clear idea of who lived and who died among all sides.

Many Sars commanded animals, and others drew upon their power of controlling plants. Trees came to life with swinging branches and tripping roots. Rodents attacked at the heels of the enemy, or jumped upon the enemy's back and sank teeth into their necks. From the deathly cries at the fringe of the battle, the larger wild beasts of the region attacked at the periphery.

Ian spotted Marcus charging toward a horde of the Primary's troops, but he soon disappeared in the melee of swinging swords and flying fists.

An arrow sliced a deep gouge in Ian's calf and stuck in Jestueax's tail. The gargoyle let off an ear-splitting shriek and Ian was thrown off her back. He landed hard against the ground. Stunned, he rose as high as all fours and shook his head to gain his senses.

A strong hand gripped Ian's shoulder and pulled him to his feet. A large man towered over him, but Ian froze, unable to tear his gaze from the soldier's deformed lower jaw. This must be Cyphir, Aeros's Lieutenant. Jaered had warned Ian to look out for him. He wasn't a Sar. But he was equally as deadly.

"I hoped to be the one to end you," Cyphir hissed. He drew back a dagger to plunge it into Ian.

With a squawk, Jestueax swooped in, but Cyphir sidestepped at the last second. One of the gargoyle's claws penetrated his shoulder, and knocked him to the ground.

An enemy soldier suffered a fatal wound and dropped his sword. Ian snatched it from the ground and fought off a soldier rushing toward him at his flank. The hilt of the soldier's sword caught Ian in the cheek. He tasted blood from loosened teeth, but managed to stay on his feet despite the blow.

Cyphir got to his feet. Blood spurted from the deep puncture wound in his shoulder as he drew his sword from its sheath. He swiped it side to side, and advanced, knocking everyone away who stepped in his path. The man's murderous gaze never wavered from Ian's face.

Ian grabbed a second sword from a fallen enemy and stood his ground. Cyphir lunged at him with a downward thrust of his sword, and Ian ducked within an inch of it finding his outstretched arm. Ian spun around and caught the man across his back.

A sickening gurgle came from his parted lips, but he didn't appear phased by the deep wound inflicted upon him. Another enemy lunged toward Ian, but Cyphir cut him down and he lay still on the ground. "Mine!" the man shouted at the motionless body.

A blur of white leapt into the air behind him. Saxon sank teeth into the back of the man's neck. Blood spurted when the wolf's incisors ripped into his carotid. He staggered, trying to knock Saxon off his back, but the wolf's death grip was too strong. The man slumped to the ground and fell face first against the dirt.

"I don't care who gets the credit," Ian said over the man's corpse. He nodded at Saxon, but the wolf disappeared into the throng without looking back.

Jestueax landed next to Ian. He hopped onto the gargoyle and guided her away from the heart of the battle. "Patrick!" Ian shouted.

Patrick's voice crackled in Ian's earpiece. "We're taking a beating," he yelled.

"Can you push them back to the top of the ridge? Maybe we can sandwich them in," Ian said.

"My Duach Sars are dispersed among them," Patrick said. "The Curse will render the remaining Sars useless if you come anywhere near."

Without being able to unite, they were no match for Aeros's most ruthless. The odor of death turned Ian's stomach. He'd led their courageous Weir into a massacre. He searched the top of the ridge, but Aeros was nowhere in sight. The idea that he might have taken his powers to Patrick's battle set Ian's blood boiling.

A heartbeat later, an idea slammed into him and he nearly toppled off Jestueax's back. "Patrick, if you can hear me, I'm bringing reinforcements. When the time comes, pull your troops off the ridge and shyft them to the dome site."

At the silent pause, Ian feared the worst.

"What's the signal?" Patrick asked.

"Lambs to a slaughter," Ian said in relief. He patted Jestueax's neck and the gargoyle flew toward the closest volcano. Ian bent low, and she dove into the crater. Just as she was about to collide with the smoldering floor, Ian drew enough power and parashyfted them.

They emerged from the sinkhole energy column on Thrae. *We need to draw attention. The kind that won't be ignored,* Ian channeled.

You are about to unleash an uncontrollable force on your world, Jestueax responded. *I hope you know what you're doing.*

"You and me both," Ian muttered to himself.

The gargoyle emitted high-pitched shrieks. Ian cupped the sides of his head and pushed the pain to the back of his thoughts. She dropped her head and headed toward the opening to the sinkhole. On their approach, Ian spotted Jaered standing at the edge of the ledge, next to Jestueax's nest. He gave Ian a perplexed stare. As they swooped by, Jaered jumped off the ledge and landed on the gargoyle's back, behind Ian.

"What the hell is going on?" Jaered shouted over Jestueax's shrill shrieks.

"We're getting our asses beat," Ian yelled over his shoulder. "I'm here for reinforcements."

Growls filled the cavern and blended with the deafening pitch. The fenris poked their heads above the vegetation and appeared between crevices in the floor of the sinkhole. Jestueax didn't let up while she circled high above the gnashing of teeth and tormented howls.

Jestueax taunted them, swooping low and slashing toward them with her talons. The fenris gathered in a frenzy, swiping at her with extended claws, but the gargoyle had enough sense to stay beyond their reach.

We need to drive them toward the energy column, Ian channeled.

The gargoyle dipped her wing and headed down the worn path straight for the pulsating power. Seconds before they approached, the pulse faded and the column disappeared.

"No!" Ian shouted. Jestueax encircled where the column should be, but it was a dark spot in the cavern floor.

Jaered jumped off her back and fell to one knee at its center. He pressed both palms to the stone and his back heaved.

"I need that column!" Ian yelled.

"Working on it!" Jaered moaned between clenched teeth. The cavern ceiling trembled as shards of rock rained about them. "Ugh!" Jaered screamed as the faintest of shimmers grew around him. "Go, I'll hold it open as long as I can."

Jestueax turned down the path, but held up then doubled back toward the column when a herd of fifty or more fenris came at them like a stampede.

Jaered had disappeared inside the renewed energy column. The gargoyle emitted her nerve-racking shriek and circled the column. The fenris lunged at her, disappearing along with Ian and Jestueax inside the column.

They reappeared at the battlefield, on top of the ridge. Jestueax raised her face to the sky overhead and bolted toward the heavens. The fenris swarmed out of the parashyft that Ian kept open with extended hands.

The fenris pounced on the unsuspecting, sinking teeth into necks and opening abdomens with their razor-sharp claws. The animals spun around and leapt in all directions, frenzied by blood lust and insatiable hunger from months, perhaps years, of starvation.

"Lambs to the slaughter!" Ian shouted, but his unprotected earpiece was fried from the electromagnetic parashyft. Oocaw rose above the tree line and batted away a volley of arrows followed by core blasts. One struck her in the underbelly, and she let loose a stream of fire upon her attackers.

Jestueax emitted her high-pitched shriek and Oocaw paused in mid-flight. An arrow pierced her leg, and her jaws parted in a thunderous roar of fire.

Ian waved to get Patrick's attention, but his focus was on his injured mount. *I need to warn them,* Ian channeled.

Jestueax dropped her head and made a beeline toward the dragon. Arrows flew by in all directions, but the undaunted gargoyle reached the dragon without one of them finding its target.

Patrick and Ian clutched their chests simultaneously as the Curse took hold.

"It's time!" Ian shouted as his attention turned to Aeros's dome.

THIRTY-SIX

The yacht came to a floating standstill. Everyone had their assignments drilled into them. There was no room for error. Timing was everything.

Eve stood by with cell phone in hand, at the ready to give the signal.

Ian stepped to the center of the helicopter pad. Eve's yacht was centered over the dome far below the ocean surface. His core kept rhythm to the splintered column pulsating and emitting energy from the depths beneath them. Breaching it was the next challenge. "Something's not right," he said. "Why aren't there any boats patrolling the area?"

"Arrogance," Rayne said.

Tara lowered the binoculars. "To keep his secret hideaway, secret."

"There's no turning back, Ian," Rayne said. "We're doing this, now."

287

Ian stepped next to her. "Like we practiced!" he shouted over the gusts of wind. He drew massive amounts of energy from Earth and it encompassed them within a widened shyft field. He was the power source and Rayne was the driver. They'd practiced reciting the details about the knoll for most of the afternoon.

They recited the shyft location, their cadence in rhythmic harmony and of a single voice, of single mind. Ian's chest blistered from the tremendous power surge. As their narrative came to its conclusion, Ian and Rayne shyfted.

Ian fought to complete the shyft, but his core was draining as fast as he could pull energy. He saw Rayne out the corner of his eye. Neither of them were solidifying. They weren't touching. Whatever drained his power, wasn't coming from her.

His focused on the scene ahead. The swirling image beyond the shyft field took shape as Ian fought to increase his energy draw. Aeros stood, watching them and diverting power from the field, keeping them in limbo and preventing the shyft from completing.

Why wasn't he halfway across Earth? Their hope to slip from the battle without his knowledge was shattered. How long had he stood in wait? Ian couldn't make out anyone else beyond the curtain of power separating them from their sworn enemy.

After several agonizing minutes, Aeros flicked his hand and Ian flew backward the instant the shyft completed. Rayne toppled over him and came to a stop off to the side, motionless.

"I have lived for eons. You are but a gnat in this universe," Aeros snarled.

"Gnats feed the predators," Ian said. "They are the ones you should worry about."

"I am a god!" he roared. "Not even a predator challenges me."

Ian rose to one knee. "Perhaps not one," he said and looked Aeros in the eye. "But I'm far from one."

The air behind Aeros brightened and expanded as a billion crimson sparks spread across the top of the hill. The splintered energy column convulsed with the draw of shyfting energy.

Ian grabbed Rayne's collar and they reappeared at the creek bed location. The air shimmered white as a group of Duach rebels solidified. They ran down the hill. The scarlet shimmer again turned to snow as the next shyfting group arrived.

Aeros shouted and took out the unsuspecting with core blasts. Gunshots rang out, but Aeros avoided the bullets as easily as playing dodgeball in a school yard.

Ian knelt over the unconscious Rayne. "Wake up!" he cried inches from her face. When she didn't respond, he bent lower, listening for a heartbeat. It was there, but faint. He needed to get her closer to the energy column, but the fierce battle had spilled across the knoll.

The sounds of battle faded. Ian stole a look. Aeros was gone. "Where'd you go, asshole?" Ian muttered.

"He won't leave," said a weak voice. Rayne stared at him. "He will want to see us defeated."

"And crush the last of us himself," he said. "We've got to find Sophenna."

"Get the hell off me and let's do this," she said.

Ian pushed back onto his heels. A core blast zipped by, singing the tip of his ear. He spun around and retaliated with his own. The blast struck Aeros's Duach guard in the center of his chest, and he fell to the ground.

Rayne rolled off to the side with her gun drawn. Her shot took out one of Aeros's Duach aiming a sword tip at a fenris who'd hitched a ride in someone's corona.

"Wait." Ian held out his arm to stop Rayne from leaving the battle. He had to witness the next battalion's arrival.

At the crest of the hill, an emerald glow lit the air, but by the time the shyftors solidified, their coronas had turned stark white. Marcus led the battalion. He gave Ian a one-finger salute and charged down the hill.

The Primary had spoken the truth. Earth's splintered core eliminated the Curse. Ian watched Duach and Pur rebels fighting side by side with the arriving enemy troops.

"Ian," Rayne said. "Sophenna."

He took a second to get his bearings. Locating Jaered's mother in the immense dome wasn't going to be easy, or timely. "We need a plan," he said.

"Aeros will keep her far away from the fighting," Rayne said. "I'm thinking the opposite end of the dome."

Ian withdrew his handgun. "Lead the way."

Rayne took off through the brush with Ian close at her heels. The battle raged behind them. The whiff of burned flesh and the metallic odor of fired weapons followed them like a swarming cloud. The urge to turn around and fight by the rebels' side was fierce, but if they didn't rescue Sophenna, this battle would be over soon enough.

Running footsteps stopped them cold and they slipped into nearby brush. Ten or so men wearing dripping scuba gear passed them, headed down the path toward the battle field. "Where the hell did they come from?" Rayne asked.

"There's got to be an opening to the ocean somewhere," Ian said.

A quarter of a mile later, their steps slowed at the sound of rushing water. They stopped on the edge of an embankment next to a wide waterfall. It disappeared several feet below them in the lower base of the dome. Ian had assumed the based had rested on the bottom of the ocean. From what he could tell, it was completely encased. There might be a subterranean structure.

Ian sniffed the air and dipped his finger where the flow came to a gentle ebb at their feet. "Salt water," he said. "He must be diverting it from the surrounding ocean. This is how they got inside."

"Can you shyft us across?" Rayne asked. "We're too far away from the column. I can't draw any energy."

The magnetic tingling grew in his chest and he reached for Rayne's hand, but at that moment, a crushing pressure magnified and it brought him to his knees.

Rayne grimaced and doubled over. "Aeros!" she rasped.

Aeros shyfted next to Rayne and with a swipe of his arm, sent her flying off to the side. She slid to a stop at the edge of the falls. He wrapped his fingers around Ian's throat and lifted him off the ground. "I tire of your antics," he said with steeled calm.

Ian pulled back and kicked Aeros in the groin with everything he had. His father dropped him and stumbled backward. Then he stiffened, grabbing his chest at the same time a shot rang out.

Rayne lay on her back, grasping her smoking gun in both hands.

A widening crimson spot covered the center of Aeros's torso. He looked down at it as the bloody edges stopped spreading. A second later, the flow reversed. With a wicked laugh, he lifted his face and confronted Rayne. "I'm immortal, you fool. You can't kill me!" He raised his hand.

Ian dropped his head and rushed Aeros. With a roar, he lifted his father off his feet and hurdled him into the current at the edge of the waterfall. Aeros cried out and was swept over the ledge.

He ran toward Rayne and reached. "Hurry!" The second she took his hand, he shyfted them to the opposite side of the waterfall.

"Ian, if we can't kill Aeros—" Rayne said.

"Not with conventional weapons," Ian said. "But first, we find Sophenna."

They rushed through the brush, zigzagging to cover as much ground as they could. Soon, the far wall rose ahead of them, but there'd been no sign of Sophenna or a place where she might be hidden. They stopped to catch their breath.

"Why hasn't Aeros tried to come after us again?" Rayne said. "Is he toying with us?"

Ian stilled as his thoughts competed with his pounding heart. She had a point. Aeros could have shyfted out of the water at any time. There wasn't anything stealth about their search for Sophenna, bending brush and snapping twigs at every turn. Why hadn't he attacked them again?

He turned off everything but his primary senses. The battle raged across the expanse. Shouts, screams, and the odor of death wafted in the air. The buzzing energy of the dome was strong. Where would Aeros have taken her?

"She could be anywhere," Ian said.

"She's here," Rayne said. "He believes he's won. He'll want to show off the dead."

"He didn't attack us until we reached the waterfall," Ian said.

"And left us alone after we took off," Rayne said.

Ian grasped Rayne's hand and with a wince at the pain it elicited, shyfted them back to the waterfall's edge. Damp footprints on the ground gave him pause. He brought a finger to his lips, then indicated for Rayne to follow.

He traced the footprints to a set of rocky steps, near the edge of the dome. If he hadn't been looking for them, he might have passed by without ever noticing them. The entrance to the underground grotto was an optical illusion, the rocky pattern blended perfectly with the surrounding rock face.

They descended the stairs. The roar of the water drowned out any noises. Once they'd gained distance from the waterfall, Ian could discern subtle variations to sound. He came to a halt and gestured for Rayne to hold back. Moans came from around the corner.

Ian pushed against the rock wall and peered around the corner. Sophenna was strapped to iron rings at the opposite wall. Mud splattered her ripped gown and her silky hair was dingy and hung in damp strands. She lifted her head and grimaced. Blood ran down the side of her face from a gash on her forehead. "Aeros, please, give up this madness," she implored. "Our children's children are slaughtering each other. For what?"

A shadow moved in front of Sophenna. Aeros stood across from her, out of Ian's sight. "My legions will squash the rebels. Your sisters will beg for your life and nothing will stop me from taking theirs."

"You may live forever, but you will be alone in this universe," Sophenna said.

"You lie!" he yelled and sent a blast of power slamming into her.

Sophenna's head bounced off the rock wall. "Ugh!" she moaned, and her head drooped toward her chest. "You've forfeited everything for the sake of nothing," she said so softly, Ian strained to hear her. "The price of your soul will be to live eternity without love."

"I will have you!" his voice filled the cave with a concussive shock wave.

Sophenna's legs gave out and she slumped to the floor with her hands dangling from the iron rings. "You will have everything, yet, nothing," she murmured. "Till the end of time."

Aeros's shadow engulfed Sophenna as he approached her. He grabbed the crown of her head and raised her face to him.

She was unconscious, but her chest expanded. She was breathing.

Aeros wailed and the walls rattled. A blinding flash. The cave grew silent.

"He's gone," Ian said.

Rayne hurried over to Sophenna. "She's alive, but barely."

"He will have joined the battle." Ian conjured the iron shackles away and gathered Jaered's mother in his arms. Rayne took off for the stairs. "What are you doing?" he asked. "You're coming with me!"

She paused. "I'm staying."

"But the fenris," Ian said.

She held up her hand when Ian made to protest. "We recruited Earth's Weir with the promise to lead them. Not leave them to be slaughtered." She disappeared up the stone steps.

Ian drew energy into his core, but he didn't stop until he'd maximized his power, hoping Aeros would notice the massive parashyft. Once he discovered Sophenna missing, Ian counted on him following. It was the rebel forces' only hope for survival, and Rayne's.

THIRTY-SEVEN

Tara lowered the binoculars. She hated that Ian was right. "Incoming!" she shouted. A massive cloud of approaching gunships, being led by two fighter jets, was bearing down on them.

She took advantage of the slippery ladder rungs and slid down to the main deck of the yacht, landing with a mad dash toward aft where she'd lined up her weapons on the back cushions like surgical instruments. She snatched one up and loaded the chamber. Eve lowered the burner cell from her ear and dropped to the deck next to Tara.

"The Primary's making good on his threat." Tara gave Eve a sideways glance. "He detests you for taking away his piggy bank."

"It's not about me," Eve said. "He has to support his brother, or deal with the consequences."

"He's a wimp and a traitor to the Weir," Tara said. One of the aircraft broke from the squad and dropped, skimming the ocean's surface, headed straight for them. She lifted the short-range missile onto her shoulder and lined up the approaching aircraft with the scope. A fraction of a second before pressing the trigger, she thought of her sister Mara and how much she would have loved this.

The fighter pilot jettisoned a torpedo, which headed for their starboard side. Tara responded in kind with a blast from her missile launcher. The kickback threw her onto her back with her life vest taking most of the brunt. Her head rung and she couldn't hear a thing, but she raised a fist in triumph at the exploding aircraft. Eve clamored for the side of the yacht and brought Tara to her feet as the torpedo bore down on them.

Tara yelled, "Take cover!" But nothing happened. When she peered over the railing, hundreds of dolphins churned up the ocean around the yacht. The torpedo had disappeared.

Eve said something. Tara shook her head and gestured that she couldn't hear. Eve leaned closer and shouted, "They're messing with the radar!"

Overhead, a sonic boom drowned out the roar of engines. Oocaw and a group of gargoyles exited the invisible energy column above the yacht. With a fiery roar, the dragon gave a tremendous flap of her wings, but reared back at the sight of modern-day aircraft.

Patrick leaned over Oocaw's neck to find them onboard. Tara gave him the okay signal, and dragon and rider took off for the circling planes. Patrick let loose a blast of power and it snapped a wing off an approaching plane. The aircraft dove into the ocean.

A deafening whine. The remaining jet came in low with a round of large-caliber shots, stippling the deck between Tara and Eve. One of the gargoyle's crashed into the aircraft's engine. In a spinning freefall, the attack jet left a trail of debris across the water's surface.

Oocaw leveled off in the middle of the battle and spun around with shooting flames, sending several boats exploding across the sea. Another gunship opened fire on her, but she rolled in midair and took it out with her tail.

Tara was sure Patrick would be knocked off and plummet to the ocean, but when Oocaw leveled off again, he straddled her, still hanging onto the dragon. He reared back and flung another energy blast at a gunboat. It was too fast for him, but he managed to cripple its gun operator.

Gunfire ripped into the port side of the yacht. A line of speedboats approached with automatic rifles aimed at them.

An enormous spout of water rose as high as the yacht and with a creaking heave, the vessel tilted out of the water, then crashed back down. The whale's wave dispersed some of the boats and upended a few others. Tara fell against Eve. "What the—"

Eve grunted as she pressed the screen on her burner cell. "Weir power over animals isn't limited to land," she said.

Whoever she was calling answered because Eve leaned off to the side. "They're ramming torpedoes up our asses!" A towering splash and a concussive blast ripped open a hole in the ocean about a quarter mile from the yacht. Tara cowered, but Eve didn't flinch. "Never mind," she said. "Carry on."

"What was that?" Tara asked.

"The whale was providing cover for my sub. When it came to our rescue, the sub came under attack."

"The explosion . . ." Tara said.

"The diverted torpedo." Eve grabbed Tara. "Look out!"

A flaming mass landed hard on the deck, knocking Tara and Eve onto the cushions. Tara's rifle tip bit into her shoulder blade. She pressed her fingers against the aching bruise and sat up, peering into the glassy eyes of a dead gargoyle with one of its wings ablaze. The smell of charred flesh turned Tara's stomach.

One of the cushions caught fire. Tara scrambled to gather her weapons while Eve grabbed the fire extinguisher and snuffed out the blaze with spurting foam.

A second later, a blast ripped into the starboard side of the ship. It lifted Tara off her feet in a hail of splinters, and she headed toward the ocean.

THIRTY-EIGHT

Ian stepped out of the sinkhole energy column with an unconscious Sophenna in his arms. Jaered rushed over and together they laid her on the ground.

"That bastard," Jaered hissed, wrapping his arms around her.

"We have to hurry," Ian said. "If I'm right, Aeros isn't far behind."

Gwynn knelt beside her sister and pressed the edge of her shirt against the gash on Sophenna's forehead. "She's too weak. Thrae needs all of us." Ian took a step back toward the column, but his mother stopped him in a commanding voice. "Rayne must return with you. Don't let her stay."

"I don't intend to," Ian said. He parashyfted.

He reappeared in the cave beneath the dome's waterfall. It was empty. Ian hurried up the stone steps and emerged above ground. The battle cries and gunplay had faded. On the surface, he came upon Wyatt and a small band of rebels. They'd grabbed some of the scuba tanks and masks. A few pieces still had blood smeared on them.

"We found the dome's control room," Wyatt said. "I've set a charge and evacuated everyone we could find. Five minutes before this place blows."

"Where's Rayne?" Ian asked.

Panic lifted Wyatt's features. "I thought she was with you."

"Get to the waterfall. There's got to be a way out at the base," Ian said. He took off, passing bodies of Weir and fenris on his dash back to the knoll. He burst through the vegetation next to the creek and came upon a bloody battlefield. Weir littered the ground with a handful of fenris scattered among them. The death toll was devastating on both sides. Howls in the distance. A couple of fenris were preying upon the injured.

A gunshot. Return fire came from the opposite side of the knoll. The dome grew silent and all was still. Fearful of what he'd find, Ian searched the mounds of fallen bodies, praying Rayne wasn't among them. He told himself he'd know if she had been killed. His core, his heart, would know.

The outline of a familiar face was painted in blood. Ian dropped to his knees and lifted Marcus's head. Stifled sobs racked his chest as he gently closed the soldier's eyelids upon a world he'd given his life to save. "Go into the good night, brave soldier," Ian whispered. "Be at peace with your son."

A rock rolled down the hill and came to a rest on its side a couple of yards from where Ian knelt. It was a fenris's severed head. The long, purplish tongue protruded from its gaping mouth. "Your army was no match for me!" The voice came from the crest of the knoll.

"But unlike you, they'll be remembered for all eternity," Ian shouted. Rustling in the nearby brush. Rayne slumped against a tree. Ian's elation was short-lived when Aeros shyfted next to her.

"Where's Sophenna?" Aeros yelled. He grabbed Rayne by the throat and squeezed. "Tell me where she is or I will end this favored whore of yours!" Aeros's mouth fell open and the flames in his eyes extinguished. He dropped Rayne, pressing a fist to his chest. "What are you?" he rasped.

"A secret weapon," she hissed. She raised her gun and shot him in the throat. Aeros stumbled back, clutching his neck. She aimed, but it clicked, her gun empty. "No!" she screamed, and pulled the trigger again and again. When reality sank in, she grabbed Aeros's hand and hung on. Blood sprouted from between his fingers. He tried to pull out of her grasp.

If Ian intervened, she'd drain them both. He stood by, helpless. "Hang on," he said. "You're draining his core faster than he can heal himself."

Aeros pulled his free hand from the wound and reached toward the knoll. A horizontal surge of energy erupted from the grassy hill and connected with his out-stretched fingertips. A heartbeat later, the gushing wound turned to seeping.

"No!" Ian yelled. He dove between Aeros and the energy stream to absorb it into his core, but it was too late. Aeros's strength had returned and he gave them a wicked smile. He pressed his elbow against the ground and pushed to stand.

Ian scrambled over Aeros, smashing him against the ground. He lunged for Rayne and they shyfted.

They appeared on the lower deck of the yacht. Rayne pushed away and leaned against the railing. "It didn't work," she sputtered. "It didn't work."

Eve groaned while tugging on a rope at the edge of the deck, pulling someone from the ocean. Ian took over and helped a drenched Tara up onto the landing. A huge splinter protruded from a wound in her shoulder. Whenever she coughed, crimson-tinged salt water spurted from her mouth.

"Where's Patrick?" Ian asked.

"Incoming," Patrick shouted. Oocaw swooped low enough for him to slide off her wing and onto the upper deck of the yacht. He took one glance at Tara and jumped over the railing, falling to one knee beside her.

The debris from downed planes and gryphon carcasses floated on the ocean's surface and surrounded the yacht as dots of confetti. "We're needed on Thrae, now," Ian said.

"Go," Tara said in a weak voice. "It's just a scratch."

Eve stuck the cell phone in Tara's hand. "Help is on the way. Hold on."

Patrick leaned in and gave Tara a lingering kiss. "Don't die on me."

"Back at ya, cowboy," Tara said.

A roar came from overhead. Jestueax had one of the Primary's elite guard in her talons. It was Komodo. He worked an arm free and he reared back, posturing to down her with one of his core blasts.

Ian was faster. His blast caught Komodo between the shoulder blades, and he went limp. Jestueax released him and he landed hard on the upper deck.

Rumbling. An enormous bubble rose from the depths of the ocean and burst at the surface with a towering cascade of salt water.

"The dome," Ian said.

A massive wave headed for the yacht. Jestueax swooped in and snatched Tara from the lower deck, carrying her to safety.

Seconds before the wave devoured the yacht, Ian parashyfted with the others.

A gust of blistering heat knocked Ian and the others to the ground. Volcanic ash obliterated what was left of Thrae's sky, which was filled with an endless, raging lightning storm. Thunder rattled the pebbles at their feet. Wide lava flows snaked their way down from surrounding volcanos.

Gwynn's coordinates had brought them to an open, desolate landscape. Rayne stared at the ground and didn't move, even when a lightning bolt struck and glinted off a massive structure hanging in the air. It was gigantic with interconnecting, towering petals that appeared to be titanium. The structure was suspended three stories above their heads. The memories of Dr. Willoughsby's experiments in the Congo

Basin filled Ian's thoughts. Painful experiments with frightening ramifications.

"It's a—" Eve said.

"Exedrae." Ian stared at the improvements Dr. Willoughsby had made to his original design. The significance of the mad doctor's experiments had come full circle. They weren't about destroying Earth, but saving Thrae.

"Rayne?" At first, Ian thought she was still reeling from shock at not defeating Aeros. When she didn't answer, he looked at what held her attention on the ground. They stood in an etched rock bed. A giant symbol identical to the Heir's Seal on his, Patrick's, and Jaered's chests. A triangle with a sun at its center.

"It's like the one on the cave wall," Rayne said. "In the Northern Colony."

A weak energy column rose from the triangle's centered sun and pulsated to the beat of the lightning storm, growing brighter with each strike in the sky, then turning dull again.

"What is this place?" Patrick shouted over the claps of thunder.

"Thrae's last hope," Gwynn said, standing at the uppermost point on the triangle.

Eve stepped to the other. Jaered stood with his mother in his arms at the third and last point.

Gwynn gestured for Ian to join her. He walked over and she grasped his hand tight. Something told him, it was for the last time.

Patrick stepped up next to his mother, and she wrapped him in a tight embrace.

"Where's my place in all of this?" Rayne shouted above the storm. "It wasn't to kill Aeros, was it?"

"No, my child. You weren't made to drain his life force," Gwynn said. "You were meant to drain ours."

She shook her head and stumbled back. "No!" she wailed.

"The energy from the lightning. It's the storm that will heal Thrae," Ian said and looked to his mother for confirmation. She nodded. "We need to direct the lightning storm's energy back into the crust!" he shouted to Patrick and Jaered.

Sophenna opened her eyes and gazed up at Jaered. A mother's devotion transformed her haggard, tortured face into a radiant glow. She placed a gentle hand upon his cheek. "It's time to let me go," she said.

"I can't," he murmured. "I've lost so much already. I'm not prepared to lose you, too."

"Don't deny me my parting gift," she said. A moment later, he lowered her legs to the ground and helped her to stand.

"Rayne, you need to be inside the energy column," Gwynn called out.

"But it'll drain you," she said.

"We've lived too many lifetimes as it is," Eve said. "I, for one am ready to pass the baton." She cupped Patrick's face and tilted it toward her. "Report me missing at sea. I've gone down with my ship. Other than a stipend for your father, I've left you everything. Promise me you'll use it wisely to rebuild not one, but both worlds." She gave him a lingering kiss upon his forehead. "I am so, damn proud of you."

His shoulders shook, and he wrapped his arms around her. "I can't do this without you," he said.

"Oh, my boy," she grabbed him by the back of the neck and peered into his eyes. "Believing that will be your only mistake."

Ian turned to his mother. "It hasn't been long enough," he said from behind a curtain of unshed tears.

"It never is," Gwynn said. She kissed him tenderly on each cheek. "You may not have been the first, but it was a tremendous blessing that you were my last." He buried his face in the crook of her neck, unwilling to let her go.

"Now, child. There's no time to waste," Gwynn called to Rayne from over his shoulder.

Ian tore away from his mother and hurried after Rayne, but she stopped and regarded Jaered. "I wasn't her," she said.

Anguish contorted Jaered's face and he shook his head. "You'll never convince my heart," he said.

Ian grabbed Rayne's hand and for once, didn't cringe at the pain it elicited, tortured ten-fold by the emotional upheaval. "There's got to be another way," he cried.

Rayne eased her hand from his grasp. "Ever since we met, you were prepared to die to save Earth. You called it your—"

"Destiny," he said.

"For the greater good. This is my destiny, Ian." The dam opened, and her cheeks were awash in tears. "We were never meant to be," she whispered. "Your mother did everything she could for us to stay apart . . . to reject each other."

"Yet, our love was too strong even for gods to deny," Ian said.

She touched his cheek affectionately. Before he could grab her wrist, she leapt into the column, and the energy consumed her.

"No!" He postured to follow, but a gentle hand clasped his.

"There's never enough time," his mother said gently.

"What do we do?" Patrick asked on choked words.

Ian turned around and faced them. "Draw energy from the exedrae and direct it into the column." He focused on the power churning in his chest. At the next lightning strike to the structure, he drew upon the energy trapped inside. A surge of blinding light raced out of the exedrae's lower opening and connected with Ian's core. He raised his palm to the column, where in his heart, stood a courageous Rayne. *Our love will endure,* his thoughts reached out to her.

Forever and always, her thoughts mingled with his.

The power surge increased as Patrick and Jaered drew energy from the exedrae and connected their cores to the column. Then the energy streams stretched between them, connecting them in a pyramid of energy.

The storm grew fierce, and hurricane winds threatened to uproot the Heirs where they stood. From behind, gentle hands came to rest upon their shoulders. *Don't stop, not for anything,* their mothers channeled as blended voices in harmonious chorus. Images played in Ian's thoughts as his mother's life flashed through his head.

Their mothers dreamt of this moment centuries earlier and gave birth to an ideal. That the Weir roam the lands as caretakers, free from tyrannical rulers. The angst Ian suffered at the onset of the power drain gave way to elation at all they achieved and gave back to their beloved worlds. Ancestors came and went, like photographs playing across the screen of his mind.

Aeros is coming. It entered Ian's thoughts as a passing statement, free from panic or alarm. *Don't stop, not for anything.*

The intense power taxed Ian's muscles and he moaned under the strain, but he and his brothers didn't drop their hands or relent on the energy pull. Aeros's image solidified between them.

It took everything Ian had to pull his attention away from the column where the Heirs sucked the life out of the exedrae and their mothers, while Rayne fed it to Thrae. It was working. Already the column pulsed stronger with steadier beats and the brilliance of the once dull light returned.

Don't stop, not for anything.

Aeros's cheeks were sunken and the flames that once made his irises blaze were clouded and hollow. Deep circles cupped his eyes and his lips were pasty and thin.

Don't stop, not for anything.

The once powerful god lifted his arm and spun around sending a blast of power. The Heirs teetered on their feet at the impact, but widened their stance, holding position against his attempt to topple them.

Don't stop, not for anything.

Aeros's back hunched, and he walked like a wounded, broken man. He reached the edge of the energy column and stuck his hand inside, but with a groan, he pulled it back and pressed it under his arm. "She's draining everything!"

Don't stop, not for anything.

"Did they tell you the truth? That this not only kills us, but is draining the life of your concubine. See for yourselves," Aeros snarled, beckoning them to approach the column. Ian clenched his jaw and stifled a sob, but held position. When they didn't budge. Aeros's back stooped lower.

A moment later Aeros swayed on his feet. He faced Jaered and lifted his gaze to Sophenna, partially hidden behind her son. "I only wanted your love, my Enna," he said. A single tear snaked down his cheek. "But you chose to give it to this stinking world!" The strength in his voice returned. "To him!" Aeros jabbed a crooked finger at Jaered.

Don't stop, not for anything.

Aeros dropped to his knees and with raised fists, wailed at the storm overhead. "I am a god!" His image grew faint in a drawn-out shyft. A moment later, it vanished into oblivion.

The pressure from Gwynn's hands disappeared at Ian's shoulders. He shuddered from an overheated core while the golden glow in his hands snaked up his forearms. Beads of sweat had turned into a drenching shower and he fought for breath.

The surrounding, spewing mountains quieted, and the rattling ground settled beneath their feet. The second exedrae was completely drained, the Heirs were released, collapsing to their hands and knees in utter exhaustion.

The energy column vanished. Rayne lay motionless at the center of the etched sun. Ian rushed toward her and gathered her into his arms. He drew energy into his already taxed core in an attempt to revive her and warm her frigid body. "Wake up!" he shouted.

Jaered fell to his knees and pressed a hand to her chest. He grimaced and pounded the ground with his fist.

"Together, we can revive her!" Ian pleaded. Jaered and Patrick's hands rested upon Ian's back and as one, they drew energy, but no matter how much they fed her, she lay still and unresponsive. Ian wailed, inconsolable, and rocked her even when Jaered and Patrick sat back and hung their heads. It was the first time Ian ever held Rayne and caressed her without worry or pain. Yet, he would never forget how icy she felt.

THIRTY-NINE

Aeros, Evelynn, Gwynndolyn, and Sophenna were gone. The Primary felt the loss of his core the second it happened, despite being two dimensions away.

He'd escaped to Smara, far from their pathetic last stand. It was a gamble, distancing himself as much as he could. It'd paid off, though, and he inwardly congratulated himself for surviving. At least for a few years longer. Without an active core, he'd continue to grow old, at a natural rate. He could accept that compared to their alternative.

He had two more mountain stashes, untouched by those thieving Heirs. He would be living the good life for the time he had left. For his first withdrawal, he'd chosen Smara's equivalent to the French Alps.

The Primary stepped away from the scenic overlook and turned toward his guide. "Onward, good man!" They finished the trek up the mountainside in under an hour. He stood at the cave entrance, withdrawing his key. His pistol would remain hidden under his jacket, provided the guide kept his hands to himself, and his mouth shut. He'd been paid a small fortune for his labor and his pack mules. The Primary didn't require too large of a withdrawal. Just enough to purchase the modest chateau nearby that had caught his eye. Close enough to his bank for the next thirty or more years. "Wait here," he barked. "I'll be back when I need your help."

He unlocked the thick, planked door and pushed it open. Rusted hinges whined and creaked at the intrusion. The rust crumbling off the hinges was a welcomed sight. It meant this treasure had not been found by the Heirs. It lay intact.

The Primary grabbed a torch soaked in creosote hundreds of years earlier and lit it with his lighter. The cavern was dank and musty. Stacks of crates were not high enough to topple, but the cavern was vast and filled wall to wall with the chests as old as pirates, some dating as far back as pharaohs. He paused, dredging up memories long buried, a time when his life had been his own, free from his brother's games and sadistic follies. Back to the years he so easily controlled others with a whisper, or with the tip of a whip.

The cavern held deep shadows and the Primary took heed of his steps. Forged metal corners on the chests could have rusted and warped. It wouldn't do for him to contract tetanus. Illness and disease were never a concern, until now. How his life had changed in an instant.

A cough came from the darkest shadows at the back of the cavern. The Primary stilled his breaths and concentrated, but the damn loss of powers had robbed him of his keen sight and hearing. Old age had taken over. He held the torch above his head. Chests stacked four to seven high stood like sentinels, rising from the floor of the cavern, motionless.

"Who is it?" he shouted and withdrew his handgun when the cough repeated itself. "I'm armed!" he yelled. Had someone found a back entrance to the cave? The lack of response grated on his nerves. He'd never known fear, yet his heart pounded, and his pulse throbbed in his neck. The gun quivered in his grip. Fear was for mortals. It was in this moment, standing alone and vulnerable in the cavern, that the Primary understood its true meaning.

Men stepped out from behind the stacked crates, one after another. In the dim light, he struggled to remember most of their names, while a few came to mind. He knew who they were, what they'd come for with their severed hands, limbs, and missing ears. The blinded had removed their patches, perhaps to make him gaze into their empty sockets.

He searched his recent memory, trying to recall the man, ahead of the others. Horace? Was that his name? It was difficult to tell with his poor eyesight and panicked thoughts.

They approached, over a hundred or so from the deepest shadows of the cavern. His executioners closed ranks with homicidal stares and determined steps.

FORTY

Jaered crouched and touched the gentle sprig of new life, poking its emerald leaf between the rocks, reaching for the nourishing rays of sun peeking through the puffy clouds.

Within days, the sun had returned and shadows grew plentiful as Thrae's rotation settled into a natural orbit. Winds swept the last of the volcanic ash from the skies and the planet's core spun and swirled with vitality. The planet set about healing itself at a rapid rate. It was the rain that Jaered cherished the most, the much-needed moisture to his parched planet. Before his eyes, the oceans grew vast with nourishing storms blanketing his world.

The unnatural rejuvenation of an entire planet would have left human scientists dumbfounded, but the Heirs understood. Their loved ones' sacrifice had transformed the dark to light, and saved a universe.

"Looking good, Mom," Jaered said, and gently touched the delicate leaf.

"I found another one," Ian shouted and waved him over. Jaered scaled the lava field and met up with him. His brother withdrew a fenris cub from between the rocks. It had a singed tail and its fur was coated in soot, but the creature purred when Ian stroked it. "It's a female," he announced.

They'd spent the first two weeks cataloguing the changes on Thrae for future generations of Weir. Ian had insisted on starting their own Book of the Weir. Volume II.

A gigantic shadow smothered them. Jaered looked up and waved. Since Patrick discovered he could channel with Oocaw during the battle, it'd been impossible to keep the two apart. A shrill squawk came from behind the dragon. Her hatchling had taken flight and proud mother showed her off to the ground crew.

Jestueax's gargoyle pups trailed behind them, nose-diving at the dragon hatchling, until Oocaw bent her head in their direction and gave them a fiery warning to let her be.

"She'll be taking riders in no time," Ian yelled.

"Patrick thinks he's in the driver's seat," Jaered said.

Ian chuckled. "He'll find out she's really the one in charge soon enough." A puff of gray smoke. At Oocaw's parting gift, the dragon banked and headed for the mountain peak.

"Sires!" One of the Weir grounds crew scrambled over the boulders and handed Jaered a note. "From Dr. Mac," he announced.

The envelope was addressed to all three Heirs. Jaered opened it and read the message. He tilted it toward Ian.

YOU'RE NEEDED ON EARTH. MEET ME AT THE MANSION IN TIME FOR DINNER.

Ian pulled out his flashlight and sent a Morse code message for Patrick to return. As an afterthought, he added, ASAP. It took a couple more attempts before a faint light flashed on and off from the entrance to Oocaw's cave. Ian stuffed the flashlight in his pack and swung it over his shoulder.

A return to civilization would be a welcome break. Jaered craved a hot shower, a warm meal, and to rest his head on something other than a dirt floor. He'd spent the last several years denying himself simple pleasures in life, believing that it would make him stronger and more resilient. The road ahead was wide open, with so many choices and possibilities. For the first time in his life, he was lost, unsure how to trust in the unknown.

Ian passed him, headed for the platform. "Come on daydreamer. We'll be back."

Several minutes later, Patrick joined them on the platform and together, they parashyfted to Earth.

The three Heirs solidified in an open field. "Where's the rubble?" Ian asked.

"Milo had a crew clear what was left of the northern vortex structure," Patrick said.

Ian glanced about. "Every time I come home, it's different."

They started out down the path, passing downed trees, uprooted vegetation, and mounds of earth. Much of the mansion grounds remained in upheaval, but a team of Thrae evacuees were working tirelessly to breathe new life into Ian's once vibrant home.

Patrick lifted his face and sniffed. "I bet you twenty bucks Milo made lasagna."

Ian inhaled. "It's jambalaya."

"If it's hot, it's heaven," Jaered said.

Still several yards from the mansion, they came to a fork in the path. Patrick veered off, away from their destination. Jaered's pulse raced and his steps came to a halt. Despair rooted him where he stood.

Ian paused next to Jaered. "He's really proud of how it turned out."

"I know," Jaered said. Sweat bristled across the back of his neck despite the cool breeze.

Ian pressed a fist to his chest. "Whenever I think of her, my core throbs, like the connection is still there."

Melancholy took a firm hold. "I'm not sure I'm ready," Jaered said.

Ian sighed. "We never will be."

They set out with dragging steps and arrived at Patrick's pride and joy a moment later. Their brother had dealt with his grief the only way he could. He'd drawn up plans for a memorial to their fallen loved ones, and recruited both Pur and Duach survivors to construct it in a show of camaraderie. Plans to open it to visiting Weir were in the works.

The memorial was in the shape of a triangle with perpetual torches at each point, representing the three sisters who saved a universe. The highest point rose at the back with the other two, lower points, nearest the trail. They never found Marcus's body, lost to the ocean when the dome imploded, but he had a marker. It stood alongside new, matching ones for Mara and Galen. At the center of the memorial, a perpetual torch spit and crackled inside a grated, three-dimensional sun.

The walls were lined with etched names of fallen rebels, more were added each week.

Jaered stood in silence, staring at the names, consumed with grief at the overwhelming loss. The ache grew unbearable, and he clenched his fists.

"They did good," Patrick said. He wandered between the markers and paused at his mother's, running his finger across her etched name. He pressed his palm against it and his shoulders drooped.

"It's perfect, Patrick." Ian held his hands out, warming them over the sun's flames. "Immortalized, as they should be."

Jaered approached the dancing flame inside the sun and read the plaque. His chest heaved and unbridled emotion dampened his cheeks. They'd added Kyre's name beside Rayne's at the base of the sun.

"It was Ian's idea," Patrick said.

"They weren't sisters in life, but they'll be forever remembered as sisters of the universe," Ian said.

It was then that Jaered realized he could face whatever the future held, with his brothers by his side.

The Heirs lingered in silence, serenaded by the birds' song and the gentle breeze. Saxon found them. The wolf sprawled out in his favorite spot between Mara and Galen's markers, and dozed.

A while later, they found Dr. Mac sitting on the steps, smoking a pipe with Milo. The two old friends laughed and were in the throes of a story from their youth. The doctor had yet to take off the bunny slippers. Jaered wondered if he ever would.

At the Heirs approach, Milo stood. "You boys look skinnier every time I see you. You won't be taking off until you've licked your plates clean." He disappeared inside.

"What's up, Doc?" Patrick said with a mischievous grin.

Dr. Mac peered at him. "You know, I can give you dysentery that will last for days, maybe weeks."

"You didn't need a summons just to get a hot meal in us," Jaered said. "The promise of Milo's cooking was good enough for me." A warm shower sounded better than a warm meal, however, and Jaered hoped they'd repaired more plumbing so he could steal away and clean up before dinner.

"Angus entrusted Gwynn with a secret a few years ago," Dr. Mac said. At the mention of Jaered's uncle and aunt, Dr. Mac earned his undivided attention. The old doctor cleared his throat. "When it became clear that Aeros was intent on ending the planet, she shared the secret with me, that day in Sophenna's quarters. It was when you and Rayne walked in on us, Ian."

Ian slowly nodded. "I remember."

"I brought a young woman and her charge back to Earth, ahead of everyone else." He descended the steps with the stooped shoulders of a tremendous weight, then paused on a step that brought him face to face with Jaered. "I don't know how to tell you this delicately, so I'm just going to come out with it," Dr. Mac said. "Your wife, Kyre. She was . . . killed by Aeros's fire. Angus wasn't able to save her," Dr. Mac said. "But by some miracle, he was able to save the unborn child."

The air grew thin, and it was as if time stood still. No one moved. "I have a child?" Jaered stared at the old doctor, and the truth stared back.

Tara appeared in the doorway. One of her arms was inside a sling, but the other clasped the hand of a young girl, clutching a stuffed bear. Jaered did the math despite the shock. The child was just shy of her third birthday, he realized. She had flaxen hair with streaks of honey. But it was her eyes, as crystal blue as the Caribbean Ocean, that stopped the beat of his heart. She was the spitting image of Kyre . . . and Rayne.

Ian's heart revved so fast, it pounded in Jaered's ears and fell in sync with his own erratic beat.

Jaered raked his fingers through his thick hair, conscious of how grimy and wrinkled his clothes were from spending the week on Thrae. He groped to find his voice and address this miracle standing in front of him.

Ian nudged Jaered from behind and he walked up the steps, then crouched in front of her. She gave him a shy smile. "I'm Jaered," he said. How scary he must appear, with the scraggly nubs on his face, smelling of campfire and ash.

Ian and Patrick joined him on the steps. "That's my bear," Patrick said.

Tara pressed a finger to his lips. "You have me to cuddle with," she said, and gave him a peck on his cheek.

"What's your . . ." Ian's voice cracked. His throat rose and fell. "What's your name?"

She looked to Dr. Mac. "Abarrane," he said. "Gwynn named her. It means Mother of Multitudes."

An odd sensation pricked Jaered's core. He reached out, but hesitated. "May I touch you?"

The rosy pink lips pulled back in a grin and Abarrane pressed a tiny hand to Jaered's chest. When he did the same to her, his core ignited with a blistering heat.

Ian pulled back and met Jaered's gaze. From the look on his face, he too, had felt it.

"What?" Patrick asked.

"She has a core," Jaered said.

They gathered around the precious child, this Mother of Multitudes. A brilliant ray of hope, for Weir generations to come.

GLOSSARY

Book of the Weir: A volume of letters and notes kept by the Ancient Weir Counsel. It is rumored to include secrets to the Sars powers and predicts the coming of the Heir.

boost: A device that draws elements from the planet, such as calcium or proteins, to aid in healing. The boost is fueled by the energy stored in a Sar's core.

Channels: A set of identical Weir twins who share a genetic marker with a Sar. The three are able to communicate telepathically or, when standing close enough together, the Sar may receive visions or eavesdrop on the thoughts of others.

core: Sars are born with a core, deep in the center of their chest. It allows them to control and contain energy drawn from the planet. Not all cores are alike and therefore, it dictates what power they yield. If a core extinguishes, the Sar dies.

core blast: It was known as the Dragon's Breath during the Dark Ages. A core power that enables a Sar to draw and manipulate energy from below the surface of the planet. Many scholars believe that it comes from the center of the Earth.

corona: A colorful gas that's created when a Sar uses a vortex. If a Pur steps into a vortex field and draws energy into their core, the gases turn green. When a Duach uses the field, the gases turn red.

Curse: An unpleasant, often excruciating reaction when a Pur Sar and a Duach Sar come in close proximity to each other. Developed by the Ancients, it prevents the Duach and the Pur from stealing each other's powers, a barbaric practice which often results in death.

Duach: *dū-ōk*\\ A rebellious group of Weir who use their powers for self-gain. They are considered the black sheep of the Weir and are despised by the Pur for their narcissistic ways.

fenris: *fin-ris*\\ A large wolf-like creature that is capable of walking on two paws and on four. Feral beasts that cannot be tamed.

Heir: The Ancients predicted the eventual decline of the Weir race and the coming of the Heir, the last Sar born to the Weir. Prophesy stated that he would be born with the most powerful of cores, and inherit all the combined powers of the Weir Sars that came before him. Since the Weir keep the energies of Earth in harmony, the planet would continue to survive.

kymera: *kie-mera*\\ On Earth they are known as gargoyles. A huge, winged creature with a baboon-like snout, forked tail and thick, leathery skin. They are intelligent and typically docile as a breed.

Mark: In ancient times, known as a Seal. A triangular image of raised skin found on the left breast of Sars. Only the Heir's mark is a triangle that houses a sun. Weir males born without a mark are powerless.

paral: Someone from Earth and someone from Thrae who are the mirror image of each other.

parashyfting: Crossing into an alternate dimension during a shyft. A powerful vortex stream or field is required. Only Sars born with the shyfting power can parashyft.

Primary: The head of the Syndrion.

Pur: \\pūr\\ Thought of as the original and longest practicing of the Weir. They continue to work tirelessly for the good of the planet and to lessen man's impact on the world and other living creatures.

The Rising: A Weir practice, designed to draw a Sar's powers to the surface. Held in the event of a Sar not discovering their powers naturally.

Sar: A firstborn Weir male who's inherited a core, granting them control over a single Earthly power. Most Sars control plants or animals. Sars born with rare powers, such as shyfting or core blast powers, are the most revered and sought after.

shyft/shyfting: *shift*\\ The ability to teleport. The Sar's core allows him to use one of thousands of vortex energy fields or streams found across Earth, and move around the surface of the planet.

shyftor: *shif-tor*\\ A Sar born with the shyfting power doesn't need a vortex to shyft over short distances.

Somex: *sŏm-ex*\\ A Sar born with the somex power can control neurotransmitters in the brain that affect consciousness.

Syndrion: *sin-drī-un*\\ The Weir counsel. Ever since the Duach broke away from traditional practices centuries earlier, the current Syndrion is made up of only Pur Sars. Representatives from each continent serve on the counsel.

splinter: *splin-ter*\\ Occurs when the planet's core energy separates into a concentrated field. As a result, energy in another location weakens and makes the planet susceptible to natural, outside forces.

Thrae: *thrā*\\ Earth's twin planet in an alternate dimension.

vortex: *vor-tex*\\ A specific location where energy fields emanate from the planet surface and circulate on invisible gases.

Weir: *wē-er*\\ Magical stewards of the Earth who have lived quietly among humans for more than two thousand years. Their purpose is to ensure harmony between Earth's various energies and all living creatures. With each generation, there are fewer Weir Sars born with a connection to the Earth. The Weirs' power is dwindling, and along with it, their control of Earth's combined energy. Thus, natural disasters are on the rise in frequency and intensity

AUTHOR'S NOTE

I hope you enjoyed reading the final novel, *Dim the Lights*, book five, in the Weir Chronicles series! To get caught up on the entire series, don't miss *Fade to Black*, book one, *Masks and Mirrors*, book two, *Sleight of Hand*, book three, and *Stack a Deck*, book four, all available wherever books are sold.

To receive the latest news about the series and other books and stories by me, visit my Amazon author page or my website at www.sueduff.com. Add your name to the fan email list to receive notices about book events, the latest information on upcoming novels, and more.

Check out my blog, A Cook's Guide to Writing, and other musings at www.sueduff.com. Follow me on Facebook at Sue Duff-Writer, Tweet along at https://twitter.com/sueduff55, view my Instagram pics and emoji strips at sueduffauthor. You can also email me at sueduffauthor@gmail.com.

OTHER BOOKS BY SUE DUFF

The Weir Chronicles
Fade to Black
Masks and Mirrors
Sleight of Hand
Stack a Deck
Dim the Lights
(available February 2018)

Short Stories
"Duo'vr"
a short story in the anthology
TICK TOCK: Seven Tales of Time

"A Mistake"
a short story in the anthology
OFF BEAT: Nine Spins on Song

ACKNOWLEDGEMENTS

Writing *Dim the Lights*, the final book in the Weir Chronicles series, proved to be quite the bittersweet experience. I've spent close to a decade with these characters, developing the worlds they lived, loved, fought, and died in. I've grown to consider each, and every one of them part of my family, and truly miss the ones who have not survived from one book to another. To be honest, I balled my eyes out as I wrote the final chapters. In part, because a few of the primary characters didn't survive to the end, and because I was so close to the end of the entire series.

I have my amazing tribe to thank for supporting me along this journey. They began with page one, and continued supporting me for more than fifteen hundred pages! I couldn't have done it without them. My awesome editor, Steve Parolini, my patient and supportive copyeditor Stephanie Viola, Matthew Woolums and his meticulous beta readings, Karri Klawiter and her incredible covers, and Sami Jo Lien at Roger Charlie for finding new and unique ways to help eager readers find my books. My writing tribe has grown exponentially throughout the course of this series as well, from the Tatter Cover critique group in Littleton, Colorado, to the women authors at Wicked Ink Books and my larger tribe at Rocky Mountain Fiction Writers.

A heartfelt thank you to my family, friends, and you the fans for giving me the encouragement to keep this series going to the end. I can't wait to dive into my next world, characters and hope you stick with me to see where my creative juices take us next!

When not saving the world one page at a time, Sue works as a speech therapist. She enjoys taking her octogenarian dachshund for strolls and stretching her creative juices in the kitchen. A Colorado transplant, she savors the incredible seasons, but appreciates that Mother Nature spares her from shoveling the driveway, too often.

Visit Sue at www.sueduff.com, on Facebook at Sue Duff-Writer and follow her on Twitter @sueduff55.

Book cover designed by Karri Klawiter, Art by Karri,
Author Photo by Liz Garcia

www.ingramcontent.com/pod-product-compliance
Lightning Source LLC
Chambersburg PA
CBHW030700120726
47905CB00001B/292